48

GOSSIP FROM THE FOREST

In GOSSIP FROM THE FOREST, as in
SCHINDLER'S ARK, Thomas Keneally
enhances a true story by delving into the minds
of the principal characters—in this case the
men who came to Compiègne to negotiate the
Armistice that ended the First World War. The
setting was unlikely: three first-class railway
carriages on a line that ran through a dark,
autumnal forest.

Six exhausted military leaders of both the
Allied and German forces meet to shape the
future of Europe: to put a stop to the slaughter
and end the war. Thomas Keneally has created
a novel of short scenes, concise dialogue and
vivid stage directions. 'This account,' he says,
'is not scholarly but merely gossip from the
forest.'

GOSSIP FROM THE FOREST

'Writing novels about historical persons and events is an enterprise of great audacity ... Bravura, however, has always been the breath of life to Thomas Keneally ... In this book, he sets himself with his usual passionate and sardonic exuberance, to study the conjunction of men who met in the railway coaches in the forest of Compiègne to sign the 1918 Armstice'

The Times Literary Supplement

'Keneally's book belongs ... with those like Solzhenitsyn's AUGUST 1914, books that delineate the past in sympathetic depth and so urge the reader to enter it'

The New York Times Book Review

'I was intrigued, excited and sure that the vivid snapshots of private-versus-public emotion would coalesce into a moving, meaningful image'

The Sunday Times

'The cunningest of documentaries'

New Statesman

Gossip from the Forest

Thomas Keneally

CORONET BOOKS
Hodder and Stoughton

Copyright © 1975 by Thomas Keneally

First published in Great Britain
1975 by Hodder and Stoughton Ltd.

Coronet edition 1984

British Library C.I.P.

Keneally, Thomas
    Gossip from the forest.
    I. Title
    823 [F]   PR9619.3.K46

ISBN 0-340-35474-7

Printed and bound in Great Britain for
Hodder and Stoughton Paperbacks, a
division of Hodder and Stoughton Ltd.,
Mill Road, Dunton Green, Sevenoaks,
Kent (Editorial Office: 47 Bedford
Square, London, WC1 3DP) by
Richard Clay (The Chaucer Press) Ltd.,
Bungay, Suffolk

To my Father

In the season in which this book was written, the French
government persisted in exploding nuclear devices above
the ocean where my children swim

Part One

Journeys and Arrivals

Fear of Trains and Forests

On Wednesday afternoon, at his headquarters in Senlis, the Marshal had a visit from the Premier of France. They read through the agenda of the meeting in the forest. When that business was finished, the Premier wanted to chat. The Marshal could tell that the old man was secretly seeking reassurance. In spite of that need, the Premier did not abandon his tone of mocking.

They sat by the fire in the Marshal's office on the ground floor. The Marshal's armies went forward up every main and country road. Although they were not used to such movement they had no need to appeal to him. Therefore few staff and liaison officers infested the park, no staff limousines cluttered the gravel under the terraces. Without hard-driven generals to salute, the chasseurs at the main steps kept a sleepy watch all afternoon. It was quiet enough and dim enough in the drizzling park to throw the night-jars into disorder. They sat in a birch tree from noon onwards, calling endlessly.

The old Marshal and older Premier could have been two semi-friends in front of a fire in a first-class convalescent home.

Clemenceau: Then how far will your train be from theirs?

The Marshal: I've never seen the place myself. But they tell me sixty metres or so. There's a siding for rail-mounted cannon. We'll take that, they can have the main line.

Clemenceau: In a train . . . in a forest . . .

The Marshal: That's right.

Clemenceau: Be careful of forests, my Marshal. Forests are full of omens. Ivy, for example. It's the symbol of womanhood. It cleans the forest floors. It keeps down the corpses of the autumns. It keeps down fallen deer. And robins. And soldiers . . .

The Marshal played a second with his moustache. He was accustomed to the Premier's bad taste and artistic vanity.

The Marshal: There aren't any dead soldiers in *that* forest.

Clemenceau: Be careful too of living in trains. The Kaiser spent a long time in his train this summer. One day he dreamt that the Queen of Norway pinned a rose to his collar. When he touched the rose with his finger-tips, he found it was a bullet-hole.

The Marshal laughed at the idea that the Kaiser's dream could with any accuracy be transhipped from sleep to awakening, and so from the Kaiser's train to the War Office in Paris.

The Marshal: I suppose your agents in Spa got the story from that drink-waiter.

Clemenceau: Yes, the Kaiser woke screaming and the waiter had to feed him schnapps. Waiters are always good value for agents. If they'd sell the best table in the restaurant for money they'd certainly sell their Emperor.

The Marshal: I never paid waiters a cent. To me it was always a matter of determination . . .

Clemenceau: I always paid. Something tangible. Bluff is intangible. That's the difference between us.

The Marshal: I suppose it may be. There seem to be quite a few differences. In any case, I have no reason to be afraid of trains. Or forests.

This pronouncement fortified the old man, or so the Marshal suspected. For soon after, the Premier called for his car and was driven back to the Senate in Paris.

Early the next morning, however, the Marshal did awake aghast from a dream of forests. Walking amongst trees he had come on some young soldiers, informally lined up in a clearing. He had presumed that they were from Castelnau's army group, resting for a future offensive in Lorraine. Those at the end of the queue were kicking a ball of rags about and stopped to salute him. At the head of the line three seated matrons worked at some task he could not identify. Their fervour reminded him of any bandage-rolling, sock-knitting committee in any town of the interior.

As he came closer to them he saw that each was busy fixing, somehow, rich military ribbons to the foreheads of the soldiers. He noticed that up to the place where the three worked so heartily and – it had to be admitted – deftly, the soldiers were the normal horse-laughing, cat-calling crowd you'd find at a de-lousing station in a rest area. Once they had their oddly placed ribbons they kept silent, not one of them speaking to another.

They abandoned their helmets and stripped their equipment away. They walked naked over the ivy, and the ribbons they had so easily accepted became bleeding wounds. He called to them. They didn't care. The forest was full of quiet seeking boys. Bloodied, they looked behind this and that elm. They were sombre children returned to a playroom after a long winter. Behind the trees, somewhere, cunningly amongst leaves, were the utterly adequate toys of childhood.

In the end all he could do was stride out of the woods, not looking either side at the mute boys who peopled it. Advancing on the woman in the centre chair, he put a hand on her shoulder. She hadn't any fear, she knew her business and her right to be there.

Woman: Good morning, my Marshal.

It was his wife's wide face looking up as he had seen it look up at the sun on summer holidays in Brittany, when the children would bring in blackberries and she would sit outside their summer-house excising the stems of the fruit with a hand plump from child-making, child-raising and honest submission.

The Marshal: But what are you doing, Julie?

The un-answer from her woke him. He lay in bed feeling, until he was properly awake, that she had somehow usurped him. Then he noticed that his bladder was full. He got out of his bed. There was a little moan, wind or thin rain, at the window. The oak-trees in the garden pressed the dark hard up against the panes.

Saying prayers for the dead he fetched the chamber-pot and wet into it, standing.

... and remember in Your Mercy Lieutenant Germain

Foch and Captain Bécourt. Both of the cavalry, now in the fifth year of their death. Dead of high explosive in the war's first summer. Hippophiles, cavaliers, innocents, dead before they found out the truth. That this war was not of the same species as all those others they studied at the École de Guerre. Amongst the shell fragments they had suffered a not unenviable delivery from knowledge, he thought. His framework had had to take in so much more knowledge that he had sometimes heard his ribs creak (though he never informed doctors or anyone else of it).

His elder girl had now been a widow more than four years. And Julie and he four years son-less.

The dream. The dream grew out of the conference he had with the Premier yesterday. Downstairs.

It made him feel more content about it to understand its external origins. To let it stop him sleeping was ridiculous. He owed his sleep to the nation. The flow of urine ceased. He covered the pot with a beaded cover and muttered.

The Marshal: Guise, la-Capelle, Fourmies, Chimay.

It was the road his enemies would travel, seeking a truce. He had bid them down that road. Even through the insulation of the battle lines, he believed he could sense the aura of those Berlin delegates, detraining by now in Belgium. Bringing their slack wills to OHL.*

And if this morning the German Emperor's poisonous nightmare had entered the Marshal's own bed and bitten him, it was a last and puny Prussian success. The toxin would not enter his nervous system. He would wilfully exclude it. He felt sure, this autumn, that he could wilfully exclude the venom of a mamba.

He scratched himself and spoke as if someone were standing at the bed-end.

The Marshal: You must be mad. If you think you can derail me so easily.

Lying, he got the covers up over his ears. The room was full of the frozen stench of his bed-time pipe.

---

*Oberste Hereesleitung – German Supreme Headquarters situated in Spa, Belgium.

The Marshal Listens to Chasseurs' Boots

A soldier woke him at six with coffee. Before he got his head off the pillow he was full of excitement. In the dim park of the château of Senlis it still rained. He could hear the boots of the GQG† company of chasseurs marching to morning parade, past the orangery, around the ornamental fountain and up the length of the façade. *That* sound. Until 1914 it had been an audible statement of the battle-will, it had some sacramental meaning, like church-bells ringing, and what it said was *élan,* dash, *volonté,* will, *cran,* guts, *cran, cran, cran.* Army boots on gravel. The crisp, monotone background scoring of all the aphorisms he produced in the classrooms of the École Supérieure de Guerre in his academic years. *If defeat can arise from moral causes so can victory . . . A battle won is a battle in which one will not confess oneself beaten . . . Victoire, c'est la volonté . . . Modern war knows but one argument, the tactical fact, battle . . . War is in itself only a matter of maintaining harmonious proportion between the spiritual and bodily elements . . .* The spies sent by the Freemasons at the Ministry of War could go back to their chief and say, That Colonel Foch talks metaphysics! But the young officers understood and he would open the windows so they could hear the soldiers drilling in the yard of the École Militaire next door. The crunch of boots made his meaning palpable to the chosen men who took courses at the École Supérieure.

The Freemasons at the Ministry of War said, he talks like a Jesuit – spiritual and bodily elements, acts of the will, faith – his brother's a Jesuit. A dangerous bastard. And popular with those fledgling staff-officers.

Tall, amorous, peasant-boy Colonel Pétain used to ques-

†GQG Grand-Quartier-Général. That is, GHQ.

tion whether *Modern War knew only one argument, the tactical fact, battle.* He cited high-explosive, muzzle velocities, enfilading machine-guns. He'd said, they're the tactical facts. It was because Pétain was a melancholy and edgy farm boy that he raised these points. He'd been right but through a defect of temperament. In the Marshal's eyes, defects of temperament were no excuse for being right.

What did it mean to the Marshal today when GQG Company B noisily occupied the carriageway and the courtyard and squared off in the rain ready for inspection? This morning the tactical, strategic, political, simple fact was: he was the most powerful man in the world. This afternoon he would take a train-ride. At the end of which he would lay down all the precedents for a new world.

The Titans of the Homefront

He had already imposed precedents on the titans of the home fronts. To detail his art in this area would take too long. But something of his manner towards statesmen should be marked down.

Throughout the autumn he spent his mornings above the Quai d'Orsay, inside or outside a small conference room on the second floor of the War Office, where only the few more powerful met. Old Clemenceau and the Welsh Prime Minister of Britain. Colonel House, the American representative, and the Foreign Minister of Italy.

Whenever the Marshal was invited to speak in this room, old Clemenceau would rest in his chair, content that French interests were now being stated or overstated. The Premier's Kirghiz eyes shifted, brooding on the river beyond the high windows. Some of the autumn haze entered his face. A Mongolian horseman dreams of the steppes, the Marshal would think ironically. The Marshal noticed too that because of the thick glass of the windows, and the autumn vapours hanging over Paris, the angle of the river he could himself see from the conference table resembled urban rivers as they were painted by the impressionists, by the Premier's old prostate-ridden familiar and master-spirit, Monet. Nature going to a lot of trouble to imitate Monet's art. Too much trouble.

While the Premier drowsed in this way, the Marshal would tell the foreign few that the enemy must not only give up the Rhineland but four bridgeheads, thirty kilometres deep, on the far side of the great river. The debate was always complicated, but never from his side, for he always stated the same argument and said, you ask me what is strategically necessary to demand. This (tapping the map), this is strategically necessary.

And whether it was or was not the map of a strategic necessity, it was the outline of what was psychically necessary to the Marshal. At a given depth of his soul, where distinctions between military and diplomatic business had no meaning, he had decided he could not sleep if this map was not fleshed out across the forests, coalfields, foundries, sweet valleys in Western Germany.

If his argument was simple, his acting out of the argument had many strands to it. He had a gift for looking at times as if his will (or the Holy Spirit) were swelling him, that he might at any instant levitate or explode like a bladder. Sometimes he would pound his horizon-blue hip so emphatically that those at table could not help becoming a little alarmed in case their generalissimo gave himself a blood-clot.

When the hairy Welsh satyr (called Lloyd George) accused him of trying to gag statesmen in debate about the bridgeheads, he could knead his jaws or paw the arms of his plush chair in a gesture of overbearing contrition which seemed to satisfy, above all, to silence everyone.

In fact, his conversations with politicians appeared in transcript to be howling melodrama. So that statesmen, reading over their notes after interviews with the Marshal, often thought, how did we tolerate such behaviour, such bombast, such bathos?

They had forgotten how the prophetic fever in the man had seduced them. He made them suspect that if they let themselves float they could be as unqualified and certain as he. It was like offering an exhausted businessman a holiday in the south.

Perilous to Health and Sanity

The Marshal could also pretend to find British demands concerning the German fleet to be perilous to health and sanity.

Lloyd George would sometimes bring with him a square and meaty British admiral called Wemyss. He was an aristocratic presence, very genial. When Wemyss sat at his side, the Welshman nagged the cabinet room about what was to be done to Germany's navy. All German submarines were to surrender, the High Seas Fleet was to be interned and stripped of arms.

Whenever Lloyd George brought up these naval terms, the Marshal took fire, clutched the rim of the table as if invisible tides of folly, set in motion by the Welshman, were about to swirl him off his chair, out the door, down the steps, across the foyer and so on.

The High Seas Fleet hadn't put to sea for two years. Did the Prime Minister of Britain want our soldiers to go on dying just because the enemy would not give up a fleet that never put to sea?

The Welshman of course pursued, defined, ranted. But the marginal imputation hung over him: that his demands were unbalanced, that he had a sickness of the mind about ships. Meanwhile the Marshal could direct looks at his blotter. What he told his blotter was the old story: The

Welshman is descending to particulars. We'll ... *I'll* ... impose our intentions on the enemy. Wholesale.

The Marshal and the Calvinist Texan

One other of his contacts with statesmen is worth recording. Sometimes in the afternoons of late October or early November 1918 he was required to go out to the Supreme War Council who had convened beneath chandeliers in the dining hall of the Trianon palace. Here Colonel House, a small chinless Texan, struggled to retain the mildness, the unvengefulness of the Fourteen Point peace plan his President had uttered earlier in the year. His task was like that of persuading wolves and tigers to take up a vegetarian diet.

Yet President Wilson was Europe's angel of reconciliation. Even the left-wing deputies in the German Reichstag praised him on the floor of the house during debates. His voice, his incarnation in Paris, this Colonel House certainly wasn't a military colonel, but was, at least, remote, seemly, no cowboy. The Marshal suspected there was Red Indian in him; he had high Mongolian cheekbones. Apart from that he looked like someone you'd find driving a lift in a very good family hotel.

One afternoon, in the dining hall, he asked the Marshal this question: if the enemy does not give in to an armistice, how long would it be before our armies got to the Rhine?

The Marshal told him four months, five. His troops weren't used to fast advances and tended to be needlessly delayed by the screens of elite machine-gunners the enemy threw in their tracks. He, in the meantime, had demanded that troops be trained to by-pass, infiltrate. But still, four months, five ...

House: It would be a great victory – to drive them all the way back to the Rhine.

The little Mongolian face suggested: and you'd be the

victor and honoured for ever. So why should you want to end the war? Therefore why should you lead the armistice pow-pow?

None the less the Marshal knew that this Texas (perhaps Comanche!) Calvinist had smelt out the most dangerous lust he carried within him. Even now, in the fifth year, his creativity cried out for a war of movement, for making a gap without losing 150,000 men, for having reserves to exploit it. By next spring there would be two million American soldiers in France.

The war had so far been a Satanic denial of talent and fire. And now that it had become possible to make war in a Napoleonic manner he was told to make a truce instead. The Marshal had now to force cease-fire terms not only on the nations but on his creative lust.

But he wouldn't admit all that to a Calvinist Texan.

Ferrason Says He Will Teach

The Marshal told the orderly to put down the razor and ring a bell connecting his dressing-room to the operations section downstairs. In answer, after half a minute, a young officer entered the dressing-room, saluting. Clever Major Ferrason. Less than thirty. Would have been a general by now if he'd been in the field. Or else dead.

The Marshal: Situation, Ferrason! Situation?

Ferrason: I'll have an immediate report written for you, sir.

The Marshal: No, tell me. Or don't you know?

Ferrason: I know, sir.

The Marshal: Righto, I'm not so old I'll forget.

The orderly's razor made a subtle turn round the limits of the old man's heavy moustache. The Marshal sat beneath the razor as marmoreal as he had lain asleep before dawn. He was *that* freak: the man whose private and public selves were one.

Ferrason: The British have cleared Bruges and are west of Ath on the Brussels Road. The Americans are going forward ten kilometres east of Le Cateau. On the line of the Aisne our forces are fifteen kilometres west of Rethel. The roads are mined and barricaded. But French forces are progressing at a somewhat better rate than the others.

He paused to signify *End of Report.*

The Marshal: A little hazy, but it gives me an idea. News of the Russians?

Ferrason: None that I know, sir.

The barber used scissors on the Marshal's hairy earholes.

The Marshal: When I see you again there will be no war. I must thank you for the walks we have enjoyed together.

Ferrason: You embarrass me, sir.

The Marshal: I hope not. We have surely shared enough . . .

In all the headquarters they had occupied, they had been walking companions. He'd acquired Ferrason when he took over IX Army in 1914. In that autumn the boy had been an adoring lieutenant, a vacant thing, a spout down which you could pour ideas about troop movement, epistemology, music, and hear them resound flatteringly. Now Ferrason was older and his own man. But they still liked each other.

The Marshal: I thank you because even if we do walk together again the quality of the debate, the urgency . . . will all have changed.

Ferrason: One can only hope so.

The Marshal: What are you going to do then? Grand Quartier General will run down. It seems a lot of its members are already harbouring plans. What might yours be? I ask myself.

Ferrason: I've been offered a teaching job at the École de Guerre. You see, they think your ideas have rubbed off.

The Marshal: I congratulate you.

The words were flannelled: an orderly was towelling and massaging the Marshal's face.

The Marshal: If it were 1872 I'd advise you to take it.

Ferrason smiled.

Ferrason: I wouldn't say your ideas were as old-fashioned as all that, sir.

The Marshal: Make your jokes. What I'm getting at is: there will be a vast allied Crusade against the Bolsheviks. Yes, yes there shall be, don't make a face.

Ferrason: I assure you, sir . . .

The Marshal lifted his thumb and for five seconds the wind surged and caterwauled in the park. You were tempted for an instant to think the Marshal had commanded and orchestrated the gale.

The Marshal: There shall *be*!

Already he had prepared memoranda. French officers would staff the campaign. And those two million American boys Pershing would have by the spring. They would have their chance in wide-open Russia.

The Marshal: I hope to be involved myself. You . . . you could be an Army commander. In a war of movement too! You can't have a static war in Russia, you know. The countryside doesn't permit it.

Upright Ferrason wore braid around the rim of his coat and was in fact crumpling it with his left hand. He gave no other sign of war-weariness.

Ferrason: With the Marshal's permission . . . I would like to pass on to the new generation the lessons of this war.

The Marshal: Don't be a hypocrite, Ferrason.

Ferrason: I wasn't aware . . .

The Marshal: You want one of those pleasant staff-houses, you want a garden of roses and your infants staggering about amongst them. You want your wife's endearments.

Ferrason: I have reasons of honour.

The Marshal: You mean then your wife's endearments don't count?

Ferrason: Sir, I know you're amusing yourself.

The Marshal: Oh no.

And the wind too thudded its dissent under the eaves.

The Marshal: You'll be a fat colonel of fifty before you know it.

Ferrason: I regret disappointing you, sir.

The Marshal: Ferrason, any damn private soldier can want to go home.

Ferrason: Yes.

The Marshal: That takes no talent.

If God were not in my soul (the Marshal told himself), if I enjoyed my power in a cosmic vacuum, and if I did not eat the Bread of Peace on Sundays, I know what I'd damn well do. I'd detach Ferrason off to Salonika to report on means of repatriating the French Army. He couldn't take his dumpling wife to Salonika. It was full of typhoid.

The Marshal: Did you go to a Jesuit College, Ferrason?

Ferrason's hand worked again, surreptitiously, at the braid. My God, thought the Marshal, he doesn't think it's a relevant question.

Ferrason: When I was a boy.

The Marshal: Of course. That's when you *do* go, when you're a boy.

Ferrason: I went to the Jesuits at la Poste, sir.

The Marshal: Astonishing. Did they teach you to make acts of the will?

Ferrason: Yes. We often talked about the Jesuits and the faculty of the will, sir. On our walks.

When the Marshal performed his bitter laugh, his overlarge head looked like a gargoyle's. Ferrason saw the mysterious ferocity of his stained teeth. Yet it was still hard to tell if the old man were playing with him or, in fact, suffering parental hurt.

The Marshal: Ah, there! You do think I'm senile.

Ferrason: If you have to have the truth I think you're the most brilliant man left standing in Europe today.

The Marshal: I didn't ask you here to talk about that. Please return to your post.

The young man saluted and went towards the door. Feeling the nausea which men of powerful fatherhood can induce in their chosen young.

The Marshal thought, if all he wanted to do was become a family man I could have strolled with someone else.

The Marshal: Ferrason.

Ferrason: Sir.

The Marshal: I want you to tell the adjutant to bring me an order for signature. That all staff officers are to be subject to the eight o'clock curfew whether or not an armistice is signed.

Ferrason: Sir, you were a military teacher until the age of fifty-eight . .

The Marshal: Fifty-nine.

Ferrason: I would not be ashamed to follow that pattern if it equipped me for war as well as you are equipped.

The Marshal rejected him with both hands.

The Marshal: Get out.

Ferrason did, the door handle moist and warm in his palm as a living organ.

The Marshal's Breakfast

The Marshal put on his winter drawers and his blue serge uniform. Simply decorated. Only two long rows of campaign-ribbons. None of the cut the English affected. The pockets rather baggy. Old Field-Marshal French, the English Commander, had once said you could tell the class of people the French generals were by the way they dressed. It had appalled him to see General Berthelot slopping round GQG in a white smock and slippers.

But we're still here, we slapdash dressers. French has vanished in spite of the cut of his suit. Because *battle* might *not* be the only tactical fact, but trim pockets weren't any sort of tactical fact at all.

The Marshal insisted on a large breakfast even though he might be what they called a fussy eater. He took it in a room on the ground floor, beside the office of the Chief of Intelligence. The lights shone on him as he crossed the lobby. No typewriters sounded, no muddy couriers ran towards the Operations Room. Only during emergencies did an HQ experience the rush of messengers, the cry for maps, the telephones pealing and staff-officers chary of picking them up for fear of what they'd hear. During the offensive of 1914 and the crisis of last spring it was not unknown for wounded men to come crawling determinedly over Corps HQ doorsteps, bringing the blame home to you.

At the breakfast table only his Chief-of-Staff, General Maxime Weygand, himself a small eater, was permitted to join him. Together they viewed the good linen and china and the delicacies.

At half past seven Weygand entered the breakfast room. Though the Marshal was half-way through a hard-boiled egg, he stood up.

The Marshal: Maxime.

Chief of Staff: My Marshal.

The Marshal: Sit down then.

Chief of Staff: Just some coffee, thanks.

The Marshal: Good ham, Maxime. Danish.

The Chief of Staff handed him some flimsies; a summary of the state of war on this, one of its last mornings. While an orderly poured him the thick-brewed coffee the Marshal favoured, Weygand passed across the table a second page. The Marshal put it flat on his hand so that it would catch all the light from the chandelier.

The Marshal: When did it come?

Weygand: During the night. Transmitted from OHL at Spa.

It was the list of German plenipotentiaries.

The Marshal: Erzberger . . . Maiberling . . . von Winter-feldt. Who in God's name are they?

Weygand: Maiberling and von Winterfeldt are obscure. But you have probably heard of the first man. A politician.

The Marshal: No, Maxime, I don't know any Erzberger.

Weygand mentioned an incident to do with Erzberger's past: some peace motion in the Reichstag. It was meant to trip the Marshal's memory.

The Marshal: No, Maxime. The Reichstag isn't my favourite house. The question stands. *Who in God's name is Erzberger?*

Painstaking Maxime (my encyclopaedia, the Marshal

called him) had read at first light a résumé of Matthias Erzberger's career prepared by political section of the War Office. He answered the Marshal's question.

Herr Erzberger's Dream

What dream parallel to the Marshal's had plenipotentiary Matthias Erzberger been dreaming all the night? In his special train, Berlin-Spa?

His boy Oscar had died three weeks back of influenza in the officers' school at Karlsruhe. Oscar had got a delicate frame from his mother, no peasant barrel-chest. He had always been weak in the lungs. Only desperate nations called on such boys.

Herr Erzberger's dreams now were a sort of seepage from that death. Therefore he avoided sleep. He stayed up till two in the morning, drinking schnapps with Count Maiberling in the saloon. The Count had been tiresome earlier in the evening. There had been berserk switches of mood. But since the staff-officers who travelled with them had gone to bed, Maiberling became a better companion. He had always had the jitters about officers: a strange phobia to show up in an aristocrat.

At two, feeling better than he had for days, Matthias decided that he and Maiberling *must* sleep, must not be blunted. Their special rolled slowly through rail-junctions jammed with troop trains. They found their couchettes in the next carriage.

Erzberger: I'm going to dream, damn it!
Maiberling: Everyone dreams. Tonight, even the drunks!
Erzberger: I dream every night.

So he went in foredoomed to do it in his own plush and enamelled compartment.

The second he fell asleep, there he was, at a summer-house in a forest – the Black Forest inevitably. The space in front of the house was covered with small wild strawberries and butterflies. Sunlight lit up all the stone façade of the house. At the door he felt very pleasantly ready for the first forest stroll of his vacation and was waiting for his wife to get her hat. Down the stairs she came but dropped the hat, the mannish straw item in her trim hand, on the bare boards of the hall. She said she'd decided to stay and cook pastries. Instead, she said, producing a treacherous umbrella, instead take this.

He had never felt threat from her before. His anger and terror were greater than anything he'd experienced in politics. For one thing, she knew after all their marriage that umbrellas couldn't be tolerated. He refused. She said yes, now that he had a dead son he must take the umbrella and go, go for his damned walk.

It was all at once out of his power. He took the thing, feeling nausea. He was now like a man under orders.

Erzberger: Kiss me goodbye.

She didn't do that but had in her hand, from nowhere, a fresh strawberry. She rubbed it along his lips. They were rather long, rather full lips, so that it took her some time to cover them – like a child colouring in. Then, more savagely, she crushed the strawberry to a pulp against his forehead.

Wife: Now do you believe I love you?

Erzberger: Yes.

Wife: Time for your walk.

He went without looking back lest she should think less of him than she did of his son. For they both knew the boy had forced his way from delirium to delirium, clear-headed about death and grappling the earth to him, since to him, drifting as he was amongst breathless constellations, it had become so small.

With such a son, you didn't look back although you were coerced to walk into the forest with a terrible umbrella.

It was a clammy and fungoid forest. It wasn't summer here. Some letting agent, too smart for his own good, must have put one over Paula by setting a summer cottage in a winter, or at best, autumn forest.

Why do I come here for holidays? he wondered. I detest stepping back into the forest, it's like going back into a womb, not your mother's but Kali's. He went on, finding the paths more and more repulsive. The elms seeped as slum-walls seep with waters of uncertain origin. His journey to the place he knew, where the path turned a full corner, took some time. But when he got there two men with black masks were waiting with repeating revolvers in their hands. He didn't like seeing them so he raised the umbrella and put it before his face. They began shooting the umbrella full of holes. He felt it struggle, was one with its panic and pains. When they'd finished he dropped it. Its wounds were blood-bespattered.

Erzberger: Why did you do it? Now I can never go back to her.

From each bullet-hole in the sickening umbrella a pale young soldier struggled. The masked men who had done the damage ran away. One of the soldiers said *it's about time* and began rapping Erzberger's skull below the hair-line.

Erzberger awoke with angina pain in his chest. Somebody was knocking on the door. He told them to come in. It was a steward with coffee. Erzberger leaned out of his couchette and raised the blind a little. Rain fell and rain-beads on the window distorted the faces of soldiers in the troop-train they were passing.

Steward: A foul morning, sir.

Herr Erzberger thought everyone must be dreaming this November. Of pale soldiers, bullet-holes, forests, seeping waters. Why do I fear umbrellas in my sleep? he wondered.

Gossip from the Forest

Since this account is not scholarly but merely gossip from the forest, the reader does not need to carry with him to Compiègne a history of the Marshal. He will find it haphazardly in these pages. He knows that the Marshal was a pontiff in Armageddon, that there is a statue to him outside Victoria Station, that his name has been given to parks, avenues and bandstands in Clermont, Birmingham, Toronto, Sydney and the republic of Chad. As a start, that is nearly enough to know, for it accords with the Marshal's monumental personality.

But Erzberger's is a name not favoured by municipalities. It has to be some way explained how he comes to be on the train to Spa with his friend, Count Maiberling.

In that November he is forty-three years old, of country stock, big-boned, plump to his friends, obese to enemies. He wears pince-nez, and the eyes behind them in the big face are delicate, and the lips are capable of being delicate. He grew up in the south, trained as a rural teacher, took to journalism and politics, organized a trade union congress and got himself elected to the Reichstag when he was twenty-eight. He had political gifts: memory, an ability to line up votes and drive wedges between people. People said he was cunning and chivalrous. From within his own skin he did not see himself as having especial gifts of cunning.

His specialities in those early days were budgetary, colonial and military matters. He did not admire the colonies, or the military.

When he was thirty-one he exposed in the house the nature of German occupation in Africa. His motives were both opportunist and visionary: that was Erzberger's nature. He caused the government to resign. His reputation was made, though not with his party (the Centre) which had had an arrangement with the government.

Like any country boy he thought, why are all these big names letting me get away with it? There was a vein of fatalism in him: he knew that one day the guard dogs that savage presumptuous rustics would catch and savage him.

Within a few years Thyssen's made him a director. They thought that he might make a grateful board member and feed them Reichstag information. It was only on looking at him a second time that they saw the fat young man made a lot of his sensible but, at its nucleus, incorruptible conscience. None the less he has been a capable director and has been able to give them sufficient expert forecasts to justify his salary.

When war started he was made director of the Office of Propaganda for Neutral Countries. It is said the press corps liked him.

He believed that the war would prove a thesis basic to European peace: that Germany could not be encircled. He also believed Germany should be permitted to annex Belgium and some coal areas on the French border.

By 1917 he had grown out of his annexionist beliefs. He was less callow now, more visibly quixotic. He was already talking peace with Russian diplomats in Stockholm, with Papal officials in Rome. In July he spoke in the Reichstag. He was a polished speaker, obsessed with grammatic correctness, though his Swabian accent was broad.

He began by detailing some special communications he had received concerning failures in Galicia and the west. It was acceptable to speak of military disasters in the house. What he said next the delegates were not quite so accustomed to.

Erzberger: Our military resources are coming to an end . . . The basis of my argument is the danger of revolution. It is no good telling me that the monarchical idea is too firmly rooted in Berlin or Vienna for the monarchs to be overthrown. This war has no precedent. If the monarchs do not make peace in the next few months, our people will do it over their heads.

What are you? some of the Conservatives whispered in his ear in the Reichstag library. A socialist? Even socialists don't talk like that.

A day or so later he moved a motion in the Reichstag: that Germany should negotiate for peace, renounce all her conquests. His party voted with him, and the socialists of all varieties. The motion was carried 212 votes to 126; it sent the Kaiser into dazed retreat at Wilhelmshohe. With his Empress, whose heart was suspect. But the advice of Matthias Erzberger and 211 others was not followed.

Erzberger Gets the Job

For this and other reasons, Matthias Erzberger was taken into the cabinet of peace-makers appointed in October 1918 to bring the war to an end. The Chancellor was a quiet Red Cross official who had married the daughter of an English duke. His name was Prince Max of Baden and his nickname was Max–Pax. Within three weeks he caught severe influenza, took too much sleeping draught and did not wake again until Turkey had surrendered and Austria sought an armistice. His ruinous re-awakening made him prejudiced against sleep. He avoided it and grew sallow.

It became clear to him and his cabinet that generals could not go to France to make an armistice. For their very names would provoke the Allies and they might also be unbending on terms.

On 6th November, in the late morning, there was a meeting of cabinet ministers in the Reichstag library. A secretary from the Chancellery acted as chairman in Max's absence. Max was trying to telephone the Kaiser who had fled a month before to Spa, to be with his soldiers. In fact he had taken up residence in the château de la Fraineuse outside the town and spent his days refusing to take up the telephone.

At the cabinet meeting in the Reichstag the secretary from the Chancellery opened his despatch case and took from it the one almost transparent sheet of paper that lay there. Only a few lines of typing stood on it; you could see that much even from the reverse side. The secretary read what was on the paper.

Secretary: Soviets have seized control of all utilities and communications in Lübeck, Hamburg, Brunsbüttel . . .

Erzberger thought of desecrated property and broken tabernacles. Schiedemann and Ebert, though socialist in name, also went numb at the word *soviet*. They were honest trade unionists, like Erzberger himself. Their idea of revolution was to give poor boys a chance to join the middleclass. Not soviets in Hamburg, Lübeck and God knew where else.

Secretary: The Chancellor appoints Minister of State Matthias Erzberger to lead an immediate Armistice Commission to the enemy lines on an axis of which Supreme Headquarters will inform him. At the earliest possible moment Herr Erzberger and other plenipotentiaries will be given their accreditations. They will travel to OHL, Spa, by special train. I wish them God speed and pledge them the gratitude of the German People.

Signed
MAX VON BADEN
Reichs Chancellor

No one spoke. Matthias Erzberger's stomach got very cold.

He thought, yes this is what is meant for me. To be told this is like coming on a lover unexpectedly in the dark. Or a murderer.

Erzberger: Not me.

A colleague called Trimborn told him he was the youngest.

Colleague: We others couldn't take on such a dangerous trip.

Erzberger: So you admit it's dangerous? Why me?

Colleague: It's your temperament, Matthias. To take on this sort of thing.

Matthias thought, you can't have it clearer. They've called me circumspect but I have no art to match that argument. *It's your temperament, Matthias.*

Secretary: Herr Erzberger, you will find waiting for you at the Foreign Office a communication received last night from the US Secretary of State. You'll take it with you as an entrée to the enemy. You don't have a lot of time – your train leaves Lehrter station at five o'clock this evening.

Erzberger: Who are the others? The other delegates?

30

Secretary: I'm afraid I don't know. I haven't seen His Excellency all morning. I was given this paper and the information about the American letter and the train. That's all.

Erzberger thought this has all the marks of dream: impossible time-tables, nebulous instructions, undisclosed fellow-travellers and destinations.

Erzberger: There's hardly time to pack.

No one bothered agreeing.

Erzberger: I must see the Chancellor.

Secretary: It may not be possible.

Erzberger: Five o'clock.

Secretary: A car is supposed to be waiting for you in the Platz. If not commandeer a lorry, a trap, anything.

Erzberger: Give me that piece of paper as authority.

The secretary seemed reluctant. Once he gave that up his briefcase would be empty for the first time in his career. At last he extracted it and laid it in the hand of Plenipotentiary Erzberger.

Erzberger Begins his Journey

Beyond the lobby and in the Platz soldiers were sitting on folded greatcoats on the steps of the Bismarck monument. Above fantastically expressive stone figures, the Iron-Chancellor thrust his granite belly towards the Generalstab Building.

One military sedan stood at the curb.

Erzberger: I am Staatsminister Matthias Erzberger. I need a driver.

The soldiers went on sitting on the steps. So close to the Generalstab Building. Admittedly protected from its windows by a bulk of statuary.

Erzberger: I am going to France to make a peace. I

demand the use of that vehicle so that I can call at the Foreign Office for my papers.

Two then immediately stood. One had an unsteady left leg, the other an annealed purple blur in place of an ear. After opening and closing the passenger-door for Erzberger, they both took the front seat.

Erzberger: Are the trams still running in Leipzigerstrasse?

Soldier: Yes. Some people are even shopping. And there's a lot of tub-thumping.

Erzberger: All right. Go by the Gate.

He thought, the most frightening rebellion is the rebellion of those with the habit of obedience. Last year when the French soldiers mutinied these men stayed docile. Their discipline made them by-words from San Francisco to Tomsk: they have visible marks of it. Why aren't they intimidated any more by the Renaissance conceits of the Reichstag Building, by the lowering classicism of the Generalstab office, by the Gothic cathedral? On 6 November 1918 army privates were surrounded by the overbearing forces of architecture and couldn't give a damn.

Three blocks down Wilhelmstrasse the sedan stopped. Here too, soldiers and factory hands from the industrial suburbs conferred as they pleased against the iron railings on the far side of the street. On the departmental statuary in front of Government buildings sat picric-tainted munitions workers and a few yellowed pretty girls playing at socialist beneath the brims of their Sunday hats.

The Foreign Office lobby was empty. It made Erzberger's breath catch and ears ring to see it that way: he felt like an archaeologist entering a ruin.

On the second floor a tall official stood in the corridor polishing pince-nez, squinting in the direction of Erzberger's passage up the marble stairs. As it happened they knew each other. The official's name was Kniege. A man of some importance, head of their legal section.

Kniege: I knew it was you.

Erzberger: Did you?

Kniege: Well, it certainly wasn't socialists. I'd imagine any socialist would run up such stairs, wouldn't he? It's part of their religion isn't it? Running upstairs with red banners.

Erzberger: It isn't part of mine.

Kniege: No. I could tell it was a heavy man. Come in. The Chancellor telephoned me. About the document you were to be given.

All the loyal clocks of *Legal Section* were banging away – they had inherited the empty offices.

Kniege handed him the document from the United States. There was jealousy, retentiveness in Kniege's hand.

Erzberger: My entrée.

Kniege: I see.

Erzberger: Could I have an attaché-case for this? My train leaves at five and I have nothing to carry things in.

Kniege: Your train leaves at five.

Erzberger: And my accreditation documents. Where are they?

Kniege knew nothing about accreditation.

Kniege: Accreditation for what?

Erzberger explained. He saw Kniege's upper lip fluttering.

Kniege: They could have told me.

Erzberger: I devoutly wish they had, Herr Kniege.

Kniege: What did they think? That I'd make things difficult for you? I've never been one of those who poke fun at your country ways. Or your clothes. Or your boots. I've never shown you the slightest condescension.

Erzberger had been member for Biberach since 1901, and was by now too used to the hauteur of the Prussian civil service to argue with it this Wednesday.

Erzberger: There must be accreditation letters.

Kniege: The Chancellor rushed in this morning. But he signed no documents. That I know of. Would you care to follow me?

He led Erzberger down a corridor of marble. Teutonic goddesses with big hips and dense frowns went on setting an example to the vanished staff of the Imperial Foreign Office. Erzberger and Kniege entered an immense carpeted Hall set with tidy desks, as if for an examination. A milky sun was already low down in the tall barred windows. The chief of

Legal Section unlocked a door at the far end of the hall. Inside, amongst dim rows of filing cabinets, stood three men in worn suits. Alarmed by the opening of the door, they had rifles in their hands. At one end of the filing room a fire had been lit; logs and full coal-bins flanked it. It spat an ember.

Erzberger was aware of the heat pressing his cheeks and could hear the hissing breath of a clerk with bronchitis.

Kniege pointed to the fire.

Kniege: In case of revolution. Documents we don't want outsiders to set eyes on. These brave fellows . . .

One of the brave fellows held his rifle by the muzzle, as if needing it as a crutch. Seventy years. Yes, seventy. Erzberger suffered a ten-second certainty of never reaching seventy and for the same period detested the old clerk's inane survival in a bad suit.

He looked a gentle and reliable old man.

A second of his colleagues came fully out of the shadow of the particular filing cabinet he was meant to protect to the death. He must have weighed 270 pounds. His face was purple.

Erzberger thought, the Foreign Office elite corps! The less trusty (it seemed), the less battle-worthy, had been sent home.

Kniege spoke to the purple man.

Kniege: Did the Chancellor deposit any documents for Herr E-R-Z-B-E-R-G-E-R this morning?

Purple Man: No sir. He signed in no documents. He left nothing for transmission.

Erzberger: You're sure? He couldn't have left it with another section?

Purple Man: This is central filing, sir. Fetch the Chancellor's file, Herr Walsmier, if you please.

The old man found a thick file in a top drawer. His purple colleague opened it to the business of that day. It was a copy of a memorandum from Max-Pax indicating that he had read the letter transmitted by Secretary of State Robert Lansing and that it was essential that copies be given or transmitted to all members of the proposed armistice commission and to General Groener, First Quartermaster-General, OHL, Spa. It was signed by the Chancellor.

That was all Max had left for him in the hot room. Am I fainting? Erzberger wondered. Bile moved in his throat. He would have put his head against the wall and been sick if it had not been for the three filing clerks, watching him so intimately, as if for an excuse to start the feverish incineration of German history.

Erzberger: My train leaves at five.

Kniege: It's nearly two now.

Matthias thought of sending one of the three clerks home to fetch what he needed for a journey of three or four nights. But he couldn't choose which one was least likely to die with his linen and toiletries, of burst hearts and aneurisms, half-way between Schöneberg and the railway station.

Erzberger: I admire you, gentlemen. I'm going to the Chancellery. If the Chancellor comes here, telephone me.

The urgency he'd picked up in the overheated annexe stayed with him in the corridors. Calling Goodbye to Kniege he ran downstairs into the lobby where four sentries from the Berlin garrison, whom he hadn't seen on his way in, presented arms. Where had they been? In the toilets reading socialist material? Or perhaps something as innocent as pornography.

Herr Erzberger and a Seditious Telephone

The car, still crewed by his two maimed soldiers, bore him back up Wilhelmstrasse to the Chancellery. All the way he inspected the state of his cuffs. I know I have no name for style. But am I meant to appear before the Marshal in a dirty collar? Something will have to be done.

Max's office was on the second floor. Only a few Chancellery officials were in sight. In this state of chaotic vacancy the imperial decor looked flatulent, an opera set the morning after the performance.

One of the Chancellor's senior secretaries went to the door of his master's office and threw it wider open to show Herr Erzberger there was no one inside.

They began a crazy and (from the secretary's side) formal conversation:

Erzberger: Oh God.

Secretary: Sir.

Erzberger: Do you realize my train leaves at 5 p.m.?

Secretary: The Chancellor is at Berlin Garrison HQ trying to compose a joint statement by telephone with General Groener.

Erzberger: Joint statement?

Secretary: For public release. Informing citizens that an armistice commission is being sent.

Erzberger: Holy God! Wouldn't it be wiser to give me my papers first?

Secretary: I think His Excellency considers it more important that people should *know* an armistice is being sought. An hour's delay here or there in actually despatching commissioners . . .

Erzberger: Have you had contact with any other members of the proposed commission . . .?

Secretary: Our Secretary in Copenhagen, Count Brockdorff-Rantzau, is the only other member I heard the Chancellor mention.

Erzberger: Is Brockdorff-Rantzau on his way? Here? Or to Spa?

Secretary: I told him by telephone to Copenhagen this morning.

Erzberger: How can he get to Berlin in time to catch the five o'clock train?

Secretary: It's impossible. I knew nothing of this five o'clock train. That was someone else's arrangement.

In Herr Erzberger's rare mood of Kismet, to find those accreditation documents and to catch the five o'clock train had become crucial objectives in their own right. The world had lost its way forever if these simple goals could not be attained.

Already it was a quarter to three.

Erzberger: Do you think you can get me through to Garrison HQ? I must speak to the Chancellor.

Secretary: Come in. I'll try.

The secretary let him into the office of Prince Max von Baden. The desk was clear of anything but a telephone – it looked as if even the blotting paper had been hidden away to save it from revolutionary hands. A photograph of an overly handsome Kaiser, dressed in the style of Lohengrin, was the only decoration to the walls.

The Secretary picked up the telephone. Inanely scabbed with *fin de siècle* ornamentation, it served to augment Matthias Erzberger's secret frenzy.

Deep in the Chancellery a single telephonist was on duty.

The secretary gave Erzberger the telephone. He seemed to be saying I've done what I could. Now I don't want to hear the noise of chaos on the far end of the line.

Voice: Hello. Major Heindorff, wine-procuring officer, Berlin Garrison.

Erzberger: My God, you're still working?

Voice: I've been at this work for eighteen years, sir.

Erzberger told him who he was, and that somewhere in the garrison buildings was the Chancellor, perhaps, sitting at a telephone. Matthias suggested that Heindorff should consider it his day for procuring chancellors.

Voice: He'd be in the communications room, no doubt. Perhaps I can get you transferred. But the privates who run the switchboard have all gone socialist. They switched you through to me for a joke.

Erzberger: Tell them it's a message for the Chancellor. About an armistice. They want an armistice, don't they?

Waiting. The secretary would not look at him other than sideways. I am the most inauspicious diplomat he's ever talked to. Yet, as if I were going to a wedding, I wish to catch that train.

And is the line dead or vacant? What tricks were the

Spartacist privates playing down that vacant well the telephone imposed on his ear?

Voice: Reichschancellor.

Erzberger: Erzberger, sir. I'm calling from your office.

Voice: Oh.

Erzberger: I can't find my accreditation documents.

Voice: Accreditation.

Erzberger: For the armistice commission.

Voice: Of course. You must forgive me, Matthias. You go to Spa and I'll send Brockdorff-Rantzau on after you with the accreditations.

Scapegoat, perhaps. But there are corners of the wilderness I will still not go to without proper papers.

Erzberger: I'm afraid I can't go to Spa without the documents. I'd be defenceless before the Supreme Command, before the Kaiser. Also Brockdorff-Rantzau will take too long to catch me up. Can't you consider anyone else?

Voice: Oh God, it's too much.

Erzberger: For all of us, sir.

Voice: Is Threme there?

Erzberger: Yes.

Voice: Put him on.

Erzberger pushed the receiver at the secretary. While Threme spoke . . . Yes, sir. Yes I have his home number . . . Matthias Erzberger watched substantial storm clouds circling at their ease in the east and below them the nameless government offices, hives of good clerks, the railings, the trees, the drifts of poplar and linden leaves, the newly insolent soldiers and lathe operators scuffing, kicking, rearranging them with their boots. It was so late in the autumn, someone should have by now swept up the dead leaves.

Secretary: I'll tell him, sir.

He put the receiver down. Minister of State Erzberger, sniffing conspiracy, had even raised his walking stick a little.

Erzberger: You hung up!

Secretary: There was nothing more to discuss, sir.

Erzberger: I'm the judge.

Secretary: The Chancellor told me to request you to catch

your train. He has decided to appoint Count Maiberling of this office to the Commission.

Erzberger: Count Maiberling is my friend . . .

He remembered a pleasant diplomat in Sofia. Together they had talked to the Bulgarian foreign minister, eaten state dinners, afterwards, drunk at their hotels, made private jokes about their hosts. For such purposes the Count made a good companion.

Now in the hollow Chancellery, a flush of paranoid fear came over Staatsminister Erzberger. Someone has cleverly marked the count and his friend Matthias for the irksome journey. Some David was choosing appropriate Uriahs. Except that Maiberling and I . . . we never tasted any regal whore. Unless you considered a seat on the board of Thyssen's to be commerce with harlots. Or took note of the few milk-white Bulgar girls the count had thrown in my path.

Secretary: The accreditations will be made out and handed to you at the train. There won't be another Spa special till tomorrow evening, you see. You will have to travel with some of General Groener's staff officers who are returning to OHL. The Chancellor is sure you won't mind that, Herr Erzberger. You always got on well with officers.

Erzberger: In the early days. Not for the past few years.

Secretary: Quite . . . I'll telephone Count Maiberling.

Downstairs the two soldiers were still waiting by the sedan. This was strange constancy by the standards of the day. Why were they so attentive? Assassins! his guts told him. Assassins are always attentive.

Erzberger told them he wanted to go to Schöneberg. He said he'd show them the way.

All the way south-west he watched the driver's luminously pink and junked ear. It shone like a rose in the half-light, like the vulva of a woman.

Erzberger tapped on the glass to break up this too clear and, for the moment, too threatening image.

Erzberger: Off the Bayerischer Platz!

The house stood behind a modest stucco wall. Unhappily there was no one in it. Paula, with Maria the spiritual adolescent and infant Gabrielle, was staying with friends in a bungalow in the woods on Grosser Wansee, where the pleasure boats used to sail all summer. November, and such a November as this, had turned it into a muted, private place. This bereaved November his own house seemed dead. It gave off cold of its own.

Old Dieter answered the door.

Erzberger: Aren't you cold, Dieter?

Dieter had once done military service and lost his left eye in Tanga. He let one believe the eye had been poked out by some tribesman. But knowing that Herr Erzberger was an expert on German Africa, never offered too much vivid testimony about the supposed battle in which it had been lost. He wore an exquisite glass eye from Bohemia, piercing and young in the old face and beside the bloodshot other eye.

Dieter: I've got a fire in the back room, sir.

Erzberger: Good. I've to pack my bag, Dieter. I'm making a journey. While I'm upstairs don't let anyone in.

It wasn't like packing for a routine journey. He handled with some hunger his toiletries, his clean linen, the celluloid collars, the neckties, the better overcoat (fur-trimmed neck). He packed them with some tenderness. The fashionable might laugh at me for my country clothes but my God, garments – plentiful and of thick weave – reassure me.

He didn't call Dieter to carry the case: he wanted to be out of the house. When he got downstairs both the soldiers were in the hall and the front door stood ajar.

Erzberger: Dieter, I said . . .

Dieter: But sir, they were soldiers. I thought soldiers . . .

Erzberger couldn't explain to the old man how soldiers had suddenly turned assertive, grown ironic about the eyes. These two seemed to be on the look-out for things to pocket. The limpy one stopped in front of a hanging photograph of Oskar.

He turned to Erzberger with authority.

Soldier: Your boy?

Erzberger: He died in training. Three weeks back.

He felt that he betrayed Oskar in being afraid to say *officer-school.*

The soldier shook his head with a sort of schoolmasterly annoyance, as if he were saying, of course, of course, tell me something fresh.

Erzberger: I have to catch the five o'clock from Lehrter.

It seemed to him he'd been repeating that formula all afternoon.

The soldiers eyed each other. They appeared to be holding a secret vote between themselves. The one with the smashed ear suddenly opened the door for him.

Erzberger: Dieter, these are bad times. Lock the main gate after I've gone and answer it only to people you know. Trot down to the police station and tell Inspector Martensen that I'm away on government business.

Dieter carried the bag. In the autumn garden the pruned roses stuck up as awkwardly as the improvised grave markers he had seen so much of. Before he lost the confidence of the officer corps and was no longer invited to the front.

The second he saw Count Maiberling pushing schnapps down in the saloon, he understood *this isn't the man I knew at Sofia.* This is too pale, too slumped in a corner chair. The long neck at full stretch; Maiberling keeping a weather eye on the staff officers quietly drinking coffee at a table close by.

He seemed to maintain awareness of them over his lowered right shoulder even after he sighted Erzberger and smiled, and offered him the flask, holding it high as a person does for an athlete who has just broken the tape.

Erzberger: I'm sorry.

He meant, for landing you here.

Maiberling: I can understand them picking you. A cabinet minister. But me? I'm no potentate.

Erzberger: Are you frightened?

Maiberling: Are you?

Erzberger: I don't think we have much to fear.

Maiberling: Bloody liar!

Receiving back the flask, Maiberling topped it and put it in his coat pocket.

Maiberling: Me? I feel imposed on. As if they skimmed off

four layers of dignitaries to unearth me. Maybe a little excited as well.

He hit the pillow behind his head. It was embroidered with a Hohenzollern eagle.

Maiberling: I like *train* travel.

At five to five no documents had come from the Chancellery. Erzberger went to see the young general who was travelling with them.

The general regretted the train had to go on the second. He was under orders in that matter. General Groener, the new Quartermaster-General, was an expert on railway systems and had decided that in view of the chaos the best hope was to be obedient to time-tables.

Erzberger decided the railway people themselves would be easier to sway. He thought he might begin with the engineer.

As he dismounted from the saloon he saw a middle-aged man in a shiny civil-service suit and wing collar crossing the tracks at a half-run towards the Spa special.

The civil servant had an envelope in the hand he extended to Erzberger. The envelope carried a red chancellery seal and a thick official nap in which the man's sweaty fingermarks were visible.

Breaking the seal, Erzberger's hand scrabbled inside the envelope for the documents. Expecting they might become butterflies and decamp across the shafts of lamplight from platform 3.

Official: His Excellency says the last two named will be waiting for you at Spa.

The document read:

1. Full Power.

The undersigned, Chancellor of the German Empire, Max, Prince von Baden, hereby gives full power:

To Imperial Secretary of State, Matthias Erzberger (as President of the delegation) . . .

Erzberger sought the railing by the carriage door. The word *President* scorpioned up his arm and bit him on the underside of his brain.

Erzberger: You go!

Official: I beg your pardon, sir.

Erzberger: You go! Anyone will do as president of the commission, it seems. So *you* go!

Official: I think you're making a joke, sir.

Erzberger: My God I am.

He climbed aboard and waved the documents towards Maiberling, who now had definitely taken on the air of a man off on holidays. All he lacked was a lumpy wife and brats.

Erzberger: They've arrived, Alfred.

Maiberling: Well. We're away then.

Erzberger: Yes.

He thought: Matthias Erzberger, reliable stall-holder in the Reichstag cowmarket, sometimes known to have given inside advice to the barons of coal and steel and chemicals if they were decent barons and his workaday conscience was not defiled. But in questions of Paula and children, in questions of war and brotherhood of nations, he presumed to strain towards idealism and vision, and even wrote books that resembled the American President's books. For though he might be a fat-arsed Württemberger, his spirit was as trim as President Wilson's. And it was exactly the gap between his knockabout commercial morals and his high conscience of the home and printing press that would not be forgiven. And for which he was put on a train and sent to be punished.

Maiberling: Sit down then. A brown study, you.

Erzberger: I was having indecent thoughts.

Maiberling: You bloody peasants. Cocks like fire-hoses!

It was not a subject Erzberger wanted to spend time on. He excused himself and moved back into the ante-room at the end of the carriage.

The whole train spat steam, steam whirled past the saloon door as a porter slammed it shut. The man from the

Chancellery still stood on the platform wiping his face. Like the last well-wisher on earth. Erzberger continued to read

. . . as President of the delegation;
   To Imperial Envoy Extraordinary and Minister Plenipotentiary, Count Alfred Maiberling, and
   To Major-General Detlev von Winterfeldt, Royal Prussian Army, to conduct in the name of the German Government with the plenipotentiaries of the Powers allied against Germany, negotiations for an armistice and to conclude an agreement to that effect, provided the same be approved by the German Government.

> Berlin, November 6, 1918
> (signed) Max, Prince von Baden

There was another thick official page.

   2. As additional plenipotentiary, Captain Vanselow of the Imperial German Navy is appointed and the name of General Erich von Gundell is removed . . .

On a third sheet, typing-paper this time, was written:

   The general and Vanselow are at OHL. Obtain what mercy you can, Matthias, but for God's sake make peace.

> Max

Erzberger found himself shivering and . . . what? . . . weeping. He tore this last message into halves, quarters, eighths, and so on, all the time hiding at the end of the carriage. Then he lowered the window and the fierce November air buffeted him. He let Max's little message flutter back down the length of the train, and saw half-blinded, the elegant suburb of Tiergarten. He felt sure that as soon as it withdrew from his vision it would reform itself into a new pattern of evocations. The same bricks would have a different meaning for a returning Matthias Erzberger. Who had always wanted to be rich enough to live there.

The Marshal Meets Some Sailors

Late in the morning of 7 November a black limousine flying a wet British naval pennon drew up at the château of Senlis.

From it stepped a rather fleshy British admiral in a top-coat, and three aides. When the chasseurs presented arms at the door the tremendous slap of boots, and of butts on palms, dislodged his monocle and he turned and laughed with his aides after putting it back in his eye socket. In his office Marshal Foch heard the barking laugh *that* race emits and knew the British Naval plenipotentiaries had arrived.

Though he made a face he was reminded of his good friend Henry Wilson, *Double-Vay*. But *Double-Vay* was an exceptional Briton, half-Irish for leavening; accused of being a frog-lover for bringing some of the Marshal's teaching techniques into the lecture-halls at Camberley. *If there's any frog I love it's you, you little bastard. Double-Vay* was the Marshal's one Englishman. So it was hopeless to look for any lasting remembrances from the laughter of British admirals.

At the moment *Double-Vay* sat with the Welsh lecher in Versailles. The Marshal thought it would have been more pleasant if the British, instead of trying him with sailors he did not know, had empowered dear old *Double-Vay* to travel with him to the forest.

The Marshal told Major Ferrason to fetch the arrivals into the office.

He thought, if I speak to them in English I won't have to tell them as much. I can be ambiguous.

When they came in he was standing with his hip hitched on his desk. He extended his hand flatly, as if for licking, to the monocled admiral.

45

The Marshal: First Sea Lord Veems. Very happy.

Wemyss: Sir. We have glimpsed each other over the conference table at Quai d'Orsay. Also . . .

The Marshal: . . . at Le Trianon. I have not forgot. Introduce me if you will to your staffs.

Wemyss took on the stance for it.

Wemyss: Admiral George Hope . . . Captain Marriott . . . Bagot here.

The Marshal: There. Yes. Bagot.

Admiral Hope and the two juniors had those amazingly *mens sana* faces the English are capable of carrying into middle age. I wonder, thought the Marshal, were they artfully chosen to demonstrate the racial pretensions of the British.

Lord Wemyss wore a beefy and more complex face.

Wemyss: We can all speak French, sir. In fact we've been rather looking forward to having scope to use it . . .

The Marshal: Your generals have little gift for the same . . .

Wemyss: An unhappy imbalance.

The Marshal: No, no, let this old man do the better he can with your jewel language. Some cognac first. For the coldness.

His moustache quivered at one corner and Ferrason poured five cognacs. Wemyss smiled a little, secretly. A these-French-are-like-head-waiters smile. Or so the Marshal read it.

Wemyss: Too kind.

They received and held their glasses till the Marshal had been served. Then the Marshal bowed to them and they began sipping.

The Marshal: A long way from the sea, gentlemen.

The First Sea Lord wagged his finger.

Wemyss: Still, the sea is there.

The Marshal: I did not mean argumentative. I just remarked. Have you any hunger?

Wemyss: We had a picnic basket in the back of the car, Monsieur Marshal.

The Marshal: How jolly.

Wemyss: Quite pleasant.

The First Sea Lord composed his face roguishly. The glint in his monocle threatened, two more sips and then we start talking about the German fleet. There was a theatricality, a straining in the new tone of the features. The Marshal resented it and was bored. He decided he'd get rid of them till train departure. Wemyss had none of the ease of wit of old *Double-Vay*, his dear British general. Who would have loped into the room saying, "Here comes the ugliest man in the British Army. And how's the little Frenchman today, how's little Monsieur Foch, where is the little bastard, is he hiding from me? . . . There he is, behind the third paperclip on the left!"

Maxime Weygand came in. Neat as a pin for the journey. Neat as a jockey in silks. Able to tell from the way the Marshal's eyes were shifting that he was to take away, entertain, buffer his Marshal from, the Royal Navy.

The Marshal: My General Weygand, these are my dear brothers in *victoire* from the Fleet of the British Navy. Will you please look to them with all care for me.

Weygand bowed and took an ushering-out stance at the office door. The First Sea Lord could tell he was being dismissed.

Wemyss: A second, Monsieur Marshal.

The Marshal spun and rushed to him, the manager of a first-class hotel rushing to an aggrieved celebrity.

Wemyss: I have to impress on you the seriousness of the naval demands.

The Marshal: I have the copy of what your Mr Lloyd George wants. Therefore it is serious enough for me. I will push the terms to the Germans.

The First Sea Lord's mouth hung a little agape; a wince of bellicose amusement.

Wemyss: It's the spirit in which they're put, my Marshal. Not that I . . .

The Marshal: I will not put it to them for the fun, Lord Veems. I will put nothing to them for the fun.

Wemyss: Quite. However, I must say I would be quite

happy to undertake the bulk of the debate on the naval terms. Under your chairmanship.

The Marshal: Yes, yes. You are the one who knows boats. Excuse me now. If you hope to rest, write letters, use some telephone, General Weygand will be happy . . .

General Weygand stirred at their flank. For some reason his decorum reminded the Marshal for the first time in months of the rumour that Maxime was the bastard of the Empress of Mexico, a lady still alive in Brussels but in bad mental health. In four years the Marshal had never had the ill-grace to ask General Weygand was it true.

From this daydream of Carlotta's widowhood (soon to be recaptured by the British Army bearing up the road from Tournai) Lord Wemyss distracted him.

Wemyss: We haven't been told where the meetings will be held.

The Marshal: The place for the armistice isn't here. This town of Senlis is taken by our enemy for small whiles in 1914. While they are here they executed the mayor and numbers of hostage you understand. So the place for the armistice isn't here.

Wemyss: I see. Might I ask where?

The Marshal: In a forest.

Wemyss: I say, this just isn't good enough sir. We *are* plenipotentiaries, you know.

The Marshal acknowledged how reasonable the First Sea Lord's aggression was by shaking his hands contritely before his face.

The Marshal: The language slowness! The place is la Forêt de l'Aigle. Seven kilometres on the other side from Compiègne. The railway siding called Rethondes. It is private and every comfort for our British brothers.

Admiral Hope spoke – a lean one, sun-tanned, perhaps from service in the Indian Ocean. A long way from the great bloodletting.

Hope: Sir. What time are the German plenipotentiaries due at Rethondes?

The Marshal: Nine o'clock. Midnight. They have difficult travel, roads all over with holes. From Tergnier they travel by the train. The saloon-car for them to sit in is saloon-car belonged to Napoleon the Third. Eh? Eh?

But the admiral's eyes remained blank before the niceness of this arrangement. If Wemyss answered at all it was only for the sake of tact.

Wemyss: Excellent.

The Marshal: You will wish to know what people are their delegates. My Chief of Staffs will tell you their names. I am forgotten them myself. They are nobody I hear of.

But when the naval men had been taken out by Weygand, his Anglophobia ran through him as a tremor and he indulged himself by repeating all four names to himself. Erzberger, he said. Herr Matthias. Maiberling, Count Alfred. Von Winterfeldt, Major-General Detlev. Vanselow, Christian name not supplied, humble naval man.

Come oh you Holy Spirit and fill the hearts of your believers . . .

Erzberger Orders a Truck

A little earlier that same morning a general and three junior staff officers, Herr Matthias Erzberger and Count Alfred Maiberling stood amongst wrought-iron fragilities that held up the station awning in the bijou Belgian town of Spa and looked about for the staff-cars that should meet dignitaries at any time, let alone a morning of downpour. The young general seemed to want to exculpate OHL.

The General: We were delayed by all those troop trains. Then the railway people probably told them we wouldn't be in till noon say. Something like that.

Maiberling still retained his semi-hysterical holiday posture, a little strengthened it seemed by a hangover. It was all a poor mask for his infectious terror. But when he spoke he sounded rosy, gratified.

Maiberling: All over Germany the time-tables are coming

unstapled, they're blowing out the window, leaf by bloody leaf. The rule books are coming unglued.

General: Not at the Grand Hôtel Britannique.

Erzberger himself had caught a dose of Maiberling's new insanity. In his brain and diaphragm the machines of urgency were burring without cease or mercy. Maiberling's indulgence in metaphor, the general's threadbare pride, made him itch with fury.

He began raking his chest with an ungloved hand.

Erzberger: There are three army lorries in the goods yard. I can see them from here. Get one immediately please General.

The general frowned.

General: There's no room in a truck. For the other gentlemen.

Maiberling: They could just hang on. They're soldiers, aren't they?

General: As you say.

Maiberling: You know, I've never driven in a lorry before.

Erzberger wanted to speak to him, straighten him up. But not in front of the general.

Now the two young staff officers marched across the railway square towards the goods yards. Rain swallowed up the authoritative clop of their boots. The general squinted upwards through the downpour. It seemed that the matt ceiling of storm-cloud wasn't much higher than the roofs of the offices across the square.

General: You don't have a good day for travel, gentlemen.

He began to wander about the railway entrance, taking different sightings on the weather, as if for the benefit of the plenipotentiaries. Maiberling called to him. Amicably.

Maiberling: You're in charge of the weather office?

The general coughed and did not look at them.

General: Chemical warfare, sir. Much the same thing.

Maiberling whispered to Erzberger.

Maiberling: Christ, a barbarian.

Erzberger wondered at the count for allowing himself

such luxuries: once we are through the French lines *we* shall be the monsters and we will be liable for the mustard-gassed and the torpedoed corpses. Whether or not we feel spasms of righteousness in the drenched railway square of Spa, no one will credit us with it.

Dead-Eye Maiberling

Maiberling wouldn't be quiet, trembling a little, pointing towards the general.

Maiberling: How would you like to have a son who . . .?

Erzberger: Shut up, Alfred.

Maiberling: Listen, in the past, when I felt better . . . I wrote letters to the Red Cross on the question of . . .

Erzberger: I know. Of gas.

Maiberling: Of gas.

Erzberger: Alfred, you aren't yourself. Why did you come?

Maiberling whispered.

Maiberling: I hate the reds. I hate the war.

Erzberger: Yes. But the generals. There aren't even cars to meet us. We have to be careful they don't treat us with contempt.

Maiberling: Don't worry.

The count put his arm around Erzberger's shoulder and pulled him close – overcoat against overcoat. From the left-hand insides of his own great overcoat he hauled a vast service revolver. He turned it about in the wet air, as if saying *our secret*.

Erzberger: Why in God's name?

The unexpected appearance of weapons always frightened Matthias Erzberger. The faint oil-and-cordite odour of the count's revolver stretched his nostrils wide. Did Maiberling know something – that plenipotentiaries would be ambushed in corridor or street or forest? By the unappeasable young officers who didn't want a bargained end to war, whose taste was Götterdämmerung?

Maiberling: I've heard nothing. But these bastards . . . OHL . . . they're a different race. (He shook the weapon.) Go armed amongst strangers.

Erzberger: For Christ's sake. Put it away.

Maiberling did so. Now that Erzberger knew the revolver was there its contour seemed a howling variation in the accepted shape of decent civilian overcoats.

Erzberger: It's pulling your clothes out of true.

Maiberling: A small sacrifice.

Erzberger: We've been promised the gratitude of the German people.

Maiberling: Words. You're a politician. You *know* about words.

Erzberger: I know. Just the same . . .

Considerately the general stayed aloof, idly reading a decree the government of occupation had posted on the station wall.

Maiberling: What are you carrying?

Erzberger: For protection? Nothing.

Maiberling: What?

Erzberger: It didn't occur . . .

Maiberling: I'll get you one. I'll lift one off an officer for you. At OHL.

Matthias exhaled his fear, his resentment at suffering fears. It all rose as robust steam towards the dripping roof.

Erzberger: Anyone might be shot these days. If they want to shoot us now or afterwards, they will. You have to be even-minded about it.

Maiberling: Sod it. I refuse to be even-minded about getting a bullet.

A military lorry from the goods yard came humming up to them. The two young staff-officers, knowing their place, were standing on the back, gaping like postilions over the roof of the cabin.

Erzberger, Maiberling, the general crushed in with the driver. All the crammed bodies and overcoats filled the cabin space with a gentle vapour smelling rather of camphor, cigar smoke and the dust they had brought from Berlin.

Maiberling again assumed his idiot-tourist demeanour.

Maiberling: These are really first class. I'm going to get one of these after the conflict. Put the servants in the back . . .

Does he actually hope, Erzberger wondered, that his small talk will winkle out the extremists, the stand-to-the-death-men at OHL? That they will creep up on him in the lounge of the Hôtel Britannique but he will whirl and shoot them down? Dead-eye Maiberling!

The Grand Hotel

The Supreme Command's hotel looked like any opulent hotel in any resort. It kept a sober face on a narrow commercial street but had the ingrained promise of high ceilings, brocade panelling, gold scroll-work, chandeliers and great fire-places. Rain pelted the Imperial eagle over its lobby . . . *Under your wings safely I can do my ironing.* The eagle and the sentries before the door could not altogether dissuade Erzberger that inside he might find wealthy men reading tranquil pre-war news and rich aunts talking about East African railway stock.

The general in charge of gas sent Erzberger through the glass doors first. In the lobby the tone of things reassured Matthias still more. A few orderlies worked behind the reception desk and by the lift a middle-aged lieutenant sat at a card-table like a waiter posted in the height of the season to take guests' reservations for dinner. In a seat by a good fire a lonely naval officer drank coffee, eyes fixed on the silver pot, and in the lounge a dozen regimental officers, called to OHL for some reason, glad to have been summoned in from the rain for whatever cause, drank schnapps and holidayed close to still another high blaze.

One of these men looked up suddenly, his head jolted back as if he could smell a politician at some distance. He was about twenty-six or -seven. He wore a major's rank. His eyes were deep-set and bruised. Matthias Erzberger knew immediately: one day in the armistice I will make, in the peace that will then be made, that boy – being beyond my diplomatic exertions – intends to blow his head off.

The chemical general told the orderlies that General Groener and the Field-Marshal von Hindenburg were absent, over at the château de la Fraineuse making a morning report to their emperor. So a breakfast tray was ordered for Matthias and the count.

Orderly: Would the gentlemen like it in here or in the lounge?

Maiberling whispered at Matthias.

Maiberling: Make it the lounge. I could lift you one of those fellows' Lugers. They're quite pissed, you notice.

Erzberger shivered. The count's brain was stewing apart like a boiled onion. Yet if I mention it I'll be given another stiff general in his place.

Erzberger spoke to the orderly.

Erzberger: In here thank you. By the fire.

Maiberling: And a bottle of schnapps thanks. On the tray.

Erzberger Meets the Naval Delegate

They found places at the fire and nodded to the naval officer. He immediately stood and approached them. He may have had an injured neck, for he carried his chin tight-in against his collar. You could barely see the Iron Cross at his collar-button for the shadow his locked chin threw.

Naval Man: Captain Vanselow from High Seas Fleet. I know who you gentlemen are.

Erzberger: Then you also know . . .?

Vanselow: About my own appointment? Yes sir. I got a cable. About midnight.

Erzberger: You'd have been told then. How we're to travel.

Vanselow: I'm not aware that arrangements have yet been made . . .

You could be sure his jaw bone clung even more strenuously to his collar.

Erzberger: No arrangements?

Vanselow: No secretary's been appointed. There aren't any vehicles allocated . . .

Maiberling: Never discount the worthy push-bike.

Erzberger thought, if it's like yesterday, the chasing-about, I'll *need* a pistol. But to suicide with.

Coffee and schnapps, rolls and butter were laid out on the table close by. Maiberling immediately poured three measures of liquor and handed one each to Erzberger and the captain. The captain received his but put it to one side.

Erzberger: Have you been here long?

Vanselow: Since Tuesday morning. As the train left Kiel I could hear shooting. It seems it was the marines shooting at sailors.

Maiberling was already draining his second glass of fire-water.

Maiberling: So the marines retained their political purity, eh? Virgins on Walpurgis Night.

Vanselow: They're more in the nature of policemen.

Maiberling: Quite.

Vanselow: It wasn't such a bad idea.

Maiberling: Idea! *Idea?*

Clearly he thought the word pretentious. But Vanselow, an uncomplicated man, believed the count was asking for a briefing.

Vanselow: The general strategy. To send the light vessels into the Thames estuary and draw out the British fleet into our minefields. Then our submarines would have moved in. Then we ourselves. The four squadrons.

Maiberling got very bellicose, as if Vanselow were pushing some naïve and fundamentalist view of the world.

Maiberling: Do you think the British would have been led by the nose like that?

Vanselow: Perhaps. It was worth a try-out.

Maiberling: Christ. It ended with Germans shooting Germans.

He was on his third double-measure. What price his trigger-finger now? Erzberger thought.

Vanselow: There were mad rumours amongst the sailors – that there'd be a duel to the death between the British fleet and ours. On the flag-deck I distinctly heard a sailor use the words "death-ride!"

Maiberling: Perceptive, I call that.

But the captain's flat jaw, backed by his collar, was proof against low irony.

Vanselow: We made rendezvous in the Jade estuary. I was with Admiral Kraft on the *König*. No thanks, not another, Your Excellency. Well . . . well, if you must . . .

Maiberling: And what happened? On this dreadnought of yours?

Vanselow: The sailors were signalling . . . illegally . . . from ship to ship. Before sailing time Admiral Kraft and I got a message from the engine-room. The stokers were threatening to put their slicer-bars into the boilers. I quite realize the mysteries of the steam turbine might mean little to you. But the stokers put in the slicer-bars, draw the coals out on to the floor plates, hose them down.

Erzberger: In brief, stop the boilers.

Maiberling: Our Matthias isn't slow!

Vanselow: That's right. Stop the boilers. Under this threat we signalled Admiral Hipper. It seems Hipper was getting the same message from all the battleships in all the squadrons. Terrible news for a Grand Seas admiral to get . . . On the *König* we had a conference on the bridge. Admiral Kraft, all senior officers. We'd armed ourselves. But the captain of the marines told us the sailors had emptied most of the arms chests amidships. We decided to pipe all hands to sea details. Sailors never disobey that . . .

Captain Vanselow gave a little moan and tears came out on his cheeks.

Vanselow: I became a cadet in 1891. I won the Tirpitz Medal at the Kiel Naval Academy. I was a liberal officer. I never hit a sailor.

Though Matthias did not expect it, the count was quite disarmed to see Captain Vanselow fall apart.

Maiberling: You oughtn't to take it personally. It's happening all over the country.

Vanselow made a fist of his right hand. A wart stood on it which he scratched dementedly. My God, Erzberger prayed. It's in our hands. Maiberling drunk, riotous, trigger happy. A weeping captain. Me, dreaming of umbrellas and hatchetmen.

Vanselow: You have to forgive me. Every time sea details were ever piped, from 1891 till now, sailors ran on deck. I'm not an artistic man, gentlemen. That was the height of art for me. Sailors. In sea boots. Answering the pipe.

Erzberger: Of course. We understand.

He nearly said *Don't labour it!*

Vanselow: That morning they ignored the order. They rushed below decks. Into the cable compartment. They wouldn't obey. They sang Red songs down there. I suggested to Admiral Kraft that we ought to pipe quarters for inspection and see if they'd obey. We did. They did. They just wouldn't raise anchor though. They wouldn't go to sea.

With his knowledge of long-standing about the war being lost, Erzberger felt peevish towards the captain, lashes still twinkling with tears, but his loss, it seemed, narrow; squadron loss, divisional.

Erzberger: You would have? You would have gone to sea?

Vanselow: I hate death. I hate pain. But in the fleet we'd begun to feel we were only paper tonnages. Statistics for diplomats to gesture with whenever they got round to sitting down with the enemy.

Maiberling: Now *you're* the diplomat. Now *you* make the gestures.

But Vanselow still answered Erzberger, as if three land-

57

locked days at OHL had left him in doubt of his power to argue sustainedly and Matthias was his test.

Vanselow: We hadn't gone beyond Heligoland in two years.

Erzberger: Don't be ridiculous. The British have been lusting for you to come out. Look at your hands. You wouldn't have them. Your eyes would be cinders . . .

Maiberling: Or hors-d'oeuvres for electric eels.

But while Maiberling was chuckling Erzberger had lost all his patience with the captain's gallantry. The sailor didn't know that soldiers were picnicking on Marxism in the Wilhelmstrasse. And where was Groener?

Erzberger: Your fleet isn't as important as Germany.

Vanselow: I'm aware of that . . . They chose a Tirpitz medal-winner to give the fleet away.

It was too much.

Erzberger: Tirpitz medal! I won a medal for economics once.

Vanselow: Of course. You'll have to forgive me.

Matthias Erzberger let his breath out at length.

Erzberger: No. You'll have to forgive me. We all have our individual stories.

Maiberling: But they're not the *total* story, are they? Eh?

The count was sneering at Matthias for being prim. Also he was challenging, seeming to say I have a story that is the whole five acts of universal tragedy. So damn you. Perhaps, it occurred to Matthias, the count's mad manners were rooted in a loss. But whose? He was a widower. His daughters and sons hadn't died – Paula would have picked it up from her daily poring of the *Deaths* columns in *Berliner Tagblatt*.

Erzberger: Where is Groener?

Maiberling: Another tot!

Erzberger: No. Not that.

Maiberling: I don't recognize your jurisdiction over my bottle.

Erberger: Then I ask you, Alfred.

Maiberling: Don't be so soulful, Matthias. You haven't the build . . . Captain?

Vanselow: No. No. I had far too much last night.

Maiberling punched Matthias fraternally on the upper arm.

Maiberling: Don't be swayed by Matthias. He's only a promoted country journalist. A little to the right of centre and to the centre of right. Still awed by officers and even by me. Oh yes. We were riding over Erzbergers, see. When Luther was a pup.

Matthias could see the captain taking literal account of what the drunken Maiberling was saying. As if it might be a serious political analysis, the captain nodded.

Erzberger: What happened then? When they refused to put to sea?

Vanselow rushed to tell them. To an extent, he said, farces. When the fleet returned to its ports the officers were surrounded and under open arrest and sailors' soviets ran the city, even directing traffic.

Maiberling: But they let you go? Out of regard for your sensitivity?

Vanselow: We had to barter with them. On the trade union model, you understand.

Maiberling chuckled and took a brief liquored tour into the skins of the rebel sailors.

Maiberling: They must be enjoying themselves, those sailors, they must be having a wonderful time. Because naval officers – with exceptions, of course – are overbearing men. Overbearing.

He tried to break wind secretly but failed and was heard throughout the lobby.

Maiberling: You'll have to excuse me. The schnapps has a diarrhoeic effect . . .

Groener – Honest Railroader

Maiberling had not long retired, bouncing off armchairs, when a group of army officers, conversing loudly, arrived one at a time in the lobby, each turning back to continue speaking or listening to those coming on behind.

Erzberger recognized General Groener's fat-hipped, mean-shouldered body, unsoldierly even when fleshed out with a trench-coat.

Matthias didn't see Hindenburg come in. He arrived, as suited a miraculous icon, without being seen to use any entrance, and for a second the ancient and familiar brute boyishness of that face froze the breath at the bottom of your larynx. Then you noticed he looked spotty and tired.

Groener saw Matthias and the captain together and advanced on them through the spinney of easy chairs.

Groener: They sent you, Herr Erzberger.

Erzberger: Yes General. I was asked for. And have been here an hour.

Groener: And at your ease, I hope. Us . . . we've been in attendance at the château since the small hours.

Erzberger: I see.

Groener whispered, dragging Matthias into conclave by the sleeve.

Groener: We talk about one subject only. That poor Willi should throw in the crown. It's pitiful, we follow him from room to room, you can't leave him alone for long because then he gets schemes. The Field-Marshal's in a bad state. He hates seeing Willi bullied. How many cars will you need, Erzberger?

Erzberger: At least . . . let me see . . . four. One to lead, one for myself and Count Maiberling . . . he's washing at the moment. One for Captain Vanselow and the general . . .

Groener: The general?

Erzberger: A von Winterfeldt.

Groener: I know, I know. An old gentleman. The Foreign Office sent him here. Goes for walks in the rain. I must say not a very handy talent but he used to be military attaché in Paris in the gay days. A Francophile. Speaks French at home, they tell me. To a French wife! I suppose it counts for something.

He called to a captain with cavalry tabs on his overcoat and asked that the general be sent for.

Taking small dreamy steps the Field-Marshal had joined them and stood with hands stretched out to the fire. The flames seemed to lap at his booted ankles – he was as close as that. His blood must be thin as coffee, Erzberger thought.

Groener slung an arm round Matthias's shoulder and drew him in close to the blaze. Fire-light on the general's face gave it a gargoyle look. Erzberger's knees prickled with the heat and steam rose from Groener's overcoat.

From this ruck poor Vanselow had been excluded, his stature emphasized: that he was a token.

Hindenburg: He won't go to the telephone when the Chancellor calls. He goes out into the garden. Sits on wet benches in the drizzle. Maybe pneumonia will take him off. I can't.

Groener: He won't let himself be told . . . the officers of his own guard find it hard to get a salute out of their men. Out at the Imperial train it's all very slack, the sentries play cards, they read. Officers can't take action . . .

Hindenburg: It's astounding. The Ruhr battalions . . . superb men . . . passing round socialist newspapers.

In small and, he hoped, unnoticed ways, Erzberger's body squirmed in the heat.

Groener: You saw the party of officers in the lounge? We hope to gather fifty altogether. Not easily done. We've spoken to thirty so far. Front-line commanders. Two questions we've asked. First, if the Kaiser were to lead the troops in a last all-out assault on enemy positions, would he be obeyed? Second, can the troops be relied on to suppress Bolshevism – or, in real terms, to shoot down seditious

Germans. Only one out of the thirty has said yes to both questions.

The Field-Marshal wandered away, blinking. Some realities were too much for him, he didn't want to hear them repeated.

Groener: By tomorrow I should have at least forty such opinions. I'll present them to the Kaiser. He'll be shocked to the wishbone. It isn't a humane method. But there we are. It's the best that can be managed.

The fazed Field-Marshal had staggered on into the lounge, as if seeking his simple regimental origins there.

Erzberger: You want me to tell the French? The Kaiser will go?

Groener: Perhaps . . . if they ask . . .

Erzberger: Certainly.

Groener: Where did you say the count . . .?

Erzberger: In the toilet.

Groener: Oh. Sick?

Erzberger: A little.

Groener: Schnapps?

Erzberger: Er . . . to some extent.

Groener: If there's any chance of his going to pieces . . .

Erzberger: He'll be all right.

Groener did a weird half-curtsy to expose the soles of his booted feet to the fire.

Groener: I asked for another man.

Erzberger: The other man couldn't have got here in time.

Groener: You both know to ask for an immediate cease-fire?

Erzberger: Oh yes.

Groener: Imperative. For the saving of life, yes. But for other reasons as well. Have you perhaps seen a railway map of Belgium, Alsace, Luxembourg?

Erzberger: Not with a professional eye.

Groener: A dozen fishing lines tangled. Individually and together. People will remember Ludendorff and Falkenhayn, the dealers in meat. My only victory will be getting the army home intact. It mustn't bleed apart, so to speak, it mustn't coagulate at the railway junctions. So you have to ask for the firing to cease . . .

Erzberger: Of course.

Groener: I know you've come to mistrust the military . . .

Erzberger: I'm not thinking in those terms now.

The little general grinned, showing his dimples.

Groener: You see, this time we really are the forces of unarguable good. Bolshevik Russia . . .

Erzberger: I'm aware. I'm aware.

Groener: Get us all the time you can manage.

Erzberger had had enough of this coaching. He beat his hip twice with his good fedora. So I am your front line now, the shock trooper for the shock troops, the diplomatic death's-head hussar.

Von Winterfeldt Takes a Walk

Groener: Von Winterfeldt! Good!

A tall officer with a thin moustache appropriate to the France of 1905 had come downstairs. Behind him walked a corporal carrying a fur-collared coat of excellent cut. He did not turn his head towards the gusts of laughter from the lounge, where Hindenburg told soldiers' stories to the young regimental officers. The ones whose opinions would finish the Kaiser.

Groener introduced the general to Matthias. Your travelling companion, he said.

Von Winterfeldt: I am aware of your political career, Herr Erzberger.

Matthias's reply was meaningless.

Erzberger: Oh well . . . there we are.

He had never got used to facing the blue eyes and sculptured faces of the *vons* of the earth; there were still movements of bumpkin disquiet in his stomach, the belly calling him back to his peasant state. As Maiberling had earlier said.

Von Winterfeldt: I want it appreciated immediately: I can handle all the speaking of French.

Groener: I'm sure that doesn't disturb Herr Erzberger.

Erzberger: No. I know no French.

Von Winterfeldt was wearing kid gloves. They seemed to have an aura of talc to them. The question of who would speak French settled, he took one off to shake Erzberger's hand.

Von Winterfeldt: I've sat at the same table as Foch. At least half a dozen times. This meeting will have strange overtones for me.

Groener: Indeed.

Von Winterfeldt: My things are packed, my papers together. I suppose there's time for me to take a walk.

Groener: I think so. Erzberger?

Erzberger: A short walk, General?

Von Winterfeldt: Of course. Long car journeys, you see, put a test on the circulation . . .

He stretched his arms out as if he might, in fact, fly and the corporal came and draped the overcoat over his shoulders. He nodded once, a violent bob of the head, and went at ceremonial pace out through the lobby doors.

Groener Offers No Guarantees

Once more Groener had Matthias by the elbow and began to walk him towards the door of the lift.

Groener: Eccentric yes, but manageable. And quite clearheaded. I can guarantee that. Now . . .

Erzberger felt a little peevish at being pushed along by the arm, as for having such a strange old gentleman forced on him.

Erzberger: Where are we going?

Groener: To my offices on the first floor. I've prepared some memoranda you might find useful . . .

The lift orderly had swept the lift-grille back for them and stood aside numb-faced. Erzberger baulked. It was terror and he sweated. He wouldn't go upstairs without Maiberling.

Groener: I'm sorry. I do haul people about too much. Even civilians, free men.

But he had in fact sniffed Matthias's fear.

Groener: I can't guarantee anything. All but one of those regimental officers, *all but one*, say their men want one thing. The end. One ... only one ... is sure we ought to battle on. But then he's a great-grandson of Clausewitz or someone.

His small pink hand went on cajoling Erzberger's left upper-arm.

Groener: Who knows what that one out of thirty might do later? To you. To me.

Erzberger felt himself reddening. An exposed coward.

Oh Dr Thyssen and all the great executives of the Disconto Gesellschaft! Who took me to your tables (board- and dinner-) and taught me about Chablis and silverware. Where have you vanished to? This is your darling guest who has become a target in a military hotel.

Erzberger: I understand. I want to fetch Maiberling.

Groener: Of course.

Erzberger: I want the cars got ready as soon as possible.

Groener: Naturally.

Groener detached himself from Matthias's sleeve and stepped into the lift. The grille closed between them. But the lift did not immediately start.

Groener: Matthias.

Erzberger: Yes?

Groener: You have my respect.

Erzberger: All right.

Seeming to understand what Erzberger thought – *you* respect me today because that serves OHL's purpose – the general pouted and was borne away upwards.

To the Toilets

Erzberger asked the subaltern at the desk where the lavatories were. Downstairs and to the right, sir.

There was only one locked water-closet and some groaning within it.

Erzberger: Alfred?

Maiberling: My ulcer. Too many quick schnapps. But what is a man to do? Journey sober?

Erzberger: Groener is here. Hindenburg.

Maiberling made a contemptuous noise and all the water-closets seethed for a second.

Erzberger: The Kaiser will go. That's settled, Groener says.

Maiberling: Oh.

Erzberger: Can I get you something binding?

Maiberling: No. Don't rush me.

Erzberger: That wasn't my purpose.

Maiberling opened the door and clung to the white marble door-jamb.

Maiberling: Poor Willi. He was all right. He liked pornography you know. Like most respectable men. I knew his supplier out in Charlottenburg. He said Willi's tastes were restrained – boots and a little flagellation and a leaning to Negresses, but nothing very unseemly. He said the nation could be proud of Willi's tastes.

Erzberger laughed.

Erzberger: I think you make these things up, Alfred.

The count's jaw hung open and, in pain, he mouthed the edge of the door; showing many gold fillings.

Maiberling: They killed Inga.

Erzberger: Inga?

Maiberling barked at him.

Maiberling: You met her once.

Erzberger: The . . . short lady?

Maiberling: Plump. She was plump. Inga.

Long ago, in the peace, Matthias had been dining at Restaurant Krziwanek. With gossipers and politicians. What non-crisis had everyone been breathless about that night? The head-waiter brought a card – Maiberling's. The count was dining in a private room and would like Herr Erzberger to come visiting for a drink. Matthias thought will I go? I don't want some tart flung at me. Temptations of the flesh always put him in a fluster, made him wonder was all the politicking worthwhile.

When he went, he found Maiberling and a fat little woman with a happy pink face. Inga. An adulteress but no tart.

Erzberger could remember thinking in some envy, they're beside themselves. The room quivered with their self-congratulations. They expected Erzberger to add his own best wishes. Erzberger can be trusted, the count had said.

Inga was the wife of some general; that's all Erzberger ever knew.

Erzberger: They killed her?

Maiberling: She had the influenza.

Erzberger: Oh yes. So many . . .

Maiberling: She got better. Very thin. End of September her housekeeper found her. Sitting up in her bath all her clothes on! Head blown off. And so bloody clever of them: pistol in her lap.

He beat at the door and dribbled down the woodwork.

Erzberger: People get so depressed after influenza. I remember Paula . . .

Maiberling: For Christ's sake don't be a simpleton.

Erzberger: I'm sorry.

Maiberling: Do you know women never blow their heads off? Ask any coroner. They prize their heads. They prize their eyes, their lips.

Erzberger: I'm sorry, Alfred.

Maiberling: Very few anyhow. Very few shoot themselves in the head. Not . . . certainly *not* . . . Inga's type.

The plumbing sighed resonantly. Perhaps the ghosts were there of invalids who had died for lack of Spa water in the last four summers.

Erzberger: What happened then, Alfred? Go on. What happened?

Maiberling: This. This happened. Her husband runs an army corps in Latvia. A hypnotic bastard – not with women, with boys, with breathless damn subalterns. And Inga and I were not always . . . not always secretive. So the valiant corps commander's honour was in question!

Erzberger: Try to be quiet, Alfred.

For the count was not chewing the partitions any more but yelling across the tiled spaces.

Maiberling: She was shot by *his boys, his* subalterns on leave.

Erzberger: Can you be sure, Alfred?

The count waved a fist at him.

Maiberling: I verified it. Do you think I wouldn't verify it? For Inga?

Erzberger: But were they seen? The housekeeper . . . did she see them?

Maiberling: What do *you* think? Their training! Of course she didn't see them.

Oh Christ, he'll shoot some staff-officer. For his dead love's sake.

Erzberger: Maybe you should try to understand . . . the depression women suffer . . . they more than us . . .

Maiberling: Sod you, Matthias. How dare you humour *me* . . .

Erzberger: You ought to wash the muck from your face.

Maiberling: . . . how dare you treat *me* as a case!

Erzberger lost his temper and spread his thick legs.

Erzberger: All right. What are going to do then? Run wild upstairs? That's what worries me. You behave like a case.

The count, upright, snatched his overcoat from its hook behind the lavatory door. Sewn into its bulk, the weapon. He'll threaten me, thought Erzberger, he's quite mad. But the count walked past him, laid the overcoat on a chair by the wall and poured water for washing. He spoke in a

68

near-whisper, a mere dry flutter at the back of the throat.

Maiberling: I know about women. I spit on all your chat about depression.

Matthias could feel the cold under his armpits; evaporating fright.

Erzberger: Alfred, we're not private men now. We're on essential business.

Maiberling: Are we? Four municipal cretins could manage it.

He began drinking handfuls of the water he was meant to wash his face in.

Erzberger: Is that your attitude?

Maiberling: If you like.

All the way upstairs Erzberger debated with himself. Will I exchange him? And, in this military ashram, for whom?

Erzberger Falls Under Siege

In the lobby he saw Vanselow, still waiting where he had been left.

Erzberger: You must forgive me.

Vanselow: Not at all. You're an important man.

A herd of gold-buttoned staff-officers moved across the lobby towards them. Soon they were encircled. An intelligence officer, about forty years old, made them a valedictory speech and offered any of his colleagues Erzberger might care for as aides.

The solemnity of the event, fat Erzberger and deep blue Vanselow in the middle, was debased by a loud young man — a transport officer it seemed — who argued by the lift-door with General von Winterfeldt.

Transport Officer: Four yes, sir. But what you ask would practically require General Groener and the Field-Marshal to walk out to the château each morning.

Von Winterfeldt: I must insist. I am the sole army pleni-potentiary. I will have special instructions from General Groener that I must read and consider in private.

Transport Officer: If you'd be so kind as to let one aide travel with you.

Von Winterfeldt: I wouldn't expect any of my colleagues to travel under those conditions.

Transport Officer: I can't provide five limousines till noon.

Von Winterfeldt: Come now. You must do better. Five. And before noon.

The bland faces corralled Herr Erzberger. Many of them spectacled, and in the lenses only a small glint of their knowledge of the landslide. Choose any of us. But which of you is an assassin?

It was beyond Matthias, or so he thought. He thought Groener must choose the aides, arrange the cars. If necessary, get the count out of the lavatory.

Erzberger: Excuse me.

He broke his way out of the siege, abandoning the Tirpitz medallist. Near the stairwell the count, his arm around a young cavalry officer. His breath reeked but he was suddenly blithe.

Maiberling: Matthias. This is young von Helldorf. Great horseman. Steeple-chaser.

The boy bowed.

Maiberling: He wants to come.

Erzberger: A horseman?

Von Helldorf: Sir.

Foch was horse-artillery. Weygand cavalry. So, no doubt, von Winterfeldt. Now this young man. A clutch of hippo-philes. To close the war that had spewed up the image of the martial horse.

Erzberger: I have to see General Groener. If he agrees . . .

Maiberling: It'll be quite a picnic.

He was on his mad swing again, from terror to gaiety. But if he's jettisoned, Erzberger thought, I'll have no one with me that I know. God help me. For I find Maiberling's madness homely this terrible day.

By the lift-door the transport officer surrendered too hysterically to old von Winterfeldt.

Transport Officer: All right then. Five cars. Five it shall be.

Von Winterfeldt: And I say, you must make it soon. History, you know, is in the balance.

The Cars Move Off

At noon five limousines arrived and halted in convoy outside the front door of the Grand Hôtel Britannique. Rain polished the Imperial eagles on their front doors; those parlous birds.

The Field-Marshal had visited the lobby to bid the delegates goodbye. He held Erzberger close to him by the elbows. The clumsy emotion of the old man, whose breath was in any case acrid with fright, made Erzberger blink.

On the wet pavement an officer told them that the first car carried a guide and the last was for aides: the count's von Helldorf and a secretary called Blauert. Maiberling asked loudly if he could travel with Erzberger. Though secretly unhappy, Erzberger agreed. He hadn't wanted the count's company to that extent, had been looking forward to solitude behind the blurred panes. As of right von Winterfeldt took possession of his vehicle and, looking about him perhaps for any acceptable companion, forlorn Captain Vanselow of his.

There were blankets in the steamed-up interiors.

Maiberling: Excellent.

He wrapped himself up and sat grunting with a sort of animal satisfaction. Not thinking of faceless Inga now, in the wet earth.

They jolted off down the polite streets of Spa. Most houses seemed shuttered. The Belgians indoors, waiting for deliverance. Soon they'd be resort people again. Soon they'd have an off-season and a season. At dark noon the mute houses wavered beyond Erzberger's rainy window in expectation of a restored clientele.

Cabbage-fields appeared, sleeping grey lanes of vegetables. Erzberger sat back and shut his eyes.

Jesus, you know this place, have been here; it's the grove of olives, crab-apples and agonies. What will you do for me?

In that moment however, the leading car developed a steering fault and slewed towards a high farmhouse wall. The row of impact split Erzberger's devout rest.

Road-block he thought. Ambush. Some Imperialist remnant *are* set on stopping us. He suffered an image of blood-bespattered automobile upholstery.

Then his own car crashed. Blanketed, hat in hand, he flew against the glass partition beyond which the driver himself had thrust his head through the glass of the windscreen.

In the long silence there was only the hiss of rain and shattered radiators.

Maiberling: Jesus.

Erzberger clung to the dickie-seat as to the only secure fabric.

Von Helldorf opened the door and made compassionate noises. He handed them out. They stood numbly with their mouths open to the low clouds. The first car had mounted a grass embankment and seemed about to topple.

Maiberling: It isn't much fun, is it? Road-accidents. It isn't much fun.

Erzberger's head was still floating high above flat Belgium.

Erzberger: Why don't you shoot the driver, eh? Why not?

The count seemed sombrely offended.

General von Winterfeldt had stepped down from his vehicle and marched up to them.

Von Winterfeldt: We can send a driver back for two more vehicles. These are quite finished. While we wait you two gentlemen must feel free to share my car.

Both Erzberger and Maiberling had begun to accede and limp towards the general's limousine. Then Erzberger stopped. To him it seemed that by physical effort he forced his gaseous brain back under the tight control of his skull.

Erzberger: We have to get on. We have to get away from Spa.

Von Winterfeldt: That isn't reasonable. Such cramping.

Erzberger: It isn't a ride through the Bois de Boulogne.

All the time he was taking account of himself. That concussion, he thought, I shall never get over. All my talents are lying about loose in my too-big body. All off their shelves. Tangled, tangled.

Von Winterfeldt: I need a vehicle to myself.

Erzberger: Count Maiberling and I will share the first car with the guide. You, General, will either ride with Captain Vanselow or remain here.

The count was kicking at shards of glass with the toe of his shoe. Frankly desolated.

Maiberling: A disaster this. An omen. A rotten omen.

Erzberger: Nonsense. They say in Swabia broken glass means good luck.

Maiberling: Fuck what they say in Swabia.

The general coughed.

Von Winterfeldt: You leave no choice. I shall join Captain Vanselow. But I cannot pretend to give General Groener's instructions full attention under these circumstances.

So it was done. Three cars edged round the wreckage and whirred away to the east. Two bloody-headed drivers were left standing numb on the wet pavis. With accidents to report.

Wemyss Reads his Dossiers

At Senlis they had boarded the armistice train.

The First Sea Lord found his cabin spacious. He called to George Hope next door.

Wemyss: Not bad, George.

Hope: No. Splendid. Just the same . . . there's nowhere to bathe.

Wemyss: Isn't there?

Hope: No. Nowhere. Marriott's done a thorough search. Just those finicking little wash-basins. Art-nouveau.

Wemyss: Get Bagot to arrange something when we arrive. Eh? A tub . . .

Hope: Maybe the Marshal has one in his wagon-lit.

Wemyss: Maybe. Can't very well ask though. If he hasn't criticism's implied.

He took a wing-collar from his suit-case and rubbed it with his thumb, speaking dreamily.

Wemyss: A bit musty, the old boy. I noticed it in the office.

Hope: Weygand too.

Wemyss: Oh yes. An eau-de-Cologne boy, that one. Long time since I unpacked my own kit, George.

Hope: Would you like help, sir? Ring for someone.

Wemyss: No, just reflecting. In any case, can't have those bilingual stewards hanging about.

He caressed a shirt.

It was so quiet in Senlis station that you could hear the shunters calling to each other through the rain.

Wemyss: You've got those dossiers?

Hope: Yes sir.

Wemyss: Remiss of political section. Been waiting on them a week. Bring them in here, will you? I've an excellent reading desk.

Hope: I as well, sir.

Wemyss: Please call me Rosy.

Hope: Rosy.

Wemyss: Hate working alone. Bring in Marriott will you? Very much concerns him.

Waiting, dinner shirt laid out on the bed, Wemyss made a hole in the condensation on his window. He saw two old women sitting on Quai 3 beneath furry lamplight.

One nattered, the other nodded, nodded, nodded. Telling and heeding some eternal woman's story: first he says he loves and must have you, then you bud with children and he's off with low women, so next you're both old and veins show and he dies of his excesses and your womb is shrunken

74

to a split pea and your sons' sons are imperilled in strange wars. A tattered man in a veteran's cap limped over the tracks pushing a handcart full of brushwood. Wemyss felt a schoolboy's pleasure at seeing while unseen.

If those people knew what this train was for the lame man would walk straight, the old women hug and dance quaint measures. The Château-Thierry local would hoot all the way to Senlis and the driver and all the passengers get drunk in the railway bar. It would be Breughel stuff.

He shivered. Hope and Marriott were at the door.

Hope: Cold, sir?

Wemyss: Not exactly the Gulf of Arabia, George. Is it?

Hope: Indeed not.

Marriott came forward with his face of grammar-school-prefect reliability.

Marriott: There's a heating device, sir.

Bending, he turned a knob.

Wemyss: We're moving.

Hope: Indeed.

Wemyss sneaked a final look at the old women on Quai 3. They did not seem even to notice the fluently departing armistice train.

As well as supplying heat, Marriott had taken the trouble to turn on the admiral's reading lamp. They all sat down – Marriott on the bed, notebook in his hand, an obeisant distance from the dress-shirt. Hope, in shirtsleeves, took from his brief-case two dossiers and put them on Lord Wemyss's desk. Wemyss turned to Marriott.

Wemyss: These are the reports of political section. Enlightening, one would hope. Concerning our two colleagues in the next carriage. You read, George.

Hope pulled his chair in close to the desk so that he was shoulder to shoulder with Wemyss. For concentration's sake the First Sea Lord let his monocle dangle and jutted his face towards the moulded ceiling.

Hope: The Marshal first. "Foch, Ferdinand, born Tarbes, Hautes-Pyrénées, 2nd October, 1851, son of a senior provincial civil servant.

Wemyss: Sixty-seven years old at the moment.

Hope: Indeed. "Jesuit-educated. Enlisted infantry 1870, saw no service. Entered École Polytechnique at Nancy, 1871, where Germans still in occupation. The Marshal affected as much as any Frenchman by these memories of defeat and occupation. Commissioned, horse artillery, 1878. Attended cavalry school. Promoted captain, age 26. Spent next ten years – apart from one year as student École de Guerre – rising to rank of major in a succession of horse-artillery regiments. Was well-known in army circles as a contributor to journals of military science. His teachings stressed morale as the great strategic and tactical determinant in warfare . . ."

Wemyss: Can you skim, George?

Hope: I think so, sir.

Wemyss: Then skim like a good chap. It's the *insights* we want. Where are we?

Marriott tried to supply the geographic answer by peering out the hazed window at a poorly lit multiple-word sign on the station they came slewing through. The too-many syllables swiped him across the eyes. He could not catch them.

Hope: "Colonel 1895 . . . professorship École Supérieure de Guerre . . . director of same 1905. Appointment due to M. Clemenceau, unexpected." Here's an interesting item. "While a teaching military scientist, Foch met and greatly influenced Sir Henry Wilson, commandant Camberley and later Director of Operations, War Office. Sir Henry a devout Francophile. On becoming Director of Operations, War Office, 1911, Sir Henry's task was drawing up mobilization plans. His work mirrored the conviction which he and Foch fraternally shared: that in the coming conflict the British should operate as the French left flank facing Germany. Through Sir Henry and others, the Marshal has had a greater influence on the British conduct of this War than any other French soldier . . ."

Wemyss: I've seen the two of them clowning in the ante-rooms in Versailles. *Double-Vay,* the Marshal calls him. Amazing.

Hope: "Appointed general commanding XXth Corps,

Nancy, 1913. Led this formation impetuously but with some skill, August 1914 . . . Commander IXth Army on Marne at end of month. Contribution crucial in turning German flank . . . 1915, general assisting Marshal Joffre . . . canny use of reserves . . . removed from post, December, 1916, after failure Somme Offensive . . ." sorry, Rosy, we'll get there . . . "planning job . . . then chief of general staff . . . German breakthrough, March this year, appointed generalissimo Allied Forces, in view his vim and aggressiveness, and signs of nervous instability, Haig and Pétain."

Wemyss: Vim and aggressiveness . . .

Hope: Ends, sir, with a brief analysis. "In accordance with his temperament, the Marshal sees war as a moral and mystical exercise. In some ways too his ideas of the meaning of the war are based on the French defeat by the Prussians in 1870. The present war has been, as it were, a replayed tournament. He is therefore either ignorant or contemptuous of the part sea-power has had in this war as also in the wars of Napoleon, about whom he is a supposed expert. Attached is a bibliography . . ."

Wemyss: Don't worry about the bibliography. It's too late for reference libraries.

Wemyss Remembers Feisal

He got up from the desk and began roving the cabin.

Wemyss: Strange man. Strange man.

His fallen monocle bounced from his chest.

Hope: Indeed.

Turning at the door he saw Marriott sitting on the couchette, bland, solemn. A *London Illustrated News* staff artist's impression of a British heavy-cruiser commander who has just given the order to ram. He thought, can we really be so simple, so much to a formula? What does he do with his wife, this Marriott? Has he got girls in ports? Or boys? Can he begin to deal with weird men like Foch?

No, no, Wemyss muttered. Identify the true enemy. Why be captious about poor Marriott? Who turned your heater on.

The one you're uneasy about is the Marshal.

Wemyss had suffered like moments of threat when faced with Emir Feisal last year. A contemptuous subtlety in deep Hamitic eyes. As if they only let us rule them, make treaties over their heads, in consolation for our own stupor.

That Lawrence, whom Wemyss had once carried on his flag-ship in the Gulf of Arabia, certainly made no bones about it: the Arabs had all the *inner* answers according to Lawrence. Lawrence himself a weird cack-handed man with inner answers!

Now Foch, the mad Arab of the Western War.

Wemyss: Saying he won't put the naval terms to them for fun . . . it isn't good enough.

Hope: It doesn't give us any proper guarantees.

Wemyss: How to corner the cocky old bastard!

For he was aware of failing to corner him that afternoon.

Hope waited long enough to be sure Wemyss wanted him to make suggestions. Unimpeachable George Hope. Little private income – some small estate near Devizes. And even in far British legations and wild caliphates, faithful to his wife's honour, calmly so, in the name of his calm Anglican God. That was real virtue. Not all the fiery sword stuff of fetid little Frenchmen.

Hope: I should imagine we introduce the subject without warning. Perhaps when the laughter dies down from one of his stories. He's a raconteur. Especially in his own eyes.

Wemyss: There's an element of spite to him. The hardest thing has always been to get him to discuss the thing on its merits.

Hope: I suggest we don't move till he *has*. Four of us. In the uniform of another country's navy. Refusing to budge.

The First Sea Lord turned absently to Marriott, who rushed to contribute.

Marriott: If he won't listen. Yes, sir.

Wemyss: Agreed then. We don't leave the office car . . .
Marriott: 2417D, sir.
Wemyss: Quite.
Hope seemed to find the captain's gift for numbers engaging, and explained it with a smile.
Hope: Marriott is a ciphers man, sir.
Marriott: For my sins, sir.
If you have any, Wemyss wanted to say.
Wemyss: We must be clear what we want. We need some sign of what he means to do should the Germans baulk about their navy. It isn't that we need his support in any absolute sense.
Hope: Indeed.
They all felt more robust now, after suspecting all afternoon that the Marshal might artfully be about to downgrade them.

And Hope and Marriott thought, Lord Wemyss is an enlightened consultor of aides, a modern and liberal lord of sea.

And Wemyss thought, this is what makes me a tolerable commander. No Poseidon, me. No great whale. It is impossible that I should ever blaze and burn out amongst clouds of mad cordite like, to name the most preposterous case, Horatio Nelson. I am First Sea Lord because First Sea Lord Jellicoe hoarded for his own decision such matters as the calibre of armament to be mounted on trawlers, wattage of Aldis lamps on minesweepers. Disappearing into his own In tray, J. R. Jellicoe had no time to tool a strategy. The cry from the Navy Board and even from Downing Street was, find someone who will deputize.

Rosy Wemyss had begun lobbying only after his name had been pushed forward. And lobbying hadn't been hard.

For he had no enemies.

Now, in the truce-train, he spoke to his flattered deputies.
Wemyss: We must nearly be there. Please, George, give us the end of the Weygand dossier.

79

All the Kaiser's Soldiers

It seemed all the Kaiser's soldiers were already coming home eastwards on the country roads of Belgium. Through the distorting window Erzberger saw an occasional gaping mouth aimed at him. What, going west? the mute mouths said. So late in the day?

Sometimes ambulances appeared head-on, moving a little faster than the soldiers. They beeped for right of passage. I'm wounded too, Maiberling would mutter inside his blanket. Beneath the privacy of his skull, Erzberger made the same claim. He wanted to let down the window and be sick in the mud. But that act, he felt crazily sure, was politically dangerous. It would outrage the mass to see Minister-of-State-without-portfolio Erzberger sick up on their familiar mud.

Light went early, and against the unscheduled clouds of men they were lucky to make fifteen kilometres an hour.

In the Car Shared by the General and Vanselow

In the car shared by the general and Vanselow, von Winterfeldt read typed instructions by the light of a hand torch. Vanselow could only presume they were documents supplied by Groener, and wished he himself had so many memoranda to steer by. He felt embarrassed to open his own attaché-case, in case the general noticed how sparse the directives were inside it, how thin the dossiers labelled *Defence and River-craft, Destroyer Flotillas, Grand Seas Fleet, U-Boats.* He sweated inside his overcoat. I am too naïve a man to be making this journey. Oh yes, all the admirals have told me my memory is good – on that account, taken me into palaces and embassies. I've been that species of aide who stands by the potted plants and doesn't drink more than the one measure of spirits all evening. If I'd stood there a thousand years no brilliant woman would have spoken to me. Nor could I have controlled my cowardice if she had. Twice I have dined with the Emperor and the Imperial cabinet and kept hysterically mute except when Admiral Müller once called on me to agree to some half-whimsical truism he uttered about the burdens of junior officers. Not for a moment did getting spoken to at that high table ease my mad suspicion that those men did not breathe the same air as the rest of us. And where is this table we're travelling to at the moment? And what awesome men will be sitting there? For midget Vanselow to face? The burdens of junior officers . . .

I am too naïve a man to be making this journey.

Meanwhile the general's eyes were stinging and he wanted to stop reading but was prevented by the imponderable risk that Vanselow might start talking.

While he shuffled the pages he thought of Erzberger. Erzberger's vanity all that morning in the Grand Hôtel Britannique. *It is not my war, I renounced it long ago, none the less I go to end it for you.* The south German and Catholic fulsomeness of fat-man Erzberger rankled strongly with the general. *I buy the dangers, sight unseen, but only if it be enacted that I am the moral primate of all the travellers.*

Memoranda? The general would like to draft a memorandum.

For the attention: Herr Staatsminister Erzberger. It might be of use to Herr Erzberger to know that General von Winterfeldt grew ambiguous about this war not as late as 1916 but even in the first days of August 1914. And that, for the very good reason that the battle-line ran down the middle of his marriage-bed. When, eleven years ago, the general, then a colonel, asked his military superior for permission to marry a delicious Frenchwoman aged thirty-five years, he was advised to marry a Jewess or a Matabele rather than. At brigade, divisional and even corps level he was pointed out as the officer who had married incautiously. If he had six fingers on one hand it would have been hard for him to have attracted a higher notoriety. Also, he and his Frenchwoman were frequently visited, surveyed and questioned by men from the Prussian War Office. I do not put it any higher than that at the start of the war he was ambiguous, and I mean by that term that he saw the event as a necessary visitation and a means to suppress quickly the hubris of British statesmen and French generals, excrescences who had nothing to do with the soft thing he held in bed. Then why did the soft thing enter a sanitarium in 1915, attack him with a knife in the new year and subside into paleness and mandragora in an expensive institution in Reinickendorf? That aside, Herr Erzberger should know that he is not the only one who travels this evening by his own consent and favour and because he owes little to the individuals who asked him to make the trip.

He had special knowledge of France and must be permitted to make use of it. Or did Erzberger want to corner *that* speciality as well?

Drinks in 2417D

They went along to 2417D brushed, shaven, their intentions locked in place. Hope, Marriott, Bagot took scotch in small sips and stood about, vigilant.

The carriage was set up like a boardroom. The dining table in the centre of the dining compartment had become a board-table – blotters had been put down instead of place-mats. The Marshal waited by a corner table on which two unconnected telephone hand-sets stood. Above his head was a thermometer to aid the wine-waiter in his decisions on when the claret should be opened.

There were small tables set in other corners for secretaries, aides, interpreters. And even a few through the door into the servery. This evening they served as places to lay aside your barely sipped liquor.

The Marshal took a chair at one of these peripheral tables. His staff and the British sailors imitated him, but Wemyss sat casually in a corner seat at the central table.

The Marshal: Your health!

He didn't waste time with his cognac. He sniffed it rowdily. He drank it quickly. He wiped his moustache with his hand, and even the rim of his sleeve. He was all head and hands — the head and ham-fists of a much bigger man stuck on the pip-squeak body. Even by these means he de-focused the concentration of opponents. As a cunning foetus in 1851 he had stopped just short of being a monster.

He told in English a funny story about one French general who made his sons pray every night that they would grow up to be like Bayard and Guesclin.

Wemyss considered. Do you always laugh at your generals for the benefit of strangers? Or is it a gesture of kindred feeling for *us*?

Marriott laughed through pursed lips, like a schoolboy sitting for a class photograph.

The Marshal told of the comic nervous breakdown of another French general four years before, during the battle of the Marne. As the Sixth Army detrained into the midst of a retreat, the poor man had ordered his aides to bring him no more bad news and gone stamping up and down the terraces of the Château of Craonne, reciting the Odes of Horace for defence.

Now? thought Wemyss. Now? The Marshal had a sort of malign radiance that brought all a man's self-doubt to the surface. Not that I have much. But some.

Erzberger at Divisional HQ

Maiberling: Guns.

Erzberger wound the window down.

He could hear guns.

At a cross-roads a sign said ←*Chimay*. Erzberger clearly saw the lettering, as if the windows were disposed to unfog whenever significant pointers to his fate arose.

Air coming in the window blew so sharp. It sliced open their fugged senses.

The headlights fell on a log barricade and a seventeen-year-old, thin in a helmet, keeping guard.

Erzberger jumped from his vehicle. Lightly and with the minor elation that goes with arriving.

Erzberger: Clear this road.

Boy: Sir.

Erzberger: We have to get to Chimay. We're German delegates to France.

Boy: I don't know.

Erzberger asked him where his officer was. The boy blew a whistle that hung around his neck. An officer splashed up from their right, pistol drawn.

Erzberger thought, Holy Christ I *do* hate those things.

The officer in his expensive trench-coat looked younger than the guard. All the fathers had abandoned the front and left their children behind.

Before Erzberger could talk to the boy mud entered his boots and, it seemed, his lungs. He began coughing. Von Winterfeldt appeared at his elbow.

Von Winterfeldt: Put that away. This is Staatsminister Erzberger on his way to arrange a truce with the enemy. Who had these logs put here?

The child in the trench-coat nominated some general. The corps-commander, he explained.

Erzberger controlled his whooping. He noticed that the pistol had remained in the infant's hand, but at a loss.

Erzberger: Do you have an HQ? Battalion? Brigade? Divisional?

The officer sneezed.

Officer: If the gentlemen will follow . . .

The general spoke to him paternally.

Von Winterfeldt: Please couch your side-arm. Couch it. Please.

Together all delegates climbed a muddy embankment following the boy. Mist blew in their faces and in the small glow from hooded headlamps Erzberger saw von Winterfeldt lift a gloved hand and sigh to see mud on the kidskin.

The western guns thumped away in a bored manner. It was hard to believe their fire came down anywhere. Machine-guns however spoke up, both sides of the road, with their old bereaving vigour. Short bursts.

Erzberger: Would you tell me how far please?

Officer: Two hundred metres.

Young as he was he found without hesitation the hole in the earth he was looking for. It was a farmhouse cellar, but the farmhouse had flown away in the autumn, so had the beasts and the farmer.

A voice asked yes?

Officer: Government officials, sir. They say.

Voice: I don't believe that. Search them for weapons.

A comic end, thought Erzberger. They find the gun in Maiberling's armpit and we get shot routinely as infiltrators.

In the after-shadow of this mad image Erzberger began to act with authority. He found he had opened the cellar-trap and hauled a vertical black drape aside. Von Winterfeldt too had taken a strong handful of the stuff. The boy was, after all, barely Oskar's age.

There was one upright man in the cellar. He was younger than Erzberger; and thinner, as it was appropriate to a field commander to be. He wore black woollen mittens and the epaulettes of a brigadier. In a corner two or three runners or aides slept industriously. A bright new map hung on the seeping wall. A telephonist sat, preternaturally stiff, at the field telephone.

General: Who are you?

Erzberger told him who, and that all the logs must be taken down.

General: Oh no. Oh no sir. We felled a forest for the road-blocks. We worked ourselves lean.

He wasn't interested in the credentials Erzberger pulled from the attaché-case, nor suspected them any more of not being the men they said they were. His mind lay all on the threat to his logs.

Erzberger: That is the la Capelle-Guise-Chimay road?

General: Yes. But of course, the French are in Guise.

The count who had come on behind and spotted the genuine dementia in the general, was all at once cool as Aristotle, making apt suggestions.

Maiberling: When we sign an armistice all the road-blocks will come down.

General: It isn't easy work, sir, once they're up. They don't fall down at a signature, you know. You'll have to go some other way.

He took a family picture from the desk. Erzberger could see its surface, framed summer-boughs and blouses and the most determined smiles. The general impassively studied the picture, as if it were someone else's family.

Erzberger: The French nominated this road. Only this road. Chimay-Guise.

General: You'd have thought someone would have told us.

Maiberling: Things are breaking down.

Von Winterfeldt: Can your telephonist get Corps HQ?

What a fine idea, thought Erzberger. Applause for the Francophile.

The general gave a nod to his telephonist.

Erzberger: While we cross over there'll be a cease-fire in this sector. Your corps-commander should have word of it.

General: Maybe, maybe. Do what you like.

He went to a heavy farm cupboard by the map and took out a flask. He poured and drank the liquor privately, back-on to the plenipotentiaries, eyes on the bright map. His necessities, it seemed, were his necessities. He couldn't spare a drop.

Erzberger approached the telephonist, and touched his shoulder.

Erzberger: Could you contact your Corps HQ?

Without speaking the telephonist arranged it and, at full stretch, elbow militarily locked, pushed the receiver at Erzberger.

Everyone in the cellar could hear the liquor travelling down the general's throat.

Taking the receiver, Erzberger spoke at last to the corps chief-of-staff.

Chief-of-Staff: I shall ask my general what he wants done.

Erzberger: I should speak to him.

Chief-of-Staff. It wouldn't be much use. He's had an accident. His telephone voice is very blurred. Excuse me.

Erzberger heard the moaning silence on the line.

Chief-of-Staff: The general would like to speak to his divisional commander.

Erzberger: If he can speak to his divisional commander he can . . .

Chief-of-Staff: Please sir, his divisional commander is able to understand him.

Erzberger took the phone away from his ear. He spoke very loudly to the meditative general in the corner.

Erzberger: General. It's your Corps Commander.

None of the sleepers moved. They might well be HQ dead, Erzberger thought, waiting for collection. But I won't ask.

The brigadier locked away his schnapps and the smiling manna of his family in the corner cupboard, pulled his coat straight, cracked a few of the joints in his mittened fingers and came to take the telephone. The plenipotentiaries saw him nod and consent to everything. Meanwhile the telephonist went about offering the cellar's three chairs to the dignitaries. They all waved him aside.

Without warning the brigadier hung up.

Brigadier: He wants you to visit him at Corps HQ. Trélon. Just two kilometres back.

Erzberger's flesh prickled in the familiar way. An urgency rash. As in Berlin, all the links of coherence and arrangement were shrivelling apart.

Erzberger: We can't waste time touring the front.

Brigadier: It will take two hours, perhaps three to clear your road. He's sending a pioneer company. Also three volunteers will go down the road with white flags. You must do what you like. You're an important man. Sit about here if you like.

When he saw that they wanted or, at least, felt foredoomed to travel two kilometres back towards Spa, he took a whistle from his desk and blew it. Out of a hessian covered alcove another boy subaltern fell; like an Italian saint resurrected from a catacomb for conspicuous innocence. None of the sleepers in the corner woke. It isn't *our* whistle, their humped forms insisted.

Brigadier: These gentlemen to Corps HQ. Good evening, your excellencies.

The Puny Range of the Count's Obsessions

Outside, in the dark arable mud, Maiberling walked close to Matthias.

Maiberling: I could see how angry you were. Bad form, failing to offer us a drink. Ill-bred bastard.

The puny range of the count's obsessions brought Erzberger to a sick stop.

Erzberger: Will you for God's sake, Alfred, understand that from this point onwards it will be all bad manners?

Maiberling: The French, you mean. Oh, the French know how to veil things. Unlike that bullet-headed ignoramus.

By accident Matthias touched a relic of St Gertrude Paula had sewn into a seam of his overcoat. It radiated no efficacy.

He thought, dinner and conference tables, that's where I've known you, Count Alfred. It was not enough. You learnt nothing of a man at tables. Fifteen minutes at the front and Matthias had caught a soldier's contempt for the way life is managed in Berlin.

So Herr Erzberger and Count Maiberling blundered towards their automobile. Well-acquainted strangers.

The Marshal's Rite of Argument

In the rolling office-car, Wemyss still meant to outweigh the Marshal by dinner-time. Not outweigh in general but in the special matter of the enemy's navy. Yet like the premiers and presidents of October he was acted on in turn, finding the Marshal's rite of argument easy to foresee but hard to manage. And though something of the rite has already been recorded we can now watch more exactly its effect on its subject.

The Marshal: Compiègne!

He stood up and crossed the compartment and looked out as the wet tar of Compiègne station rolled by. Shepherds waited at the railway gates.

The Marshal: There!

He indicated with energy an exact spot amongst the town's blurred lights.

The Marshal: Jeanne d'Arcq our little general. Captured just there. Dragged off her horse there by the railway bridge. Well, well.

He turned and smiled at Wemyss.

The Marshal: She knew how to make people swallow things whole.

Wemyss thought, let him know now! That he can't get away with his Jesuit legerdemain.

Wemyss: I don't have that trick, sir. But I have instructions to stick by the naval clauses. As they stand in the

89

agenda. The disarmament of every ship. The internment of specified vessels. You shall have to swallow that whole. If I may say.

Soul-brother to Feisal, the Marshal kept his large face bright and mantic. The way all Wemyss's small knowledge of the man would have him expect. He thought, I could not have known it would rile me so quickly. The old man was a sort of mad chemical that ate into the small lock-up safe of a man's rationality and foamed at the front of the brain.

The Marshal: The last day of May in 1916.

Wemyss: I don't follow, sir.

The Marshal: I am naming the last time the German High Seas Fleet put to sea. Your government requires millions of soldiers to go on risking their persons? For a fleet that never puts to sea?

While Wemyss replied the old man flattered him with the full power of the old eyes but occasionally bent at the knees, exercising himself, implying, I can deal with this at something less than all-in concentration.

From the bright lamps on the wooden moulding of the ceiling, the Admiral's lens caught light and signalled sea-wisdom to land-locked Foch. But this was small magic. The Marshal, bobbing slightly every two seconds, evaded it.

Wemyss none the less made his speech.

The British blockade had done what could not be done on land. It had destroyed the enemy's supply line. It was true, wasn't it, that German soldiers during their spring offensive had been depressed by the quality of stores they captured in the French and British trenches? This disparity of supplies was produced by the British success at Jutland and the continuing control of the Baltic by the British Navy.

The Marshal went on doing his varicose exercises. Though Wemyss felt his blood rising he knew you couldn't threaten to walk away from the conference table just because an old man bent at the knees and looked flippant.

It wasn't too much to say, Wemyss said, that the war had been decided on the sea – if the Germans had not declared unlimited submarine warfare there would have been no declaration of war by America. But for the convoy system

devised by the British Navy there would have been a failure
of raw supplies to British and French industry . . .

The Marshal had begun to stare at Wemyss more slyly,
pretending to have been overtaken by some new presenti-
ment. As if he understood that Wemyss's polemics were a
cover for a more primal and unhappy itch. As if, in fact,
what Wemyss might in fact be asking was that whores
should be laid on.

The Marshal: What do you really want, Monsieur Admiral?

Though he had had a French nanny, it wasn't in
Wemyss's temperament to abide these foreign skills, this
powerful nonsense. His hands itched at his sides. He had
never been more tempted to try strangling a man.

Wemyss: The truth is; I *won't* sign . . . I am not *permitted*
to sign any document that yields on these issues.

The Marshal went steaming up and down the length of
the main compartment. All his aides' eyes followed him
except Weygand's which coolly remained fixed on the First
Sea Lord's pink face. The First Sea Lord was aware of it.
Quite a team, these two, he thought. They give off potent
emanations of success. They must be terrible creatures to
army and corps commanders who have no fleet to go home
to, no court of appeal from small villainous men.

Wemyss saw the Marshal part his lips in his mandarin
way. The thick-grown passionate moustache had gone
sandy from tobacco on its under-side. The strong teeth too.

The Marshal: Perhaps you don't understand: you are a
very political race, reasonable, you make arrangements.
We, on the other hand, we will never make arrangements
with the enemy. When we get him at this table we will make
him choke down all the terms at a gulp.

Wemyss: Like Jeanne d'Arcq perhaps.

The Marshal: The lady is true to the French temperament.

Wemyss: That's all very nice but the German delegates
are free men. How do you . . . *we* . . . intend to make them
swallow terms whole?

The admiral suffered a moment's impression that the
Marshal was expanding or perhaps rising off the floor. At

the same time as Wemyss hated the illusion he felt intimidated.

The Marshal: We shall do it by the extent of our perceptions. By the dominance of our ideas concerning the true nature of the. event. We shall do it through a harmonious proportion between physical and bodily elements.

Hope and Marriott frowned at Wemyss. Appalled by the onset of mysticism in the Marshal.

Wemyss: I don't quite follow, sir.

The Marshal waved his hand in the air, exactly like a teacher erasing a blackboard, beginning the demonstration all over again. For the slow children's sake.

The Marshal: It will happen. *They* need the peace, we don't need it as they do. They will swallow it whole because I will demand it of them.

Wemyss: I still fail to see any necessary . . .

The Marshal: I shall *exact* it from them. I shall not accept the hypothesis of failure. My Admiral, you are not to worry. I don't wish to see my British brothers stamping away in anger through the forest.

The train was slowing. It stopped. There seemed to be no sound from the engine or undercarriages, only the soaking murmur of rain amongst trees.

The Marshal stood still, his legs together, his precognitive passion all at once folded away as neatly as a beetle's wings. Even before he spoke he had again taken on the airs of someone half-way between host and hôtelier.

The Marshal: I think we have arrived, gentlemen. I believe they still have to back us from the main-line into an artillery siding. But that will take mere seconds. In the meantime I must go and inspect the hors d'oeuvres in the dining car. I have a name for being a fussy eater and only the finest will do for my British brothers.

When he had gone Weygand sat forward and stared more keenly still at Wemyss. Over-bright eyes, over-tended moustache, Weygand was the British child's conception of a gendarme.

Weygand: I hope the Marshal has satisfied Monsieur Wemyss.

Wemyss understood it was dangerous to get angrier. Or feel foolish, even a little, in front of George or Marriott or the other fellow, Bagot. They had to live together many days yet.

General Weygand's face grew foxy in its corner. A brother's bright pride was there too, for the ungovernable talent of brother Foch. Or a son's bright pride for a father, a lover's for the wild beloved.

Wemyss ached to say aloud: you disgusting little wog!

The General Who Swallowed a Hook

At Trélon, Corps HQ lived in a good two-storey house with shutters. The doors were adequately marked: *Operations, Intelligence, Administrative, Signals;* and people went in and out of the doors. So it was a going business. Not like that room in hell they'd come from.

An aide took them straight into a ground floor office. There the corps general sat behind a desk. His hands were joined. He was bald. He stood up. A tall man, with a high-located paunch, right under the breast-bone. His stiff walk increased the impression of pregnancy.

General: Gentlemen, I welcome you. This is Colonel Bayerling, my chief-of-staff. I couldn't manage without him. Now I have to tell you . . .

The voice was thick; the general had not bowed and had generally kept the left side of his face towards the plenipotentiaries.

Maiberling therefore whispered to Erzberger.

Maiberling: Another piss-pot!

General: . . . tell you that three of my officers have already gone across to the French lines under flag of truce to arrange the cease-fire in this sector.

Matthias thought, the drunk and the mad, perhaps I'll never get out of their hands.

By accident the general turned full-face on. A palsy had taken hold of the right side of his face and was dragging the corner of his mouth downwards. To counteract this pull he wore the ear-piece of a pair of spectacles hooked into the pink lining of his mouth and attached by wire to another hook around his ear. The tension in the wire was savage; his gums improperly exposed, his mouth threatening to slough off its pink membrane in the hope of saving itself.

Maiberling relented on his false judgement. The susurrus of his commentary filled Erzberger's ear and even the room.

Maiberling: Christ, a championship trout.

It sounded like a cruel image to Erzberger, even if it was the metaphor plaguing the minds of everyone in the office, perhaps even the general's mind. But if the military had defaced Inga in her bath you could not absolve them just because a hideous palsy took hold of their faces. The count was this far consistent. A dim small augury of consistency at the conference table.

As if he *had* overheard Maiberling, the corps commander decided before their eyes not to say any more. With a movement of his hand he yielded place to his chief-of-staff, limiting himself to lifting a telephone on the desk and saying a few words into it. For a lunatic second (of the type that had been recurring all day) Matthias wondered if he was alerting assassins. The likelihood thankfully fell apart. This general must have found out only an hour or so before that delegates would come his way. He had not had time or means to alert his divisional generals. Even if he *were* dead-centre of a group of extremist officers he would have found it hard to arrange for an ambush in such a little time.

He did not look as if he were dead-centre of a group of extremist officers.

Chief-of-Staff: A company of pioneers are clearing the Guise road of land-mines. It is only fair to tell you that our engineers have planted delayed action mines indiscriminately over there. On the roads you'll be using, that is. We do not however count the danger high . . .

An orderly had brought schnapps in and poured six glasses, placing one at the desk. Then he served one to each of the delegates and last of all to the chief-of-staff.

General: For your journey, gentlemen. I'm sure it will be safe.

God how cold I am without knowing it, Erzberger thought. He drank his schnapps in one intake. The orderly waited with the tray for each of the drinkers to return the glass. Maiberling gave his up without any patent regret.

The general suggested they all wait in the officers' mess — there was a decent fire-place in there while in the office nothing but a stand-up heater gave warmth. The delegates were taken with the idea of a fire in a fire-place. As the colonel showed them the way, the corps commander asked if he could have the honour to speak to Herr Erzberger.

When they were alone Erzberger felt uncomfortable looking the general straight in the face. There was so much improper stress in that line from mouth to ear.

General: Sir, can you tell me? What's happening inside the country?

Erzberger squinted. Trying to catch sight of the correct wary terms. But tiredness moved upwards through the muscles of his face and he could manage only something near to the truth.

Erzberger: The sailors of the Grand Seas Fleet have mutinied but the Cabinet hopes to bring them to a settlement. There are rumours that a general strike will commence on Friday . . . when's that? My God, *tomorrow*. But Ebert, who's an old trade unionist, says workers will never start a general strike on a Friday — it's pay-day you see. There are soviets in Kiel, Lübeck, Brunsbüttel, Düsseldorf . . .

General: Please sir, I don't want town names. What are they all doing? Don't the dead mean anything to them?

Erzberger cast up his hands: the general confused him as much as rebels.

Erzberger: I think people have been seduced. Not in wanting an end to the war. But in taking Bolshevik directions. You see. For example, they tell me at Spa that even the Ruhr battalions have been corrupted.

The general cupped his crooked jaw in one hand, and protected his right ear with another.

General: Please sir. I'd be grateful now for no more details. I have details enough of my own.

He lifted a flimsy typed sheet, synthetic-looking, from the table. He offered it to Erzberger.

General: You see. Details.

It was the return from the day's roll-call for the 101st and 193rd Divisions. It listed the day's casualties, which seemed heavy, of offensive proportions. But his soldiers were fighting no offensive. The 101st had been reduced to 349 effectives, the 193rd to 437.

Erzberger: These figures are correct?

General: Correct.

Erzberger: They couldn't have been caused except by a great battle.

The general soothed his desk with the palm of his hand. It might have been a restless animal.

General: We have been in this sector for six weeks.

Erzberger: Even so.

General: Desertion is a word I will not countenance.

The wire tugged wildly and even more of the mouth's lining was pulled into view and thickened his words. Erzberger thought, if I were not a Minister of the Empire he would hit me.

General: I tell my officers to mark down the deserters as dead.

Erzberger: I see.

General: It is a spiritually exact description.

Erzberger heard boughs scraping at the window. Perhaps the general read that sound as the damned trying to beg their way back into the house of the saved.

Erzberger: What can I say?

General: I would be grateful sir, if you conveyed nothing about events in Berlin or Kiel to my officers. Some of them . . . such special talents.

A father begging that his favourite sons should not be corrupted. That was the general, needing to believe all his boys were political virgins. After all the fear and killing, his knowledge of men as narrow as some boarding school chaplain's.

Erzberger: Perhaps they know.

General: Know?

For a second, tired Matthias felt a visceral urge to hit out at the man's deformity.

Erzberger: Perhaps they haven't told you. Out of politeness.

Erzberger Meets a Swabian

As they turned on to the main Guise road a soldier jumped in front of their vehicle, both arms stretched wide.

It seemed to Matthias that an expectation of assassins had been racketing in and out of the heads of all the delegates, though Vanselow and von Winterfeldt had not admitted to it. Now it possessed Maiberling yet again. He went squirming for the revolver in his coat's left armpit.

Erzberger: No!

The loud monosyllable made the count slump.

Erzberger: You'll have to toss that revolver. The French will search us.

Maiberling: Of course they won't. We're diplomats. Immune.

As the car slowed they could hear the driver calling to the soldier and the soldier replying in the accent of Matthias' home hills. Swabian, wide as a farm-gate.

Soldier: I got put here to tell you, sir, there's a cease-fire along this road at the moment.

Erzberger felt a sentimental but powerful impulse to speak to one of his own race. He wound his window down.

Erzberger: You speak the Swabian tongue?

Soldier: Yes sir. Where are you going this time of night? A decent Württemberger.

Erzberger was gratified by this country oddity: although the soldier must have stood all-night watches at the front he

97

still had a peasant's view of movement after dark: that it was somehow disreputable.

Erzberger: We are going to make a truce with the French and English.

The soldier could see only the front car.

Soldier: What? Just the two of you?

Erzberger rolled up the window, laughing. The convoy drove on and, a little maudlin, he told the count how the good frowning peasant had been amazed that, though it took millions of men to fight a war, a few car-loads of delegates could end it.

Maiberling: For Christ's sake, spare me the country wisdom.

Erzberger: Pitch that revolver.

Maiberling: No.

Erzberger: Alfred . . .

Maiberling: Listen, I know how these things work. It'll be all right.

For the first time Matthias noticed his gloves were full of freezing sweat. And now that visibility would have been prized, the hooded headlamps lit up nothing but particles of mist.

He thought, we won't get far because this is long travelling, it's Dante's hell and all we can expect is a further circle. And the worst thing is I have no Alighieri stature. I'm just a happy glutton with a head for figures and a little wife.

Like a cardiac spasm he suffered again the terrible bereft sense that there was nothing in his background that justified this journey. Treatises on united Europe, heady speeches in the chamber – they aren't the true Erzberger. At its most high-flown the true Erzberger's mind wasn't far off steak and red wine and Paula's warm and undemanding bed.

A Night's Lost Sleep

Wemyss's discontent had broken up under the genial effect of shrimps and some Chablis, rôti and some Beaujolais.

Everyone at table seemed to understand that the Marshal and Wemyss were to exchange stories of sea-war for stories of land-war and that the stories should not be sombre or of loaded intent.

Wemyss told the story particularly well of how Lawrence, long melancholy face reduced almost to femininity by white Arab robes, had visited the flagship in Jedda and tripped on his skirts while coming down a companion-way to the main deck. The First Sea Lord spent time on the idea of the prophet in mid-air flying in his finery, army boots and hairy legs bared by the pace of the fall.

At nine o'clock the Marshal demanded dessert and news of the German plenipotentiaries. A telephone call was made from the scullery to Tergnier, where their train waited for them. The train is still waiting here at the Tergnier station, said a transport officer. They have not arrived. It is credible they've been held up by cratered roads.

Though this information did not puncture the Marshal's vivacity at the dining-table, he began to speak of his sleep. For him, sleep was as studious a matter as any other.

The Marshal: I don't think we should wait up for them. We all need our rest. Do you know, Lord Admiral, that I have lost only one night's sleep in the whole of the war.

Wemyss: I didn't. No, I wish one could say the same.

The Marshal: Weygand has made it possible for me. I am useless without sleep.

The First Sea Lord knew what dutiful question must be asked.

Wemyss: And might I ask what kept you from your bed the night you speak of?

The Marshal and Weygand looked at each other, their eyes mutually softened. For a second Wemyss felt appalled by the intimacy of the two Frenchmen. A mouthful of sorbet wafted the shock away.

The Marshal: It was more than four years ago. During our offensive on the Marne.

Weygand: One could never forget. The night of September 10th, 1914.

The Marshal: Thank you, General. I transferred a colonial division from my right flank to my left. It took longer than I thought and when it got into action with its new corps, it captured the town of Fère-Champenoise. A pleasant little town it used to be. Its little *Mairie* was like something out of a toy village . . . That was already midnight, when we got into Fère-Champenoise. We were able to settle down in a room on the first floor of the town hall. On mattresses. No covers. It was a very cold night and after *that* summer we were still wearing our lightweight uniforms. So we found it very cold. People came and went on the stairs – you see the corps commander had set up his HQ in the place. I don't know if he liked having his superior officer on the premises. We were just dozing off about one o'clock when someone blundered in to tell me I'd been made a Grand Officer of the Legion of Honour. I said what do you think I care about that at this hour of the morning?

Maxime Weygand's eyes glistened with his special knowledge of the event.

The Marshal: So we dozed a little, for an hour or so, and then an officer came in with a present of cigars from Marshal Joffre. I said what, does the Marshal think I've had a baby? The same man had blankets. A rarity. The army had thrown their blankets away that summer. So we sat up the rest of the night wrapped in the blankets, smoking cigars, and people continued to come and go on the stairs. The least I could do was ask them if the bridges over the Marne were clear and intact. Within an hour all communications were being brought to us. Our bedroom became army group HQ.

Without any noise, Weygand again laughed. Though a secretive man, he showed nakedly now his gratitude for that oddly shared night in the war's first autumn.

The Marshal: Will they be here before dawn? Who knows? I intend to go to bed at the usual time.

A Trumpet and Faces

As they went forward a trumpeter jumped on to the running-board and hooked his left arm into the driver's compartment. What he blew on the trumpet was meant to be the cease-fire, but the shattered road jolted him so much that it sounded like a student rampaging on Walpurgis Eve with a hunting-horn.

Then Erzberger saw German soldiers crowding in on the car. At first he though they were mobbing it, but that was only the narrowness of the road. They were in fact lining the way. They seemed silent. Erzberger thought he saw a boy, raising his hand to wave them well, fazed out of it by the anonymity of the peace-makers inside the vehicle. In the refracted light all the helmets seemed too big for all the heads. All the heads therefore seemed under sentence. Like faces in a Gothic propaganda poster – one devised by someone clever on the other side, and dropped on our lines.

Erzberger: What's wrong with them?

They should have been laughing at the frantic trumpeter. Their lack of sane laughter turned Matthias's heart cold. He might have been travelling his own funeral route.

Then he was aware of a newcomer's horror in the count and thought, of course he's never been here before. And never seen such faces.

Erzberger: You were never invited?

Maiberling: Not exactly. I didn't want to come.

Matthias wanted to say, they're as innocent as Inga, some of these men. But he didn't want to start the count on that line again.

The trumpeter blew tar-ant-ah and then the notes slewed.

Maiberling: Boys home on leave, twenty-one-year-olds, twenty-two, twenty-three. They began to look so knowing. I wasn't so knowing. So I never came.

Erzberger: Yes. Knowing. That's the word.

He remembered his nephew whom he'd gone to look at in Pankow military asylum. Private Pieter Erzberger, son of a postman, split ear-drums, split nerve-ends. From an artfully orchestrated artillery barrage at Arras. Pieter Erzberger and fifty other men, filing into a dug-out, lifted by a great current of blast and laid down in crooked positions. Pieter stayed some hours amongst the forced, scorched smiles of his blast-dead colleagues. The shelling passed over and returned, over and back yet again. When fetched by stretcher-bearers Pieter Erzberger had nothing to say, an attitude he had now maintained for three months. And though his eyes stood wide-open like a gibbon's, what they swelled with was knowledge. A glut of knowledge had seized up the mechanisms of his throat.

Erzberger: Yes. Knowing.

Arriving

Maiberling: They're gone.

The soldiers had vanished.

Maiberling: What now?

His knees jumped. The car bounced and the inane bugle-call went thinly ahead.

Matthias felt exaltation like static electricity in his skull and hands.

Erzberger: I can't believe we're arriving.

Maiberling: No man's land?

The words scratched up the count's clay-dry throat. Matthias could tell he got no joy from arriving amongst the armed millions of the German-phobes.

Erzberger: But think, Alfred. You're safe now from all those German officers.

He counted to seven and there they were: a convergence of French soldiers. Holding their rifles slackly, by the muzzles; as had the old clerk defending the records in the Foreign Office.

Erzberger's door was opened and torch-light took him full in the face; then Maiberling. A very young French officer held the torch.

Officer: Les Plénipotentiaires allemands? The German plentipotentiaries?

Erzberger: Oui. Yes.

Officer: Trumpeter! Go back.

He made broad gestures with his free arm.

Officer: Back! Back to your lines!

The trumpeter made a wide passage round the outskirts of the torchlight. He began to shamble through the mud in Germany's direction. A second or two and he couldn't be seen, but he blew the cease-fire all the way back, in case he caused the war to begin again in that sector.

Helmet off, the French officer got in with Erzberger and the count. He pulled down a dickie-seat and sat forward. He had a flat, seducer's moustache. One could well suspect it had been drawn on the callow face for a comic purpose with blackened cork or boot polish.

Erzberger noticed that a French bugler had mounted the running-board in front. Meanwhile the boy with the theatrical moustache had been joined by another officer who might have been as old as twenty-five. This one also pulled down one of the retractable seats and spoke to Matthias and the count in rehearsed German.

Officer: I am Captain Huillier, commanding 171st Infantry Regiment. Please tell your driver to go on, following the signposts marked La Capelle.

Erzberger passed on these directions.

The vehicle pitched and yawed and the two French officers smiled at each other and the Germans on account of its wild movement. At every jolt, it seemed to Erzberger, the concussion of the accident outside Spa revived in small ways in his body.

Officer: An evil road. Many mines.

The bugler blew, taking the shocks, bending at the knees. A little jockey of a man.

Erzberger thought, perhaps this will become a simple journey, more direct now that we have come into the well-organized half of Europe. But it was a foolish hope.

He read the roadsigns. They were in Gothic script: this stretch of France had been German for four years and had only last week ceased to be so. Where the mist frayed Erzberger saw a dressing-station and a priest in surplice and purple stole burying a poilu. It seemed improbable that the dying could not hold on in a cease-fire, could not bide a truce.

The road rose out of a cutting and was all at once strewn with bricks, looking soft in the rain, like crumbled bread.

Someone had painted an art-nouveau sign in cursive Roman script and stuck it, enhanced with an asterisk, in rubble. *La Capelle,* it said.

Poilus crossed in front of the headlights without adverting to the Kaiser's eagles on the bonnets, the Imperial guidons in the flag-holders.

Matthias saw electric light in an estaminet on the left and two slim women dancing beneath it amongst the soldiers. They were only girls, and Matthias felt a minor reverberation of concern for them. In an armistice they would suffer mounting by hundreds of poilus. Each pounding in the point: here I am, alive, and no one's ever going to take aim at me again.

Officer: Here! Here!

They were in a square, and a pocked municipal building of the Second Empire stood shuttered in front of them. It was still labelled *Kaiserliche Kreiskommandantur* in studious German script. Clusters of French flags hung sodden from its balconies.

All three vehicles nosed in towards the municipal building and the officer told Erzberger to get out.

The German party stood on the muddy cobbles. Von

Winterfeldt moved from Vanselow to Maiberling to Erzberger, speaking softly.

Von Winterfeldt: Pardon my saying. We must not look confused or lose our dignity.

Maiberling: Thank you. Very valuable.

Von Winterfeldt: If there's anything the French respect in us it's our composure.

Maiberling: Jesus!

Von Winterfeldt: Leave it to me to explain why we're late.

A staff-officer strolled down the steps of the building marked *Kreiskommandantur*.

His face and limp were thoroughbred. He moved with the aristocratic boredom that either angered Matthias or rendered him fearful. There is no doubt, thought Erzberger, this man has been sent to meet us and be up to our weight. Where have you vanished, pleasant Captain Huillier and your boy-subaltern?

Von Winterfeldt moved forward to the man and made a salute. He introduced himself and began to speak volubly in French. Erzberger thought, he's really enjoying himself, they'll begin discussing vintages very soon.

But the staff-officer's eyebrows began to rise in the light from the vehicles. The subtlest arrogance invaded his face.

Staff-officer: There is no need for any of you to speak our language. I have made arrangements for you to speak your own and to be understood.

He implied, of course, that he was denying them access to a special tongue. Von Winterfeldt became rigid, did not move, might never move again. Just to show that he had sang-froid in the face of unreasonable prejudice.

Staff-officer: Herr Erzberger.

In fact he had addressed Count Maiberling.

Erzberger: I am Herr Erzberger.

Staff-officer: Major Bourbon-Busset. I am to take you to the meeting-place.

Erzberger: Where exactly . . .?

Bourbon-Busset: I am not permitted to say. There are many reasons. Your safety is one. And in the matter of safety . . . your party cannot travel further in German Imperial automobiles. They will be kept here in the transport pool. The drivers will be fed and looked after and you will pick them up on your return journey. You are welcome to dry yourself at the fire inside while we wait for the French vehicles.

Von Winterfeldt still waited irrelevantly stiff, facing the blank doorway of the municipal building. The rain hissed down, which made his game of hurt honour, his mute back, seem even more precious and astounding. It was when the rain began that Erzberger noticed, by the sound of rustling ground-sheets, that they were surrounded by French poilus, young boys smooth-shaven and men of thirty-five or more with heavy rustic moustaches. With them too, Erzberger thought, the middle areas of youth have been destroyed. They scarcely talked, they did not poke fun at von Winterfeldt, perhaps because they did not understand his gesture. They were engrossed, like recruits say, watching the dismantling of a machine-gun. They seemed to have no more hate than cattle.

Lapsing from grace, Matthias saw that von Winterfeldt and Major Bourbon-Busset were more of a common nationality than Bourbon-Busset and these Frenchmen. But to think that was a dirty Bolshevik thought. Erzberger suppressed it by conscious effort.

Maiberling was already half-way up the steps and called to Matthias.

Maiberling: How are you enjoying the Third Republic?

In the waiting-room three German officers in muddy uniforms stood beneath a wall-high portrait of Napoleon III. They were the ones sent ahead with truce flags and they were pale and kept their voices low beneath the statuesque vulgarity of the painting.

The count nudged Matthias and pointed to Vanselow. The captain surveyed, in his stiff-necked way, the lower reaches of the masterpiece.

Maiberling: Perhaps sailors don't see much art.

But there was an edge to the comment and his eyes returned to the three officers. As if they proved the killing pervasiveness of the German army by being here, so deep down a road they had already given up.

At nine o'clock Bourbon-Busset came back. There were to be five cars and no two plenipotentiaries were to travel in the same car. It was for safety's sake.

Outside, the near-silent crowd had invaded the machines, standing on the bumpers and the mudguards. A military photographer exploded a flash-powder at the base of the stairs. The powder charred an umbrella the photographer's assistant held over it and when Erzberger could see again the assistant was inspecting the fabric in a melancholy, any-thing-for-art's-sake manner. Umbrella umbrella, thought Erzberger.

Matthias told the count.

Erzberger: I'm going to protest to this Bourbon-Busset. He's got too many little shocks arranged for us.

Where, for example, had this further crowd come from? Had Bourbon-Busset cleared out the estaminet and ordered all the poilus to HQ steps?

Matthias, though he knew it wouldn't profit him, attempted to impart to his heavy body movements of crisp, jolting protest.

Bourbon-Busset: Make way there.

As Erzberger turned to his car the poilus came crowding around him. *Finie la guerre?* they asked quietly, flatly. Just perceptibly they pulled at his coat. *Finie la guerre? Finie la guerre?* Bourbon-Busset did nothing to protect him from their exhalations, which were of sweat, excreta, mud, death, cordite, sperm. An old soldier asked him *Cigaretten, Kamarad?*

Erzberger: Excusez-moi, je ne fume pas. Je n'ai pas rien cigarettes.

A few laughed quietly at his tourist's French. Someone said, *Eh bien, vive la France!* From disappointment over the cigarettes.

The drivers were speeding their engines but still the broad peasant faces, the damp factory-hand moustaches blocked him off from haven amongst the upholstery. *Finie la guerre?*

What's French for perhaps? his brain cried out. Is it

peut-être? And how do you say *eu* in French? Without turning Frenchmen hostile?

Erzberger: Peut-être. Maybe. *Peut-être finie la guerre. Je ne sais pas.*

Then the car doorway presented itself. Bourbon-Busset sat up in his pill-box hat. Erzberger pulled himself inside and the poilus shut the door for him.

A playful voice from amongst the soldiers called *Gang nach Paris* and there was a little laughter.

Bourbon-Busset: The general!

Von Winterfeldt still stood, back on to poilus and the whole mêlée, in the spot where his French had first been rejected. Had he stood there, unheeded as a piece of municipal statuary, all the time they'd been inside? Maiberling yelled to him from the second car and called again. The general made a regimental turn and walked, tight-faced, straight to the vehicle and in its door. No poilus bothered asking him for predictions or hand-outs.

Bourbon-Busset had taken the count's corner – no dickie-seat deference for him. He rapped on the driver's glass.

Bourbon-Busset: Driver! Straight on to the left!

Out of a sudden loose encirclement of whistles and catcalls the vehicles escaped. *Nach Paris.*

Bourbon-Busset smiled privately.

Bourbon-Busset: Your friend the general likes to speak French.

Erzberger: He has a name for admiring your country.

Bourbon-Busset: Oh?

His eyes significantly took stock of the rubble across the street.

Bourbon-Busset: We'd better give him his head a little. Eh?

Smart Jew Mayer

Beneath his used cheese-plate the Marshal found a note. All at table observed him finding it because the discovery was enacted in the midst of some sentence, not a significant one since Wemyss, disarmed by the cognac, immediately forgot what they had been talking about. As the Marshal glowered at the note, Wemyss took the chance to smile at George Hope.

The smile said, those poor Germans out on the cold roads now, or jolting along behind a locomotive driven roughly by some hostile French patriot. They're not being amused like us.

But it was only a marginal smile. You had, out of artistic respect as much as for diplomacy, to give the mass of your attention to the thunderous performance of the Marshal.

The Marshal: The same insult!

He gave the note to Weygand. Weygand bent his compact face to it.

The Marshal: That smart Jew Mayer! Could he have managed the war though? Could he, Maxime? Could he have conducted campaigns?

Weygand: No. Not that I knew him personally. But by report, the practice of war was beyond him.

Wemyss thought, do the French ever really speak like that? The Marshal and Maxime sound like historical melodrama. In rehearsal at that.

The Marshal's ham-fist took the note back from his chief-of-staff.

The Marshal: My friends must forgive me. I cannot expect them to know that in the remote past I published *The Principles of Warfare*. A work of faith rather than of science. Clever Jews don't understand these things. A clever Jew called Mayer was one of my chief critics. Mayer had made a grand study of your Boer War, and such. Someone – I don't know who – has written an opinion of Mayer's and left it here under my plate.

He bowed to his three officers.

The Marshal: I know it is none of my staff.

They returned the bow over their coffee-cups and the fragments of wafer and Gruyère.

The Marshal: And of course not my British brothers.

Feeling with some justice that he was being forced into some alien stock-part, Marriott bowed as awkwardly as an Etonian third-former in a Nativity play.

The Marshal: Someone has gone to the trouble of copying out in their own hand Mayer's prognostication. "A great European war will put face-to-face two human walls almost in contact, separated only by a strip of death. This double wall will remain almost inert despite the will to advance on one side or the other, despite the attempts that will be made to break through." And the second paragraph. "One of these lines, baffled frontally, will try to outflank the other. That, in its turn, will extend its front; there will be competition as to which can extend the most, so far as its resources allow. Or at least, this would happen if it were possible to extend indefinitely. But nature presents obstacles. The line will come to a halt at the sea, at the mountains, at the frontiers of a neutral country. The families of soldiers will grow tired of seeing the armies marking time without advancing, if not without suffering grievous losses. It is this that will put an end to the campaign . . ."

The Marshal raised his eyes, his forehead and jaw had somehow grown more delicate, like the face of a monk.

The Marshal: "It is this that will put an end to the campaign rather than the great victories of other times." Captain de Mierry, do you think that this is a true forecast of what has happened in the last four years?

The captain answered with valour, though the valour too sounded rehearsed.

de Mierry: It has a certain . . . *limited* validity.

Weygand: It is easy to be right in the privacy of one's study.

The Marshal: Could you call in the chef and his assistant, the wine-waiter and both the servants?

All the naval men felt that they had blundered into the annual general meeting of a club to which they did not belong and whose rituals might prove disgusting.

Wemyss: Would you like us to excuse ourselves, my Marshal?

The Marshal's face coruscated with furious attachment to all four Englishmen at table.

The Marshal: Please, my friends, you mustn't leave the table. This will quickly be attended to.

Wemyss nodded. He was beaten by the man's blatant use of unction, such as he had beheld only during productions of *King Lear* or once when he went with his mother to the burial of a High-Church peer (his uncle) and listened to a frenzied panegyric given by some homosexual pulpit orator.

The French nanny, who had raised him, taught him his French and what his father's lowland relatives considered effeminate and continental ways, had never behaved so perfervidly.

Wearing an apron, carrying his hat, the chef was let in.

The Marshal: Do you read military journals?

Chef: No, my Marshal. I know the crêpes were a little too dry round the edges.

The Marshal: Crêpes? I'm not worried about crêpes. I want to know, do you read military journals?

Chef: I went to work at the age of ten. I'm afraid I never was much of a reader.

The Marshal: For God's sake, do you read military journals? Do you follow debates on strategy?

Chef: I know I ought to try. After all, I'm a soldier.

He was middle-aged, pressed into service from some good restaurant somewhere, maybe Bordeaux or somewhere in the Marshal's part of the country. He had the same Spanish look and the same hint of excess in the use of his hands.

The Marshal: You misunderstand me, it isn't my purpose

to criticize your reading habits. Have you lost sons in this war?

Chef: One. I only had one. Four daughters.

He began sniggering at the idea of this imbalance in his breeding pattern.

The Marshal's voice grew more intimate.

The Marshal: He was killed?

Chef: Ages ago. Artois. July 1915. I think.

His hand made wary scooping movements as if he were actually digging through the strata of more recent corpses to get some memory of his son.

The Marshal: Do you feel bitter about it?

Chef: He was missing, thought dead. So we hoped. All his sisters hoped. There's no bitterness while you're busy hoping. By the time we got over the hope a lot of other people had lost boys. We had to look to them. It keeps my daughters busy, sir.

The Marshal put his hands palms out, concessively, towards his cook.

The Marshal: There should be better things for girls to do.

Chef: Better, sir?

But he looked more at ease, seeing the Marshal's persona swing to become that of Father of Unhusbanded Daughters.

The Marshal: It isn't good for young women to be Sisters of Charity. Unless they feel called . . .

Chef: No. There's no one for *my* girls. No one left. To speak of.

The Marshal: Do you know someone called Mayer?

Chef: Claude Mayer, sir. Assistant Dining-room Manager at the Metropole.

The Marshal: No. Not him.

By now the enquiry had grown idle. Already the Marshal visibly considered the chef his brother in loss; his face, blazing all evening with idiosyncrasies, went blank, so utterly bereft that for a second Wemyss felt his own breath detained at the bottom of his wind-pipe. What is it: grief, victimhood, death, lunacy? Wemyss felt he must know if his breath were to travel ever again with ease.

When the illusion died he understood his honest lungs

had not considered seizing, but noticed other men at that table looking obliquely at each other, wanting to verify their fellow diners were not fading.

The Marshal: When you go, send in your assistant.

Chef: Yessir.

The Marshal: I lost my own son, you know. And my daughter is a widow.

Chef: Of course, sir.

The Marshal: Sufficient to the day is the pain thereof. Eh?

The chef went back to his kitchen. You could then see the Marshal settle himself, workmanlike, in his chair, for the next interview.

Wemyss thought, it's indecent to go on watching. It was like the rigmarole of interrogations and ownings up in the house-master's study at some school. The air in 2417D, as in the best of schools at scandal-time, was full of the master's moist and obscenely sweet paternal rightness.

Wemyss: I think perhaps, my Marshal, it is a domestic matter. I must repeat that if you want us to withdraw . . .

The Marshal: You are disquieted, Lord Admiral?

Wemyss: No, I wouldn't put it so strongly . . .

The Marshal: And you haven't finished your cognac.

His thick finger pointed to the ceiling.

The Marshal: We are getting through it, don't you mind.

And so the others were brought in and questioned. The drink-waiter and the assistant chef could claim no personal loss. None of them admitted that they had any knowledge of the halcyon controversy between the School of *Offensive-to-the-limit* and its opponents.

All the time Wemyss grew angrier and would not drink more brandy when the young French interpreter brought it around, treading faintly so that the Marshal's tight questioning of the head-waiter should not be distracted.

The First Sea Lord telegraphed his discontent to his staff by various movements of the mouth and by socketing and unsocketing his monocle. The Anglo-Saxon grimace and mouth-gape that went with the bunching of face muscles around a monocle were useful to him now. This isn't our sort of game. But stick it out for the sake of the naval clauses.

Once one was reconciled, the whole act had its interest and was at least quick. Within ten minutes the Marshal had the combined dining-room staff back in again. He held the clever Mayer's opinion between his index and second finger, as if it were about to receive its last mention of all time.

The Marshal: If anything like this appears in my presence again I shall have you all, every one, charged and interned in a military prison. You know I have the power. Without trial, mind you. My displeasure is your trial.

The men looked secretively at each other's faces. Christ, we've got a clever bastard amongst us! A socialist! A *reader*! He to whom I pass the dishes has betrayed me. But which one?

The Marshal: Go back now. To your work.

When they filed out the Marshal sat again with an apology and flicked Captain Mayer's statement away down the table. It nosed into the fruit bowl.

The Marshal said aloud what he always thought and said of his percipient enemies, of Pétain and Mayer.

The Marshal: If Mayer was right it was out of a flaw of character. A flaw of character doesn't show up in a military journal but, my God, it shows up in battle.

And Weygand sang the antiphon.

Weygand: In battle, the moral stature of the commander is the deciding consideration. No one denies that.

Wemyss thought, these men are as remote from me as Cistercians. Thank Christ I served with men who thought that the range of the enemy's armament, and the diameter of the shell he could send seeking you, were questions to be considered above all others.

After coffee, served a little tremulously by the assistant-waiter, the Marshal begged permission from Wemyss to go to bed.

The Marshal: You might remain. More coffee, cognac. And you must forgive the unpleasantness.

Weygand stayed a little while to say, it's raining. George Hope agreed and they all cocked their ears in the strained way of people with nothing more to say and heard rain crashing on the roof with a sound like static electricity.

Hope: I hadn't noticed it was so heavy.

Riedinger: The sentries will be cursing.

Weygand: No. It's better than the trenches.

Riedinger: There's that.

Weygand: They can shelter beneath the trees.

Wemyss thought, with an A.B.'s pithiness, they can put their heads in the mud and whistle Annie Laurie through their arseholes for all you care.

He picked up the sheet of paper quoting clever Jew Mayer from amongst the North African oranges. He was aware as he glanced at it of a submerged pulse of disquiet in General Weygand. He inspected the hand-writing – a fast, professional hand, more likely a staff-officer's than a waiter's. He would have liked to take it away and set Bagot to finding whose hand it was. Yet the paper remained still, in some way, the Marshal's special property.

He returned it to its bed amidst the fruit.

The Marshal's Friendly Relationship with Sleep

In his compartment the Marshal exercised his friendly relationship with sleep. Chin up, arms out, hands flat, he floated on it. Ears full of it, he did not hear any more the rain or understand that as in last night's dream he was encircled by the ivy and elms.

In this state he prayed for the perfidious Mayer, yet again for Captain Bécourt and Lieutenant Germain Foch, and for all the lost sons of his staff. Behind his ears yet again the Spirit flexed its wings. Without you I am nothing, the Marshal signalled to it. Gave one kick of his left foot and went under.

Erzberger at the Railhead

Still sharing the back-seat with Bourbon-Busset, Matthias suffered heart-burn from a fast meal they had eaten in Homblières. He now felt like a bored tourist, somehow committed, by the food he had gulped, not to complain any more about the itinerary, yet wearied by the continuing view of the ruins.

He needed to sleep off the disastrous meal.

He put his hatted head back against the upholstery and adopted the secret childlike face you needed for sound sleep. Three inches from his nose the passionate and alien rain broke and ran in a film down the pane.

It was nearly an hour before the major woke him.

Bourbon-Busset: Tergnier, Herr Minister.

Erzberger: Where are we?

Bourbon-Busset: Tergnier. The railhead.

Erzberger: But there's nothing here.

Bourbon-Busset: No. The vehicles can't go any further. There's a walk. A hundred metres.

Outside, the delegates bunched as prisoners-of-war are known to do. In the thin rain Erzberger could hear the others swallowing the malaise that had come up their throats during sleep in the ill-aired limousines.

Bourbon-Busset: This way.

In front of them went a driver with wire-cutters. He snipped a way for them through three barriers of wired rubble.

Bourbon-Busset: Round here.

Wreckage of red bricks, foliate iron-work and roofing rose five metres in their path.

Maiberling: Hell!

For his trousers had been torn.

Maiberling: Are those drivers bringing our bags?

Erzberger: Of course.

Maiberling: Thank Christ.

On their right and across two tracks, an old locomotive, at first sight a casualty of war. It was, if one looked more closely, on its rails, and hissed softly. But no engineer stood on its plates, no furnace glowed.

Erzberger called to the major.

Erzberger: Is this our train?

At the loud German syllables arc-lights popped on and blinded all of them. Matthias raised his arm against the carbon-stench and buried his eyes. Even closed, they went on stinging from the blow of arc-filaments. He heard a military order given, a crash of feet and butts. He thought, it's all right now, I greet the bullet.

When he looked up he saw even Bourbon-Busset shielding his eyes with an open gloved hand. In the bilious light a company of chasseurs presented arms amongst holed tarmac, sandbags, indefinable wreckage.

Behind the vacant locomotive three first-class wagons stretched. Bourbon-Busset, Vanselow, von Winterfeldt took the salute. You had to admit: professional military men knew how to recover from shock. Von Winterfeldt accepting the military compliment, being placated by it.

Whereas Erzberger wanted to attack Bourbon-Busset's long bones with his finger-nails.

Bourbon-Busset: You are free to board the train, gentlemen. The saloon-car is in the centre. Excuse me, I wish to reprimand the electrician.

The first track was broken by a hole, filling with water. Von Winterfeldt delayed Bourbon-Busset by questioning him about it in French. Bourbon-Busset explained the crater. The general nodded. In-talk. Then von Winterfeldt gathered himself and spoke in German so that the other delegates could hear.

Von Winterfeldt: The Supreme Command never authorized destructions on this scale. It is very regrettable and must be the work of isolated people.

Bourbon-Busset: A few million of them perhaps. I must speak to the electrician.

The Prussian general stood on the cinders groaning and crumpling his gloves. Had there been a Europe once where professional officers had been a race without frontiers? Old von Winterfeldt, betrayed that way by his diplomatic career and French wife, thought there had been and felt its codes betrayed by Bourbon-Busset.

Erzberger wanted actually to begin arguing with the general, to say, look here there *is* one Europe, but not in that old way.

The count was already aboard and stood in the entry-way rubbing his gloved hands.

Maiberling: General. Matthias. The heating's working.

The general let Erzberger go first.

Beyond a staid entry-way their coach was draped with blue and gold satin.

Maiberling: There should be a first-rate tart somewhere.

Indeed it was a style of decoration not unknown in the whore-houses safely visited by Reichstag deputies.

Where the wall-panelling coalesced to form sconces, a flowering N embraced a florid Roman numeral: III. Cuspidors, brocade, plush.

Erzberger: Napoleon III. Look. This is an imperial carriage.

Maiberling stiffened; he might renounce it, the warmth, leather, genial lighting. Then a giggle shook him loose and he fell into a superb armchair.

Maiberling: This is what passes for subtlety, I suppose. This is Gallic wit.

Matthias let himself down into the plush and Captain Vanselow sat restrainedly on a corner of the sofa.

Appalled perhaps by this slackness, von Winterfeldt in his high-collared coat tried to firm them up with some special information.

Von Winterfeldt: The hole in the other track was a delayed-action mine laid by our army in retreat. They say there may be some under our track.

Dr Blauert, military secretary and bookish by nature, sat

forward. But Count Maiberling worked his buttocks even more deeply into the imperial leather.

The general walked to a wall and read the Emperor's insignia on the cornice.

Von Winterfeldt: Have you gentlemen ever been in the Kaiser's train?

Maiberling: No.

He sniggered, considering it a preposterous question.

Von Winterfeldt: In better taste than this. Everyone can laugh at Prussian grossness. But the Kaiser's train is in better taste.

So (Erzberger thought) the Prussian General compares the styles of two dead empires and their jettisoned pharaohs. For, give a day or so, the Kaiser would be forced into his tasteful train and, at best, sent over open points to limbo.

As Bourbon-Busset marched in and wished them comfort they could hear steam being got up.

Maiberling spoke in creaking French (he had, after all, once been German Minister in Switzerland).

Maiberling: Très joyeuse. Merde sur la tête de l'empereur.
Bourbon-Busset: Eh bien. Quel empereur?

Our Last Viewing of the Marshal

Now that the monolith is asleep, we can take our final view of him. From this time onwards we shall more accept than examine him: acceptance will be our only recourse, for he will not change or sprout unexpected limbs at the conference table. Knowing that he sleeps deeply as a child, we feel there is time to hunt about the dark cabin for signs of his fallibility and age. What was he reading at bed-time? And where are his teeth stored, and his old handkerchiefs?

The books are well back on the writing desk. Three only. A novel about Brittany in the 1850s. *Meditations on the Humility of Christ* by Monsignor Dupanloup. Antoine

Jomini's *Summary of the Art of War*. The Breton novel stands there in preparation for a return to life in Plonjieu next summer. He knows he will sit in the sun in the kitchen-garden with his women about him, wife, two daughters (one spinster, one widow). Vegetables in their laps, beans from the kitchen-garden sleeping in sunny colanders. He still desires his wife for the good reason that she is humorous and he finds a droll woman appealing; and because he wills to love her. Sexual disorder makes inroads on a soldier's power of decision, his sword of honour and truest gift.

The book of meditations hasn't been opened in nights. But if he had time to meditate he could, as effectively as any monk. He has certain psychic powers. Once in Flanders, for example, he felt – personally – machine-gun bullets entering the bodies of some three or four French soldiers advancing on Mericourt. Sitting in a chair in a villa at Hersin he felt the sideways tearing of the four sets of organs. Pain is the least and he felt no pain. Only the worse things: the last panic of the bowels; encounter with the fastest creature, so quick and ruinous in chest and throat and belly; the May sky winking once and shrivelling.

He has already confessed this experience in writing, but has little talent (would not want to have!) for setting such private knowledge down. He has managed this much in his journal: "I saw with an almost physical clarity the sacrifices my soldiers would be called on to make . . ."

Which is nothing at all like fore-dying their deaths.

The Jomini has always been with him, an 1837 edition bought at a high price by the Marshal's father and given to his son on his commissioning day.

Even this sparse travelling library testifies to the influences that have made him: the father, the schooling, the religion, the wife. You would think there were thousands of French officers like him, *revanchiste*, right-wing, Mass-going, wanting to be a Marshal under Napoleon. But there is no one like him. No French army or corps commander, no one on the staff or at the War Office. For he is consistent utterly to the factors that bred him. More than any army or corps commander, anyone on the staff or at the War Office. More than Mordacq, Debeney, Mangin, Pétain, Gamelin, Weygand. More than Field-Marshal Haig or any of Haig's people. If consistency were talent then the Marshal is a genius. And his training disposes him to see consistency as the greatest human talent. Therefore the Marshal believes he knows what he is.

There are no teeth missing except two he lost in a motor accident one springtime. Their substitutes, stuck on a partial false-palate, are slung on the washstand, do not inhabit a glass of water. There are no spectacles about. They are not needed.

The face is so firm in sleep, confesses so little doubt. Already a first-rate brain surgeon has written in the *Journal des Études Neurologiques*: "The discipline of Foch ought to be taught to children and applied to the treatment of the mentally ill."

Tonight as any night and even in the dark there is a faint nimbus (having to do with innate success) about the head.

He turns over and shows us a scar under his left eye. His thumb rubs another under his jaw. Won the same day he lost his two teeth.

That was in May 1916. In that month the British wanted to make a great frontal assault to the north of the Somme. The French command required Foch to use his army group as well, along the north and south banks of that hazy country stream. It would take pressure off the French salient at Verdun, the crumbling fortresses, redoubts, caverns that were too old-fashioned in 1880 but had attained a sanctity like Notre Dame's in Frenchmen's minds. The unreality depressed the general (as he was then). He admitted the depression only to Maxime and told no one at all that he feared he might once again be given pre-experience of the deaths of poilus.

As well he believed, for soldierly reasons, the Somme attempt could not work. In his lecture-room he had spoken not only of *élan*, dash and drive, but also of *sureté*, material, fire-power. By May 1916 he had come to respect *sureté*, and the fact that the enemy had a bunker system which could withstand much of it.

As well, a third of his divisions were transferred from the Somme and sent down by train into the tragicomical bulge the French insisted on keeping at holy Verdun.

By way of staff-officers, the Marshal (or general) leaked this more professional discontent with the plan into the offices of the highest – into the office of the President of the Republic. Then he was himself invited to give voice to it, and he gave voice to it. (See, says the thumb, now an inch from his jaw and barely discernible over the rim of the blanket, the growth in knowledge.) Leave it till next year, he'd said in May and June 1916. That's a unilateral policy, he was told. The enemy won't wait till next year.

He'd said, attack each defensive line separately, giving each a preliminary bombardment. Don't expect Western Europe to open like a can of peaches and according to your wish. (He could, in fact, sense it was *wish* not *will* that had led his brothers and elders to make these summer plans.)

On 16 May 1916 Foch's car went into a skid on a road flanked by drainage ditches. *Meaux 2 km* a local signpost said. It was a touring car and above him the limpid spring sky which, without being seen to inhale, breathed down mad ideas of invulnerability on all the allied bivouacs from Labroye to Guiscard now began jerking like a ballooning muscle, a frightful lung. He believed therefore this was going to be a bad crash. When it was clear the ditch couldn't be avoided, the driver seemed to want to swing the car head-on for it, as if *that* were his favourite way of entering ditches. He was thrown over the windscreen and General Foch took his place face-first at the driving wheel. Two staff-officers were also thrown about in various ways.

When he was clear again a senior medical surgeon was suturing his face under a lamp in the hospital in Meaux. The damage was small by the standards of what could happen to soldiers. General Foch thought then, in a concussed way, that the sky had never meant to impose a serious accident on him. The rips in his face had been given him so that he could remember, while touching his skin or being shaved, that he had tried to argue away the offensive on the Somme. (The suspicion lasted through concussion into clarity and is very strong with him tonight, even while he sleeps.)

He needed the feel of his scar-tissue at the end of '16's summer when the British and French had advanced eight kilometres on a front of thirty-five and lost between them 630,000 men. He needed it in the winter when they took him off the battlefield and forced him to a notional job in an office. Perhaps he will need it in an era of peace.

Here, in the wagon-lit, there are no papers, no family letters from his wife. Only the books, the two-tooth plate, the scars. His baggy uniform is hung away. Beneath the blankets the body is quite small under the large head. We feel he is a partially deflated manikin.

The window jalousies rattle a little because the window beyond them is open some way. Not even cold air from the forest breaks up the cabined smells of his sweat and tobacco, the persevering tang of his manhood.

Asleep in the Plush

When Count Maiberling said he thought he would sleep as he was amongst the plush, Erzberger felt grateful and knew he himself did not wish to sleep alone that night. Only von Winterfeldt and Helldorf went off to the sleeping car.

The count laughed and suggested they might have an indecent purpose. Erzberger and Vanselow unlaced their sodden boots and did not join in the joke against the military.

They hung the furnishings of the imperial saloon with wet socks and overcoats. Since it was quite warm they also shed their suit-coats. As they stretched amongst the cushions an orderly came and took their cognac glasses away.

Major Bourbon-Busset, upright in an armchair to see that

no shutters were opened, sent him to get blankets for the dignitaries.

As soon as they had settled down the Major, like a dormitory prefect, switched off the main lights. Matthias felt some shame at not forswearing the saloon and Bourbon-Busset's supervision.

Maiberling: Take care, Major. As soon as you're asleep I intend to raise the window. And read the calibre of your raindrops.

No one laughed. The count muttered amongst the opulent leather.

Maiberling: Good suspension. A nice ride.

Christ, Erzberger thought, in two hours the Büttenhausen clever-boy Matthias must speak up to the victors. He would have consented to ride on on the good suspension, under the rain and even under the Major's direction, for eternity, his feet cramped and blanketed in the plush, his brain blinking and nuzzling in its burrow.

Maiberling: Matthias. Can you hear me?

Erzberger considered lying.

Erzberger: Yes.

Maiberling: Do you have a mistress?

Erzberger: No.

Maiberling: Should I believe you?

Erzberger: Of course. How could I keep a mistress? With my background? It would be in all the conservative press.

Maiberling: I suppose.

Erzberger: Let me tell you, Alfred. They hire detectives to find such things out about me.

Maiberling: You'd like to have a mistress. If it were expedient.

Erzberger: This isn't profitable talk.

Maiberling: Paula doesn't satisfy you.

Erzberger: Don't force me to be angry.

Maiberling: And you have no mistress. So you come on a flirtation with the great whore History.

Erzberger: Go to sleep.

Maiberling: I understand these things.

Erzberger: You have a mistress!

For some seconds the count kept a poignant silence, as if he had not forced Matthias to make the barbarous claim.

Maiberling: I know you, Matthias. And this sort of journey is typical of men your age. Ardent bastards who know they'll never be satisfied. The bull goes to be pole-axed.

Erzberger: I won't believe it.

Matthias Wakes at First Grey Light

When he woke up all lights were out. Wakeful Bourbon-Busset stood by a window smoking without interest through his long nose. First light from an unshuttered window fell across his chest and hands. Oh dear Jesus, Erzberger thought. Arrival.

He sat up, resentful about the state of his mouth. He began putting his boots on and noticed they'd been cleaned by invisible orderlies in the night. He did not like the idea of Frenchmen padding around his couch while he slept, and watching his open mouth. However he was grateful for the polish.

The boots were dry and solid, as if they'd been put on a hot-plate. When he had them on he walked up yawning behind Bourbon-Busset. He saw small trees and a farm two fields away, stained with moss.

Erzberger: Where are we?

Bourbon-Busset: At the edge of the forest.

Erzberger: What forest?

Bourbon-Busset: The forest where you'll meet our dele-gates.

Erzberger: I thought it had perhaps a name on the map.

His dream of the winter forest and umbrella struck him as his irony faded. He made a small cry Bourbon-Busset did not hear. That instant, a few kilometres away, the Marshal woke and went to his window, interested to know what sort of colours the day of the triumph of will came dressed in.

Bourbon-Busset: We'll be there by seven. From that hour breakfast will be served in the dining car. You'll find your baggage in your wagon-lit. The attendant will bring you shaving water.

Erzberger would not be dismissed but stayed on to watch the forest pass. Its floor was lower than the railway line and matted with ivy. He saw a hunting trail, well kept. Therefore we are well into France. Near Paris? Fontainebleau? Germain-en-Laye? Mists kept station behind beech trees.

He found a sleeping-cabin marked with his name. Quite comfortable; he'd been mad to spend the night in the saloon. A steward came with shaving water. Erzberger tried French.

Erzberger: Where are we please?

Steward: I don't know, sir. You see I'm from the north, I don't know this line.

Erzberger did not know how to state disbelief in French. He changed his shirt and socks and went to the dining car.

Erzberger: Where are we please?

Waiter: I don't know this line, sir. I'm from the north.

The line branched and the slowing train took the right hand track and stopped. Off to the left, about seventy metres away, another train waited. Solid republican first class, no imperial coaches inset. Duckboards ran over the mud, amongst small elms, between the trains, and two poilus chatted by them in long blue trench-coats. Erzberger sat panting over his coffee, trying to exhale all the tensions of the journey. Von Winterfeldt came in. His riding boots glistened and he began speaking to the waiters and asked that the cook be also brought in. The debate grew. At last the general gave it up and approached Erzberger.

Von Winterfeldt: They say they don't know where we are.

Erzberger: I know they do.

Von Winterfeldt: They're lying.

Erzberger: Yes.

Once more the general seemed humiliated that his special Gallic knowledge had no currency in *this* France. That he might as well never have made friends with the French subjunctive.

Von Winterfeldt: I ought to tell you. General Groener wants me to stress the matter of rolling-stock. He wants me to read out a statement . . .

Erzberger: After I have spoken.

Von Winterfeldt: Of course.

The general sat and received coffee and raised the cup to his sculptured lips. Matthias thought, I must try to speak to him, I must not treat him as Prussian small beer.

But before Erzberger could open his lips, the general turned to the waiter and, as if for companionship, conversed with him in French. Even Matthias could understand the first sentence.

Von Winterfeldt: I have a French wife . . .

Part Two

2417D

Over the Duckboards

Nine o'clock. Knowing where they were and that they could even walk on a radius of two kilometres into the forest (though not enter the other train unless invited), the German plenipotentiaries climbed from the rear door of the saloon straight on to the duckboards. Bourbon-Busset led them. Matthias and the count. Von Winterfeldt, Vanselow and the aides. At the edges of the clearing winter birds made much busy small-song. The air was raw. Matthias saw his breath making vapour. We have at least been recognized by the foreign climate.

Poilus came from the trees to watch them cross the duckboards. Matthias thought he saw them come close to shrugging, as if they would go back to their wet tents saying, after four years they might have sent us faces that meant something.

The duckboards led them to a restaurant car. They boarded it. Inside it seemed as republican as it had looked at first light from the other track. Window-drapes cut close beneath the level of the sills; a heavy dining table. Its only cuisine, blotters and government paper. Matthias and the others were perhaps meant to climb in here and be unmanned by the bourgeois virtue of the fittings, the little tables in the corners, the simple yellow lampshades on the main table, dreary lampshades, stylized blossoms inverted over the electric bulbs. Perhaps we are meant to think where is the renowned French decadence the Kaiser called on us to destroy? Perhaps we are meant to have our moral wires crossed.

Bourbon-Busset: You will find your names on the left hand side of the table. Would you please stand behind the place tagged with your name. Captain von Helldorf can sit here at the bottom of the table and Captain Blauert at the small desk in the corner. I think you will find pens, paper and all you need.

He left them. They could hear faintly the high voice of an army telephonist beyond a glass partition, testing the line. An orderly took their hats and overcoats and hung them by the entrance-lobby. Maiberling refused however to give up his overcoat.

They found their places at the dining table.

Maiberling: Like a wedding.

Erzberger: Do you think so, Alfred?

It is the unhappy tumour of my apathy, Matthias thought, that lump the count carries in his armpit. And now, it seems, I shan't be seated by him to restrain his arm.

For the seating arrangement was: Vanselow nearest the door, Erzberger, the general and, at the table's end, Count Maiberling.

While they stood by their places, Matthias watched and was unreasonably annoyed by Vanselow's jaw locked down over his collar.

Erzberger: A battle injury, captain?

Vanselow: A fall, Herr Erzberger. Down a companion-way.

Erzberger: And nothing can be done for it?

Vanselow: The spinal column was damaged.

Erzberger: Ah!

On his white blotter, the captain made emphatic movements with his hand, careful lest Erzberger should imagine screaming gales off Heligoland and ice on all the rungs.

Vanselow: It happened in dock. In Wilhelmshaven.

Erzberger: Unlucky for you.

Vanselow: At first they thought little damage had been done.

Erzberger: Oh?

He was tiring of the captain's neck.

Vanselow: They had to be persuaded how serious it was. They don't know everything. Doctors.

The count, an eye on the telephonist's back, risked a calm

glance down the row of chairs on the far side of the table. He was half-back to his place when a small French general came in, said *Weygand* and that he would let the Marshal know they had come, and walked out again.

Maiberling reported his observations.

Maiberling: The seats aren't labelled.

Erzberger: Four places.

Maiberling: The names of the arses. That's the question.

Von Winterfeldt had no doubts and reeled names off.

Von Winterfeldt: Haig, Pershing, Foch, the King of the Belgians.

Forlorn Vanselow would not agree.

Vanselow: There must be admirals. British admirals.

Maiberling: The King of the Belgians? Small beer.

The count drummed the back of his chair. One of those fits of breeziness that were thin placenta to his loss of a mistress and his terror.

Erzberger: I don't think we should suffer too much. I don't think it's required we be anxious.

As he spoke, he still looked at his sweating hands, their stewed appearance, like the hands of a laundress or kitchen-hand.

Erzberger: We all know what our tasks are.

They had apportioned tasks at a meeting after break-fast.

Erzberger: It is a comforting idea that we are in the position of envoys, and envoys carry everywhere with them their immunity.

The count grunted and felt his armpit.

There was a small noise of leather boots in the entrance way. In an instant and too soon the Marshal stood opposite Matthias, staring him in the eyes for a few seconds, letting him taste the ocular fire. General Weygand arrived on one side of the Marshal and two British admirals on the other. A pair of junior naval officers took a table in the corner which, unlike Blauert's table, was equipped with a telephone. Two junior French army officers passed through into the servery and took the table beyond the ornamental glass, sending the telephonist away through the kitchen. Everyone was so

quickly, crisply in place; it was such a well-oiled position-
ing.

No American, no Belgian, no Italian. Only the Marshal,
Allied focus on earth, and the admirals with their will to
blockade.

Looking at the ceiling, the Marshal spoke. The two
interpreters, von Helldorf at one end of the table and a
French lieutenant at the other, talked at each other in both
languages, nervously seeking the sense of the utterance. In
the end young von Helldorf was ready to tell Matthias.

Von Helldorf: The Marshal requests your accreditation
papers, Herr Erzberger.

Opposite the sea-captain, Weygand had his right hand
out to take Matthias's documents.

The Marshal hooked spectacles on to read them and then
spoke again in French.

Von Helldorf: The Marshal and Lord Admiral Wemyss
will withdraw to examine the credentials. No delegate can
sit at the table until he has been accepted. He requests that
we all wait here.

The statement had been quite literal: only the Marshal
and the admiral left. While they were gone Erzberger took
from his attaché-case the communiqué from US Secretary of
State Lansing. After a few seconds' doubt he carried it to
Maiberling.

Erzberger: You're fluent in English?

Maiberling: Oh yes.

Erzberger: Could you read this if it is required?

Maiberling: Yes.

Little General Weygand watched them out of the corner
of his compact face as if he might at any second revoke their
right of communicating.

To Sit and Smoke

In the saloon compartment next his sleeping cabin, the Marshal invited Wemyss to sit and smoke. Seating himself the Marshal packed and lit his pipe, unfolded and read once more the accreditation papers, brushed ash from them and handed them to the admiral.

The Marshal: All as on the list. Let them think for a while. Perhaps you think it's wrong to delay things even a little?

Wemyss: I wouldn't go so far.

The Marshal: It will get better terms in the end. And more lives thereby saved than would be lost while a man smokes a pipe. Do you ever go in for pipes?

Wemyss: I'm used to tailor-made.

The Marshal: Turkish?

Wemyss: Turkish, yes.

He did not however produce one. He sat back with eyes almost closed. Hoping the Marshal could not tell how much he wanted to get back to the table.

The Marshal: This is a North African tobacco. Strong, yes. But I like its smell.

Wemyss: Very aromatic.

His lids still down, he put the German documents on a leather-tooled coffee table. To indicate how easy he felt.

Wemyss: We mustn't forget those.

The Marshal: What?

Wemyss: Those accreditation papers.

Hope's Letter to His Wife

Meanwhile Admiral Hope had sat at the table and begun a letter to his wife:

> Darling Nora,
> By the time you receive this the news it carries will be public knowledge . . .

The German plenipotentiaries watched him, the goats watching the sheep on judgement day. Admiral Hope did not look up at them or, in the ferment of the occasion, think it a strange time to write to one's wife.

> . . . The German delegates are in front of me at this moment. They represent the final cowardice of that Empire. None of their notorious leaders have come to face us. Instead a minister without portfolio, a decadent count, an out-of-work general and a mere captain of that great Imperial fleet!

None the less he realized all at once he did not want to be there, was close to a sort of vertigo.

> Nonetheless [he wrote] I feel the heavy onus of being placed here by God and Britain. Our responsibility, to balance demands for proper precautions against mere lust for vengeance, to destroy the mechanisms of the German Empire without destroying young and old indiscriminately. I believe that never since Pentecost has a descent by the holy spirit of wisdom upon mere men been so necessary.

And with the writing of the words he began, in fact, to feel Pentecostal, infused: and his breathing eased.

Of course, one suffers a bit from that old recurring question: why me? There are so many generals, so many admirals, so many nations to speak for. It is exactly the way one feels in battle while timing the flight of enemy shells. Why should this ship of all the British ships in all the British seas be the one to go sailing amongst the vapours of death?

You and I know the answer: there is no arrangement that is not divinely arranged.

How are Catherine and dear little Edmond? I'm glad that at last Major Henderson has stopped calling on her. I think he's an insensitive man, a common enough kind of regimental oaf, not up to Trevor's weight. On the other hand, there is really no need for her to go about dressed as a widow all the time – three months black is enough these days. Now that I have seen the front, there is something I wish you to pass on to her. Tell her that if it was meant for Trevor to die it was best it happened quickly, as soon as the German artillery began firing. On our way here I met Horace Turner who is commanding a division near Amiens. He told me that when our retreat began, men trampled over the wounded in the rain, became mad things shut off from each other, lost to brotherhood. He says he saw a shell-shocked subaltern walk calmly down a line of wounded shooting through the head whoever groaned loudly. This is such a terrible war that we cannot be sure it was not precisely such a destiny that even an upright young man like Trevor was saved from by his instant death. Do I sound too callous? France is a running graveyard, my love, from Calais south but, because I cannot believe that God refused to admit to his light any of the young who died here, it follows that there are worse things than death. There are living hells and the memory of living hells. As painful as it may be to say, it must be said. There are men alive now who would gladly take Trevor's place in quick and honourable oblivion. How to say this to Catherine? I can't say. But I rely, my darling, on your tact and wisdom . . .

Reading of Terms

The Marshal and Lord Wemyss returned in a faint tobacco sourness. Erzberger was asked to indicate his party, the Marshal introduced his, the nervous interpreters referred to each other for the spelling of names. Von Winterfeldt at centre table had sense to know they would not like his aid.

All this settled, the Marshal signalled that they could take their places and with a similar bare gesture of his left hand that Erzberger should speak. Phlegm impeded Matthias's throat and could not be easily expelled. When he could talk his words were breathless, the voice furry.

Erzberger: I have come to hear the Allied proposals for an armistice.

Laperche translated to French, the Marshal answered, Laperche transmitted, in merely viable German, the answer. That was the pattern.

The Marshal: I have no proposals to make.

The count put a combative elbow on the table, in the manner of sane diplomats.

Maiberling: We wish to enquire as to the conditions under which the Allies would agree to an armistice.

The Marshal: I have no conditions to propose.

On Erzberger's left von Winterfeldt exhaled, expelling perhaps his last residues of Gallic enthusiasm. It wouldn't be of any use to remind the Marshal that they had once dined together. Beyond von Winterfeldt however Maiberling, glowering at his hands, showed the most urbane anger. Now that diplomatic contact had been made he seemed a man of exquisite protocol and sense. The idea of his extracting his armament from the overcoat and putting a bullet into the Marshal's stiff neck was no longer probable.

Erzberger: President Wilson informed our government

that *you* have authority to state conditions. I would like my colleague Count von Maiberling to read our last communiqué from the government of the United States . . .

The Marshal permitted it. Perhaps he had not received a copy himself before leaving Senlis. Perhaps the American President did not honour his allies with copies of all state papers exchanged by Germany and the United States. Perhaps that was why the Marshal had permitted no American here.

Maiberling began to read, pausing at the ends of sentences for the French interpreter.

Matthias watched the Marshal haul furiously at the ends of his pipe-stained moustache. And Wemyss, ample face concentrated on the keeping of his monocle in his right eye, taking from his pocket first one pair of spectacles, then another. A regular Cowes review of his optical armament.

How shall I speak to them? It is almost beyond belief that they manage to speak to each other.

Maiberling finished the reading of the American communiqué.

The Marshal drove his body forward in the chair. Out of furious goodwill he would sort out their clumsy overtures.

The Marshal: I am here to answer you as to terms if you require an armistice. Do you require an armistice?

He drew the possibility in the air as if it were a remote and theoretic one.

The Marshal: If you do, I can *acquaint* you with the terms. I cannot *make* them myself. That is the work of the governments I represent.

He stored his tongue in his left cheek and held it there, something cleverly achieved.

Matthias and the count both spoke at once. Eager to be acquainted with terms.

General Weygand began to read from the document before him. Even in French it sounded ruinous to Erzberger, doubly ruinous when Helldorf translated. The massive terms rose, sucked oxygen out of the air, made Erzberger dizzy, gallows-gay.

They wanted Belgium, France, Luxembourg, Alsace, Lorraine evacuated in *fourteen* days. They wanted repatriation of all natives of the nominated areas in fourteen days. These demands stung Matthias on the raw side of his conceit – he wrote on the paper provided, *Der Volkerbund,* Chapter IV. It was as far as he could go towards telling them: in the book whose title he had just noted down he had chastely written against expatriation, and now felt insulted by the punishing time limit.

They wanted five thousand heavy and field guns given up in good condition. Thirty thousand machine-guns (good news for the soviets), five thousand trench mortars, two thousand fighters and bombers.

Von Helldorf translated impassively; perhaps he was happy if the regimental horses were not touched.

They wanted evacuation of the districts on the left bank of the Rhine. And across the river from Mainz, Coblenz, Cologne and Strasbourg, bridgeheads thirty kilometres deep. From the end of the table came the noise of choking. Captain Vanselow had begun to weep. Was he a Rhinelander? Erzberger could not help feeling the captain was off cue. Weren't his tears supposed to be for the fleet?

Matthias himself was being watched by Lord Wemyss, who noticed his pained mouth and the way that, at each clause, his eyes slewed up and down the table. Wemyss thought, he believes he's in control but in fact is well under, two-thirds gone. I ought to be pleased . . .

Clause V, the army had twenty-eight days to get out of the Rhineland. Clause VI, no one was to be harmed by the evacuating armies and no food or other stores destroyed.

There won't be time for any vandalisms or other barbarities, Erzberger could have promised. They'll be all trying to get out by mule or bike or even by catching a train. Even the notorious Death's-Head Hussars, featured Herod-style in the American press as baby-roasters. No time for a single baby-barbecue for the hussars this November.

Clause VII. Five thousand locomotives and one hundred

and fifty thousand wagons in good repair to be delivered to the Associated Powers within thirty-one days.

Surely I can depend on Maiberling now to turn earthy and scream: Famine-mongers! Dealers in scrofula!

But Maiberling stayed cool and business-like.

Clause VII brought forward its other surprises. Ten thousand lorries to be delivered inside a month.

Innocuous Clause VIII. The German Command shall be responsible for revealing within forty-eight hours all mines or delay-action fuses disposed on territories evacuated by German troops . . .

Genial Clause IX. In the east, all German troops to withdraw inside the frontiers of Germany as they existed on 1 August 1914.

It was possible to breathe amongst such clauses.

Vanselow had now got himself under control and packed away his handkerchief.

Financial clauses: Reparation for damage done. Return of the cash deposit in the Bank of Belgium, return of Roumanian and Russian gold . . .

Such a gambling race we are. Now all the bills will be called up at the one time.

Naval clauses.

Don't go to pieces again, my captain.

Vanselow listened mutely.

'Immediate cessation [read Weygand] of all hostilities at sea and definite information to be given as to the position and movements of all German ships . . . To surrender at the ports specified by the Allies and the United States all sub-marines at present in existence (including all submarine cruisers and mine layers), with armament and equipment complete . . . The following German surface warships which shall be designated by the Allies and the USA, shall forthwith be disarmed and thereafter interned in neutral ports, or, failing them, Allied ports, and placed under surveillance of the Allies and the USA, only caretakers being left on board, namely:

  6 battle cruisers
  10 battle ships

8 light cruisers
50 destroyers of the most modern style.

All other surface warships (including river craft) to be concentrated in German naval bases to be designated by the Allies and the USA, completely disarmed and placed under the supervision of the Allies and the USA. All vessels of the auxiliary fleet are to be disarmed."

Matthias watched the captain's hand skid across his notepaper, leaving deft shorthand in its wake.

The Killing and Numbing Clause

Clause XXVI was the killing and numbing clause. In fact Erzberger heard very little of Clause XXVII onwards after Clause XXVI fell on him.

> The existing blockade conditions set up by the Allied and Associated Powers are to remain unchanged, and all German merchant ships found at sea are to remain liable to capture.

Erzberger found himself dipping his pen into ink and writing according to his futile Reichstag rhetoric on the virgin paper set for him. "We will let you [he wrote] render the army helpless, destroy the fleet. The Rhine can be your sewer. But you want to strike at the grocers' shops and soup-kitchens."

He noticed that Admiral Wemyss, who had gone on tampering with his spectacles all through the army, territorial, financial clauses, kept his hands emphatically still throughout the reading of the naval terms. Lest anyone think he didn't mean to impose them.

It was one of those especial moments, Erzberger realized, when the diluted emotions a politician (*this* politician, Matthias Erzberger) takes with him to any conference table are reduced to unity and all he wants to do is scream across the table, *Murderer*. For he finds, in spite of all the self-doubts and secret pride that drove him to the hustings, that he is one with the apolitical others – the people with ration books.

When he was conscious of the men at the table again he found he was being watched, though the Marshal's face was clamped down tight over the Marshal's curiosity.

He saw too that he had covered the page with feverish writing. There were a lot of exclamation-marks.

He sat upright, turned the littered page face-down.

Weygand finished reading and dropped the armistice document to the table. Erzberger could see across the table that there were typing errors in it, many words X-ed out.

Helldorf reported that the duration of the Armistice was to be thirty-six days. With the option to extend.

The Marshal as Exegete

The Marshal: Well?

Erzberger thought, I'm the one who has to speak. What do I say that will show up against those mountainous propositions? As an outsider and with disbelief he heard his own speech.

Erzberger: We wish to appeal for an immediate cease-fire while the terms are considered. Our request is not a military stratagem, Marshal. I can tell you only that our armies are in a state of Bolshevik anarchy. We had such difficulty crossing our own lines. I could certainly provide the Allied pleni-potentiaries with a list of cities where Bolshevik revolutionaries have taken control of local affairs. We ask for a cease-fire not only for Germany's sake but for the sake of Western Europe as a whole.

Wemyss sighted the white paper with his right eye and wrote, *A little late to go pan-European.*

The Marshal: Rebellion is quite normal in defeated armies. Western Europe can look after itself.

Von Winterfeldt begged to read a memorandum he had been given in Spa. He read it in his smooth French and between sentences looked up at the Marshal and Weygand as if inviting approval of his accent. It spoke of those who would die during the consideration of the terms who would otherwise be restored to their families.

The Marshal: There will be a cease-fire when the terms are accepted. That is the whole rationale of the terms.

Erzberger's ears still rang.

Erzberger: I appeal to your president.

The Marshal: There's no sense in such an appeal. The terms are strategic matters and the business of soldiers. Therefore you are here as military deputies. You cannot appeal to a president.

The count advanced a well-ordered face in front of von Winterfeldt and stared Matthias in the eyes. I'm with you, said the eyes. Matthias thought without comfort, so you are.

Erzberger: I must of course seek your permission to radio the terms to the Imperial Chancellor and to OHL in Spa.

Foch: The terms can be transmitted by radio in code. If you are worried about revolution in your army we can't very well send them *en clair*. Any radio operator who picked them up could pass them on to other soldiers or even suppress them. If you don't wish to use coded radio you may send a courier, one of the German officers you have in your party.

From the table in the corner Captain Blauert had risen and dropped a slip of paper on to Erzberger's blotter. It said, *Impossible for us to encode such detailed clauses. Possess no cipher books.*

Erzberger: Our departure was so hurried we could not gather the requisite cipher books to encode the terms. On the other hand it will take a courier at least twelve hours to reach OHL at Spa. Therefore I request an extension of one day to the deadline for acceptance of terms.

The Marshal: I have no authority to do that. The deadline

stands. Seventy-two hours from conclusion of this meeting, say 11 a.m. That makes the final hour for acceptance 11 a.m. on Monday.

Everybody at table, except the Marshal and the interpreters, wrote it down: 11 a.m., Monday.

The Marshal: My staff will arrange for your courier's safe-conduct and provide him with maps that indicate our requirements in the Rhineland. You yourself are free to inform Spa and your Chancellor that the courier is on his way. You should present any messages to my staff who will be on duty in this carriage.

Weygand: You may seek further general or individual meetings with members of our mission.

The Marshal: I do not advise you to look for any softening of terms as they now stand.

Do They Take in Wuppertal?

He stood. Can I stand? Erzberger wondered. Have they left us our legs?

The British admirals, the French generals abandoned the table. Climbing down to the duckboards Erzberger felt his calves tremble as if he had had a hard day's walk with hills and some rock climbing. Not looking back: some staff officer had no doubt been set to watch them and behold them fall into a terrified knot of strangers bickering amongst the low elms. He heard Maiberling whisper *Jesus* and the nearly devout word blew over his shoulder as a short puff of vapour.

They sought the deep chairs in the saloon and wallowed, panting; they had gained the summit of the German defeat. Four climbers from seventy million. Von Helldorf and Blauert, who had had their work to do in 2417D and were in any case young, stood by, lithe, ancillary, remotely sympathetic. General von Winterfeldt, having got his breath back, went statuesque again. Captain Vanselow called for paper, wrote a proposition or two for use in the face of the British admirals, lifted his pen after a few lines and spilled tears on to what he had written.

Maiberling: Are you a Bavarian, captain? A Rhinelander?

Vanselow made a gesture with his hand that said it doesn't matter, I beg you to believe me brave. And not to report my behaviour to historians.

Erzberger thought yes, how disastrous for a professional naval officer. To be known for having wept in front of the Marshal in the forest of Compiègne.

An orderly crept in and asked them if they wanted coffee.

Maiberling: Cognac. Cognac, gentlemen?

Von Winterfeldt: These bridgeheads they want? Do they take in Wuppertal?

Erzberger: I don't know. They'll send us maps.

Von Winterfeldt: I knew a very fine family once. In Wuppertal.

Major Bourbon-Busset entered from the direction of the dining car. They glanced at him, he nodded, sat, took account of their misery whose symptoms he must strictly report to the Marshal. As yet more fuel and staple for the Marshal's theory of will.

Radio Flimsies

In the Marshal's saloon they needed no stimulants other than the offered morning coffee.

Hope spoke quietly in English, privately to Wemyss.

Hope: That naval chap crying . . .

The Marshal hammered his pipe riotously on a metal smoking stand. You got the impression his short legs had been drawn gnomishly off the ground and that he might hug himself.

Reidinger brought him a radio flimsy. He read it, nodded,

held it face out to the Admirals, though they could not read it from the place they were sitting. A new degree of brother-hood, he implied by this gesture. Nothing to hide.

The Marshal: From the War Ministry. The Italian govern-ment insists that Bavarian troops evacuate the Tyrol.

Wemyss laughed. The modesty of the request! He too was suddenly full of blatant gaiety.

The Marshal threw an order over his shoulder.

The Marshal: Mark it on the agenda.

At a quarter past eleven maps were brought to the German delegates' train. In one envelope maps for the information of Erzberger, Maiberling, von Winterfeldt, Vanselow. In the other, sealed, copies to be carried by von Helldorf to Spa.

Erzberger was first to inspect the maps. The others sat about a small console, pens in hands. Expecting to be shown, as they would have to be. But Erzberger hesitated to hand them their copies. What would it produce? Gunplay from Maiberling, tears from Vanselow, inane and gentle-manly hurt in von Winterfeldt?

The cross-hatching on the maps covered the Rhineland and crossed the Rhine and swelled, three neat goitres thirty kilometres deep, eastwards. At least Wuppertal's nice fami-ly did not fall inside these ruinous bridgeheads.

When he handed out the maps the others considered them indolently; directors well into a routine board meeting. Von Winterfeldt delivered some statistics evenly, like a clerk recording mortgaged land.

Von Winterfeldt: So they take our Rhineland. Twelve thousand square miles. Five million people. German since 1814. So they take it.

Von Helldorf, recent translator but courier now, had already begun packing his satchel.

Seeing him, Erzberger spoke to the others, saying they couldn't wait a day or more for answers from Spa and Berlin whenever a courier was sent through the line. The only quick method was to send a radio message. In it, to ask if Max and the generals believe that the terms must be accepted, they should authorize their men in the forest, *us* that is, to sign at once. Getting what concessions we can; from that old man.

The others would not answer, their hands ran over the maps like mice. At last, the general.

Von Winterfeldt: Could we code such a message?

Erzberger: Blauert says not.

Vanselow: No. It would be too hard. And finish full of mistakes.

Von Winterfeldt: The Marshal would read it before it was sent. He would know we're willing to accept his terms. In principle, as they say.

Maiberling: As they say. What's the use, trying to play diplomats. He has us by the balls.

Yet he seemed placid about the fact.

Erzberger: If he *does* know . . . it's the best means of softening him to make concessions.

Von Winterfeldt: He isn't easily softened.

Erzberger: Our best strategy is to make him see that Western Europe is endangered.

Maiberling belched.

Maiberling: It's endangered. Yes.

Von Winterfeldt: He hasn't eyes for such propositions.

Yet the message was taken to 2417D to be transmitted. When the Marshal had inspected this message he immediately drafted a communiqué to the War Office in Paris. It said that the German delegates accepted the terms in principle. Later the Marshal was told that that decadent old sentimentalist Clemenceau had wept when he saw the flimsy. Of course, the Marshal thought. His intent that they should accept wasn't as strong as mine. On the battlefield the will can be baulked by tactical facts: mud, gas, machine-guns. But in 2417D it was just them, us, the terms, no tactical surfaces, no blockages.

Over the Soup

At lunch in the German dining car everyone felt better.

Maiberling: This afternoon. That's when the important work will be done.

Over the soup they felt eloquent, they breathed in the soup vapours as if they might nourish their powers of negotiation.

Erzberger felt happier than ever before with his three colleagues. At one o'clock Bourbon-Busset brought news that transport and safe-conduct had been arranged for von Helldorf. Von Helldorf put on his overcoat and had an attaché-case locked to his wrist. He remained a second in the saloon, looking for best wishes. A well-tailored messenger to that Empire, already dim in outline, that Erzberger had left only yesterday.

The young horseman travelled by army truck to the Noyon road, where a limousine waited for him. Alone in its back seat he played somewhat with the chain about his wrist and raised his arm. Testing the weight of his country's certificate of chaos.

The Gods of Agenda

Erzberger spent the afternoon in the saloon writing expansive notes and submissions for the plenary sessions. He started with energy but apathy got into his blood about three o'clock and he went to a window and looked out at the scene that had already got tedious for him, as a suburban garden gets tedious. In *this* garden grew mud, vaporous drizzle, guards in duck-egg coats, and varnished coaches.

It was getting dark and his tongue itched to make small talk to someone. We won't see the sun again today. But there was no one about. Even Bourbon-Busset had gone to his cabin to sleep off his earlier vigilance.

In 2417D, the count and the general were arguing with Weygand.

Maiberling: One wonders if the Allies draw up such severe terms just to have the Germans refuse them?

Weygand: There is nothing hidden about the Allied intentions.

Maiberling: Do the Allies intend to make the armistice fail so that they can go straight on to a discussion of peace terms?

Weygand: If you knew the jealousy of our politicians! We are forbidden to speak of peace terms. Peace terms are their business. For us, just the settling of a truce.

The count still behaved with ceremony, appearing to believe as much as anyone in the gods of agenda, minute-paper, conference-table.

The general and he argued in tandem, in the manner of genuine colleagues.

Maiberling: A truce is necessary. To save ourselves. But to save Europe as well. There are already soviets in Hamburg, Cuxhaven, Altona . . .

Weygand: Yes, yes.

Von Winterfeldt: We came to you through the wreckage of units. You know as I do, General. The German army could not recommence fighting once the armistice is signed, once the withdrawal starts. The war began with railway time-tables and will be finished by them. *Our* railway time-tables, taking over inexorably. Making us incapable. You understand this. So the severe terms are wasted.

Maiberling: You must understand that the surrender of thirty thousand machine-guns would weaken the army too much in the event of its having to take on the Bolsheviks in its own ranks and in the interior.

Von Winterfeldt: If the army isn't kept intact for fighting these rotten elements, Germany will be lost and incapable of paying reparations.

Maiberling: So it is to everyone's advantage that the army should be given time to march back in an orderly fashion.

In these and other terms they chorused each other like brothers. While Maxime Weygand kept tidy notes of all they said — section heading across the page, indented a's, b's, c's — in a small hand. Generally they spoke to his brushy scalp. In the end they felt their diplomatic eloquence sapped by Weygand's mute bobbing head.

Maiberling: In poorer parts of east Berlin and Hamburg and a number of provincial towns, people are getting as little as 800 calories a day in the form of corn-meal or potatoes.

He saw Weygand write down 800 faithfully.

Maiberling: The state of famine is already established. Therefore the clauses touching the continuation of the blockade and the surrender of five thousand locomotives and ... what is it? ... 150,000 wagons? ... are inhuman.

Weygand: The bridgeheads!

Maiberling: The bridgeheads?

Weygand: Are they inhuman too?

Von Winterfeldt: They take in such cities as Mülheim, Solingen, Remschied ...

Weygand: We are aware of what is taken in.

The tufty head of hair jerked a little impatiently before them. I suppose this is the way the unemployed are treated at poor clinics, thought the count.

Weygand laid down his pen slowly, as if seeking for it a particular and exact axis.

Weygand: The Marshal wishes the German delegates to understand that these informal discussions are merely exchanges of opinion.

Maiberling: What is your opinion though? After all, you are obviously intended to give your opinion.

Weygand: It is my opinion, based on a knowledge of the statesmen who framed the terms on the advice of military experts, that you would be mistaken to look for substantial concessions.

They went back to Napoleon's saloon and had cognac and coffee with Erzberger. Matthias had been already infected, from across the mud, by their despair.

Erzberger: We have to work. We have to say the same things over and over.

They switched on the lights as more autumn rain fell into the forest. They began work on a submission called *Some Observations on the conditions of an Armistice with Germany.* But the count wrote only a few headings and tossed his pen down.

Maiberling: It's only basket-weaving, this. To keep the inmates happy.

And he glared at Matthias and the general and the opulent draperies. Wanting a fight.

Von Helldorf and Enfilading Fire

North of Bohain, Captain von Helldorf was taken down into a shallow French system of connecting trenches. He could smell careless latrines in the support trenches where unshaven poilus slept on crumbling ledges in trenchcoats and beneath especially fouled blankets. Did they fight the whole war like this, like Armenians?

His guide: a middle-aged captain, synagogue-Jewish to look at. Someone had impressed on him that Hauptmann von Helldorf must not be shot. He kept exhorting the cavalryman.

Guide: Head down please, Captain. These trenches are mere drains, so rudimentary. The speed of the advance hasn't allowed . . .

He was a gentleman and an obvious civilian. He implied a certain carelessness on the part of his people in that their spade work had not kept pace with their victories. In his elbow he carried an exactly rolled white flag for von Helldorf's use.

Guide: A hundred metres on our right.

They had to crawl in the front line, which was made of shell-holes and connecting entries scraped in the mud. In the holes men slept or lay at ease. Machine-guns worked regularly from both flanks and from the German lines as well. The noise seemed to encourage them in their repose.

Von Helldorf's Jew found the appointed regimental officer. A young man with a cough. He excused himself every ten seconds and turned to one side to spit. He'd been told they were coming, he said.

He took out a whistle, blew it, spat uselessly. Down the line other subalterns blew whistles. The French machine-guns stopped. A runner on his side in the hole heard the cessation in his sleep and woke enquiringly. His thin slum-child neck stood out at full stretch.

The machine-guns in the other lines spoke out again. The spitting officer nodded at von Helldorf.

Officer: Your dogs are still barking, sir.

His right hand on the side of the pit for balance, von Helldorf believed he could feel, as vibrations through the mud, the impact of bullets.

Officer: They've been told?

Guide: By radio. They've been informed. At divisional and brigade level.

Officer: Command is very broken up over there. That's obvious. Eh!

He coughed. It sounds tubercular, von Helldorf thought in a corner of his brain.

Officer: It'll be too late when I get pneumonia.

Von Helldorf asked for the flag. The guide gave it up reluctantly.

Guide: They're in a dangerous mood. Like anyone asked to offer himself up . . . they don't care who's offered up with them.

The runner was standing, sensing there would be calls on him.

Von Helldorf chanced his flag over the rim of the hole and scrabbled up the embankment.

Guide: Careful!

Officer: It's his funeral.

Guide: That's the armistice he has in that bag.

On his knees in the open, von Helldorf saw the mud spitting to his left and reaching to take him in. He let himself glissade back into the hole. He still had the flag. The retention of it gratified him as a professional.

His guide was scribbling a message for the runner. A droll sergeant strolled up and spoke to von Helldorf.

Sergeant: What's the difference between a staff-officer and a vase?

Von Helldorf: I don't know.

Sergeant: Nothing. They're both decorated before they go under fire.

There was no malice in him – he simply offered the foreign gentleman a little joke to take back to OHL.

Routine machine-guns from the French lines had started up again. But everyone in the shell-hole seemed buoyant and brotherly, pleased that a hopeful thesis was being proven by the German gunners; namely, that the enemy could not pass messages from brigade to his outposts. Or if they could, the outposts no longer understood. They had become foreigners to each other.

Guide: The runner is being sent back, Captain. It won't take long.

Von Helldorf however insisted the cease-fire whistles again be blown. The consumptive officer did his dry spit and blew. Whatever pitch he blew at, there was immediate obedience, not only up and down the line, but from the gunners on the German side.

Von Helldorf rose out of the hole, not saying goodbye to anyone. He held the truce flag wide of his body, free of the mud. In the last daylight he walked three metres but could then hear two lines of fire moving to nip him dead.

Launching himself forward into a mud-hole, he got sodden at the knees and the palms of his gloves. He muttered about what sort of army it was over there, and remembered the twitching generals he'd seen last night.

In a silence he yelled his name and status. He had mud on his chin and rain began to fall, dissolving the authority of his call. Will you answer? he yelled; I demand an answer. He believed an answer was framing itself warily over there amongst the sacrificial gunners. We will sacrifice successive screens of very brave men, Groener had announced. The successive screen ahead of him was tremulous about his voice. He thought they're full of the dream of slipping away in the dark to some unassailable knoll. All their thoughts rearwards, they don't easily listen to me calling on them from the wrong direction.

The guide jumped on top of him and the gunners fired.

Guide: I had orders to verify that you were safe.

Von Helldorf: That's most unfortunate.

They lay as close together as lovers in that little sump. The guide had sour breath and began to sneeze.

In the next silence and the one after that von Helldorf called to them and at last someone shouted the words. Come! You alone.

He went, without looking once at his guide. The guide however was frightened that von Helldorf might be shot in the back from the French lines and called cease-fire exhortations to his rear. There were a few indolent replies but soup canisters had been brought up and even von Helldorf out in the mud could smell the poured and savoured soup and understand why they would not bother sniping at him.

So they let him go forward with the offer of exorbitant peace chained to his wrist.

The Softer Version

Towards dinner-time the Marshal sent to see Admiral Wemyss privately. But when he reached the saloon, Wemyss found the Marshal's concept of privacy to be eccentric. For Weygand was also there.

Wemyss: Shall I send for Admiral Hope?

He put as much side to the question as he could.

The Marshal: No. I could send Maxime away. There are no notes to be taken. But I am so used to thinking of him as a limb.

Little Weygand seemed improperly pleased to be named part of the Marshal's mystical body. The rump, Wemyss thought.

Wemyss: The general is welcome to stay.

The Marshal: I thank you. Sit please, Lord Admiral.

Wemyss sat. The Marshal gestured with his pipe.

The Marshal: About the news of their courier.

Wemyss: He had a problem, I believe. Crossing over.

The Marshal: I would like your opinion.

Wemyss: Oh?

The Marshal: It seems to me we can tell the story two ways. First, we can take their courier's difficulties —

Wemyss: The fact that he was shot at.

The Marshal: Yes. We can take it as symptom of a decay of authority inside the German army.

Wemyss: The outbreak of Bolshevism?

The Marshal: If you wish to use such terms. On the other hand you can take them as a purely local breakdown of communications, natural here and there along the front of an army in retreat. You see, two different stories.

Wemyss: Two extremely different stories.

From the veins around the Marshal's eyes a humourless irony was secreted. Christ, I hate these reptilian generals!

The Marshal: The question I ask you is which story should we tell to our heads of state?

Wemyss: I shall inform Mr. Lloyd George that there was a local mistake.

The Marshal: Very good.

He began to smile in a parental way, the way he would have smiled at a naïve cadet who had just uttered the academy's version of truth. And so powerful was the Marshal at touching off the sonship glands in other men that for a little time Wemyss felt stung. His brain leapt to prove itself full-grown.

Wemyss: What then will you tell the Premier?

The Marshal: The softer version. The Premier lacks certainty.

Remembering Clemenceau's ferocious certainties, Wemyss wondered if the Marshal were speaking of the same man.

Wemyss: You believe what Herr Erzberger says? About chaos? About Bolshevism?

The Marshal: Herr Erzberger colours it rather highly.

He smiled.

Wemyss: My Marshal, I understand this: they are Imperial plenipotentiaries, the men on the other track. If by tomorrow we discover there is no longer any Empire their powers are void. I would be very surprised if our statesmen did not understand this. No matter what version of the courier's problems we send them.

The Marshal: It's a matter of sustaining their faith. And the same with the German gentlemen.

Wemyss sought his reading spectacles, for he could not tolerate seeing the Marshal's impish square face too clearly. My God, he thinks he can sustain the Empire in being until he no longer needs it – say till eleven o'clock Monday morning. He thinks those German delegates are here at his nod, accredited by his certainty.

Beneath the thick brows, in the Marshal's eyes, sat a fanciful or perhaps serious proposition: Everything will go the way it ought if you will simply accept for a day or so that I am the God of Moses. And can part the waters.

Bedtime Childishness

It was ten o'clock before Matthias and the others heard that von Helldorf had passed through the lines in a less than promising manner. They all became short-tempered, since the news foreshadowed what they all feared. Germany would not afford them an easy re-entry.

The count gave up the little work he had been doing, handed to von Winterfeldt the few pages he'd covered, said good night to no one but Matthias and went to his cabin.

The general stood up amongst his cluttered submissions.

Von Winterfeldt: The count must be fetched back, Herr Staatsminister. Our document has to be ready for morning.

Erzberger: I could fetch him back. Perhaps. But he would tend to be disruptive . . .

Von Winterfeldt: It's a sort of desertion. To go away like that.

Erzberger: Perhaps he can't write any more. I doubt if I can myself.

The general's hand crumpled the corner of a written page.

Von Winterfeldt: We have no business taking account of our limitations.

Ignoring him, Erzberger looked around the saloon for Captain Blauert. The young man sat in a corner marking papers with coloured pencils and laying them on the floor in piles – blue with blue, red with red. Tranquil as a school-teacher in the mountains.

Erzberger: Captain Blauert, are you tired?

Blauert: No, Herr Erzberger.

Erzberger: Can you type?

Blauert: Ninety words a minute, sir.

Erzberger: Wonderful. If the gentlemen and I left our observations on the terms with you, could you edit them? Remove the repetition?

The general beat his papers with his left hand.

Von Winterfeldt: I believe some of the phrasing of my arguments must be retained.

Blauert: I have already begun editorial work on some of the memoranda Herr Erzberger has given me. I can assure the general I shall try to retain his polish.

The general put his hands in his lap.

Von Winterfeldt: Come and take what I have.

The naval captain followed Erzberger into the sleeping wagon, called after him in the corridor.

Vanselow: Herr Erzberger, can you tell me? Must our consent to the terms be unanimous?

Erzberger: I hadn't thought of the problem.

Vanselow: I have decided I cannot consent to the naval clauses. So I ask.

Erzberger: The Chancellor will tell you to sign.

Vanselow: My son is four years old. What sort of name would I pass to him . . .?

At the base of his neck, Erzberger could feel a devouring exhaustion, and in the calves of his legs.

Erzberger: Abstain from signing if you want. Don't come round me behaving like a child.

The Captain moved his feet in the manner of a boxer but his head lay squarely locked down on his chest.

Vanselow: It's hardly fair to mention my uncharacteristic tears of this morning.

Erzberger: I don't give a damn for your tears. Abstain if you wish.

He turned away and staggered towards his cabin. As unevenly as if the train were moving.

Vanselow: It's different with you three. You're all fat with rank and wealth. You're simply paying for what you've been given . . .

Erzberger felt so threatened by this talk.

Erzberger: Paying? Where do you think we're at? A grocer's shop? *Pay*ing!

Vanselow: Why should I pay as you do?

There was saliva on his chin and his teeth looked very sharp. Erzberger whimpered.

Erzberger: Abstain, stay in your cabin, have the vapours. I'll make your excuses to the others. But don't give me trouble.

Matthias was permitted to go on his way towards bed, but the sailor still followed and harassed his flanks.

Vanselow: I didn't expect my defiance to be treated with such contempt. Thank you, thank you, Herr Erzberger, for indicating what you think I'm worth.

Erzberger: Go to hell. Eh? Go to hell.

At last the captain ceased barking at his heels and turned back towards the saloon. Perhaps to cry? Erzberger wondered.

The Count, Gun in Mouth

Hoping for a companionable word before bed he paused at the door of Count Maiberling's cabin. From inside he heard a heavy and well-oiled click of metal. At first he thought the count was working at the metal clip of the window shutters but then understood that he had heard the mechanism of the service revolver at work.

He opened the door wide. The Count sat on his bunk, looking askance above the mouthful he had made of the revolver barrel.

Erzberger: What's this?

The Count pulled the trigger and swallowed the metallic sound from the unloaded chamber with apparent thirst. Then he took the gun away from his face, making a moue at the faint taste of oil he had got in his mouth.

Maiberling: I'm just getting used to the situation.

Matthias could not but believe the three of them had planned their bedtime childishness.

Erzberger: Don't you realize the delays involved if you had an accident?

Maiberling waved his left hand.

Maiberling: A man has to have some outlet.

The blood quaked in Matthias's hands, at the rims of his ears.

Erzberger: I wish you'd all damn well stop. The general vain about his bloody prose-style, Vanselow old-maidish about his navy, you play-acting with your revolver. There's no room in this business for such pettiness.

He could see the diplomat was hurt and laid the pistol

down as if it were an excusable luxury he'd been asked to give up, against all reason.

Maiberling: Pettiness. It has many faces. Don't you remember the *spätzle*?

There was all at once a buoyancy in the arches of Matthias's feet that offered to pitch him, claws-first, at the count's throat.

Spätzle

Because of the business of *spätzle*, his favourite dish, Erzberger had been given a public name as a gourmandizer.

It had happened this way. Two years before, Herr Angele, a member of the Reich Barley Administration, had been dismissed from office during a north German conservative movement to cull as many south German liberals as possible out of positions of leverage. Angele appealed to his local member, a man who had taken on the northerners often enough and survived to talk about it, a man with a temperamental weakness towards crusading. Herr Erzberger.

One afternoon Angele called at the Erzberger house in Schöneberg and found that Herr Erzberger had not yet come home. Paula Erzberger, small, restrained, pretty but motherly, also a southerner, though of a better family than Matthias's, broke open like a flower to the sound of a Württemberger accent and invited Herr Angele into the kitchen where she was cooking.

They spoke of the food shortages. Matthias is a steak-and-red-wine kind of man, Paula told him. But I can't get eggs to make him *spätzle*. Herr Angele told Paula that, since he owned a malt factory in Herr Erzberger's constituency, he could help Paula out with food parcels from the south. So for eighteen months the Erzbergers' larder was enriched by Herr Angele's shipments of sugar, butter, geese, flour, ham; and eggs for the *spätzle*. Erzberger himself, working his sixteen-hour days on every day but Sunday, was scarcely aware that his house was a special sphere of plenty in blockaded Berlin. He ate absent-mindedly, relished absent-mindedly, absent-mindedly grew fatter.

Early in the new year of 1918 Paula was handed a summons for receiving food illegally. She was sick with grippe at the time and had to be handed it in bed. The shame, she said. Her delicate hand made a fist. It's that Mrs. Dittman.

On 25 March 1918 in the local court she was convicted and fined 200 marks.

The Berlin conservative papers made much of it. Reformer Erzberger fattening on *spätzle* while his not so much younger fellows gnawed hard-tack in the mud.

Now Maiberling, who had telephoned him at the time, and offered him fellow-feeling!

Erzberger: You yourself? You never ate more than a citizen's ration?

Maiberling: I'm not saying that.

Erzberger: Do you know that *they*, those Junker bastards, have never forgiven me. Not for eating *spätzle*. But for telling people how we were treating the Africans.

Maiberling: Yes. Yes.

Erzberger: I told the house that a Prussian army shot thirty thousand East Africans in one year and burned crops so that another quarter of a million starved. These are *recorded* deaths.

Maiberling: Yes. Yes. I know you —

Erzberger: I told the Germans that General von Trotha ordered the shooting of every male Herero in South-West Africa. And drove the women into the Kalahari.

Maiberling: I know, I know, I know. Don't boast. It made your career when you were very young. General von Trotha was a gift from God.

Erzberger: Is that the kind of mind you have?

But even behind his fury he was thinking, yes, that's the size of it. There's so much fat politician in me. Even if not enough to make life always comfortable.

Maiberling: What were you? Thirty? Thirty-one? The

bloody Hereros set you up for life.

Erzberger: Stand up and tell me that.

For the count still sat on his cot, the revolver on the coverlet while Matthias pawed the basin and bent above him.

Maiberling: Go to hell.

Erzberger: Let me tell you. Everyone warned me it was political suicide to bring up those African scandals. Everyone told me I'd be a victim for life. Well, I got away with it, but ever since they've been after me, that rat-pack . . . And all they've been able to find out in ten years is that my wife received food parcels from a malt-brewer. Great scandal, that! Eh? How would you have come through the last ten years, Count Maiberling? With your mistress, with your harlots in lovely Bucharest and that woman — what was her name? — Frau Blesniak in Sofia.

Maiberling: You want to make me angry, I suppose.

Erzberger: I want to sting your bloody hide.

Maiberling: Soon Matthias I'll take you up, I'll demand satisfaction.

He did, in fact, as rehearsal for that time, offer the service revolver butt-forward to Matthias. Matthias sniffed at it.

Erzberger: The trouble with your class is that you think even death is an aristocratic ritual.

The count laughed.

Maiberling: A regular Bolshevik yourself, Matthias.

He began unlacing his boots.

Erzberger's Happy Dreams

In his cabin he suffered a *happy* dream of taking his daughters for a walk in the woods near Munderkingen. They were more or less lost but he knew throughout that a climber's cabin would occur and kept joking his four-year-old, whom he carried on his shoulders, out of weeping. The cabin presented itself, beyond a fringe of pines and full of lamplight. He lit the fire with the breath of his paternity and vivified little Gabrielle's hands against his heart and saw tall Maria, an ample woman in anyone else's terms, undress by a bunk. Kind Jesus, he said, don't let her be a nun.

But where is Paula? he thought. Who cooks my *spätzle*? Why have I cut Paula out of my happy dreams?

The First Sea Lord had never known his father, had lost him two weeks after being born. It had happened in as Gothic and ancestral a way as any fanciful child could have hoped for. On the north side of the Firth of Forth Wemyss Castle is found, a building as glowering as all the other Scottish castles travellers find ruined throughout Scotland. But by some special arrangement with the British navy, Wemyss had survived the ruinous first half of the eighteenth century when warships used to sail up firths and lochs and bombard Jacobite structures.

One wing of the castle had been made comfortable and classic terraces ran away from it downhill towards the Firth. In a twilight in the summer of 1864, Lady Wemyss went up to her room to rest because she was nearing term. Lord Wemyss and his sister sat at the top of the terraces watching the Firth change colour as the light lasted and lasted from the west. Very remotely they could hear young men and women from the village of East Wemyss laughing too continuously in a pack on the road towards Kirkcaldy. In hope and terror of what the eventual darkness would do to them.

It should have made Lord Wemyss feel very seigniorial on his terrace. In fact he had been melancholy throughout his wife's pregnancy. He had been invalided out of the Royal Navy for heart and respiratory weakness. The family ran to admirals – his father, grandfather, uncles, cousins. He had been raised to become one. Everyone said that's why he's so restless; he has lost his direction.

That still evening, on the lower terrace, without any encouragement from wind or rain or lightning, the paving split loudly as a cannon. Stone flags, gods and Roman senators, balustrades and urns slid away, grinding and breaking.

Lord Wemyss said, "That's it. I'm dead."

His sister said what nonsense. She pretended to be angry only with the Kirkcaldy landscaper who had done the work under contract. But that did not distract her brother.

Lord Wemyss said, "Whenever an Earl of Wemyss is about to die, his death is announced to him by the sound of falling masonry."

When Rosslyn Wemyss grew to be a boy he could never forgive his father for responding so pat to the omen, like any of the non-people who inhabit ghost stories. Wemyss's outrage still expressed itself in his sleep.

Throughout the night of the falling terrace and the next day, the laird appeared resigned, not frightened. This seemed to the womenfolk to be the most dangerous state of mind. The family doctor could not talk him round. He suggested that since they intended to travel south to London for the birth, to their town-house in Buckingham Gate, they should go as soon as possible.

When the child was born a boy and called Rosslyn, Lord Wemyss looked at its face and said, "This is the last child I shall beget." Rosslyn Wemyss would develop the bitterness any child might feel who served his father only as a spur to that father's numinous self-pity.

After ten days, Lord Wemyss the father died in his sleep of heart failure.

Thirty years later Lady Wemyss reported the event to the Society of Psychical Research. They had broadly similar cases on record: people (generally aristocratic) who had died of omens; such as the sighting of certain untoward animals or combinations of animals, of certain stains or patterns.

When young Rosy Wemyss came home from prep school he heard his mother complain of servants. She said, they now think they're their own lords and ladies. Perhaps they had come the full way by 1914. It was then as if they all heard or saw some great communal omen, having become their own aristocrats, and went off and died resignedly, as his father had. *Noblesse oblige*. Women of Britain say Go!

The First Sea Lord dreamed of the fallen terrace, the jumbled stonework and his father so unnecessarily reading death there. He took his father brutally by the elbow, saying it isn't the old days, you are no clan-leader with a need to answer portents. Up and down the Firth and all over the decaying myths of the clans, brewers and mercers and shipwrights are building and see no presages amongst their profit and loss columns, yet are more important to the working of the world than any laird. Though not to me they aren't. Not to me.

Wait, he always begged. I've never seen you. Though I've seen masonry fall. In Lemnos and the Dardanelles and when I relieved Feisal's Arabs in Akaba, I saw fallen masonry then. Did I lie down? So wait.

But every time Rosslyn bullied him, his young father seemed self-absorbed.

Necessary Love-Making in 2417D

In the morning Hope came in and told him, in an oddly disarmed sort of way for a man who did not like fornication, that the French had found a woman's handkerchief in 2417D and a sergeant had been arrested.

Wemyss too smiled and hoped nothing too bad would happen to the sergeant.

Wemyss: I thought I saw a woman amongst the elms. Night before last.

He was happier about 2417D. The woman and the sergeant had humanized it for him and it wasn't too much to say that he felt grateful.

He would never discover what happened to the sergeant or if a woman was apprehended. But in Compiègne and amongst old soldiers the event took on the marks of a fable. People would tell you this: that a French sergeant in the infantry regiment camped in the forest felt impelled to bring a Compiègne woman, appropriately a young war widow gone reckless with loss, through the perimeter running west south and east around the sidings of Rethondes.

The widowed girl had to bike it four or more kilometres from her house in town to the ruin of a stone cottage along the Compiègne-Soissons road. Here a dry corner would have suited her and the sergeant. Except they were impelled towards 2417D and no other surfaces would do them.

If they met any sentries the sergeant told them he was taking the girl to one of the delegates. The officers were all in camp beds and tented against the rain squalls. The sergeant and the widow came to the blind side of 2417D and found it quite unlocked.

He had thought she might be awed in a sight-seeing way but Compiègnoises are not easily impressed that way – Louis XIV, XV, XVI had lived more or less amongst them, at the Palais de Compiègne on the end of the town. Napoleon Bonaparte, Napoleon III. For two hundred years they had worked in royal households or supplied them with candles or coal, soap or pheasants. The girl's uncle had owned a patisserie whose handmade chocolates had ravished the Empress Eugénie. Even lately the Palais had been HQ for renowned soldiers: Nivelles who had killed her husband, Pétain . . . She simply put her hand on the neatly laid out blotters. *So!* was all she said.

She wasn't there for the sights.

He began to caress her. Her skirts were wet to the knees. He moved one of the acanthus-leaf lampshades to a safe place down the table, also an ash-tray and cut-glass ink-stand. Then he pitched her backwards so that she lay between the notepads of Vanselow and Erzberger on one side, and Weygand and the Marshal on the other. The leather table-top was at first very cold through her dress.

Even if they had not already had their minds on it, they would have found coitus the obvious recourse. Simply because it was insufferable to think that in such a little space, round a table no bigger than a family dinner table, with notepaper and pencils, it was possible for eight men to weave a scab over that pit of corpses four years deep.

It was clear that the notepads flanking her reminded her of vacant memorial stones, set either side for soldiers still to die. For they found in the morning that she had written *R.I.P.* and *Pour la Patrie* on them.

Dressing they could hear noises in the next carriage, where the duty wireless operator and the night telephonist talked and yawned. It occurred to them how dangerous their little rite had been.

She shook her skirts together quickly, mute but not regretting. The seed now travelling in her was necessary seed.

The sergeant replaced the inkpot, the lamp (using his handkerchief to polish its brass shaft), the ash-tray, but missing the pencilled-on pads.

He helped her back to the Soissons road.

Rumour of them dies there. No child is said to have come from the penetration of 2417D – no drunkard or poet, deaf-mute, whore, violinist or other symbolic offspring.

Simply that in the coming world people would now and then nominate the sergeant and the widow as the wiser visitors to 2417D.

Off to See the Frocks

At the breakfast table, Wemyss heard that overnight there had been utter silence from Spa and Berlin. He was not enlivened by the coffee he drank opposite pert Marshal Foch.

The Marshal: The Kaiser might abdicate? Yes. But that is not a revolution. That is the triumph of the healthy cells.

Like Erzberger, even Wemyss considered for a moment that he might be – for puckish or other motives – denied the truth. He turned to Weygand; sphinx-in-chief, he thought.

Wemyss: No message at all?

Weygand: None.

Wemyss: Could it be the weather? Transmission problems?

He thought less of himself for grabbing at comfort in front of these two.

Weygand: That isn't possible, Lord Admiral.

The Marshal: Well then, I'm off to see the frocks.

It was his term of contempt for statesmen.

A staff limousine heaved down the forest track to collect him. As it made for Senlis the mist grew streaky and fell away and a high wind broke the cloud apart. Quick smart it travelled eastwards. The sodden poilus at the front would be pleased to see it shredded like this.

On his arrival, his staff stood to attention in the hall of the château. He saw tall Major Ferrason who was about to take to the academic life.

The Marshal: Did the Kaiser give up while I was on the road?

Ferrason: His five sons have all taken a vow not to succeed him as regents. That's all we've heard.

The Marshal: And the Salonika front?

Ferrason: The Bulgarian surrender terms are being enforced. The typhoid epidemic has worsened amongst our soldiers.

The Marshal: Cold, isn't it?

Ferrason: The fire is lit in your office, my Marshal.

At his desk, he heard the honour guard clash to the salute for the arriving premier.

The Marshal: Ferrason, I want you to stay and take notes.

To enter the château, the old Prime Minister held a thorn stick well down its length, implying he might dare beat the Marshal or perhaps lesser soldiers should they mislead him. As well he wore gaiters as if on a trip to the front. His lean secretary from the War Office, General Mordacq, an army man who had backslid amongst the frocks, kept watch at his side.

Clemenceau: A fire, my Marshal? Let's all sit round it. I said to my PT instructor that after twenty-five years of daily calisthenics I've found there's nothing tones a man up like a blaze.

His eyes avoided the Marshal's and his lips were well hidden behind the strands of his Confucian moustache. So he didn't seem to wish that his intuition about toning men up would benefit anyone in particular.

Clemenceau: What's this officer doing here?

The Marshal: He will take minutes.

In fact Ferrason was shifting chairs at that moment into the fire's ambience.

Clemenceau: My God, we're not going to take things down in evidence are we? Aren't we friends?

The Marshal: Of course.

Clemenceau: I don't want him making notes. He can stay. But I don't want notes.

The Marshal: As you wish.

The Premier took his seat slowly and the Mongolian eyes now settled on the Marshal. Mordacq sat by his master. Mordacq and the Marshal were, of course, well-established enemies. Mordacq, the freemason, the agnostic, pretentious about strategy, pretentious about politics. A keeper of secret files on enemies actual or possible, on people who could be used for advantage. Very much in the old man's image.

The Marshal knew what the old man would talk about and was not surprised.

Clemenceau: I'm very concerned, my Marshal. The men you have in that train in Compiègne are Imperial pleni-potentiaries. If the German Emperor abdicates today, if there's a republic proclaimed, they won't have any power to negotiate . . .

General Mordacq spoke exactly to the middle air.

Mordacq: The written authorities on the basis of which those Germans in Compiègne are working have a very exact diplomatic meaning.

That's meant to be information for the crude soldier, the Marshal thought. He grew pugnacious.

The Marshal: They're waiting simply on word from Spa. I refuse to believe that so close to signing they'll be emptied of their authority.

Mordacq: Not everything is a matter of believing or refusing to believe. Faith isn't the rails diplomacy runs on.

The Marshal put his large hand over his yawn. He decided to speak exclusively to the old man.

The Marshal: You might remember there was some fear – the British Prime Minister, that Colonel House – that we were asking too much. What happened in the train is an answer. They will give up armies, navies, territories. They argue in small ways but you can see in their eyes they've already given them away. They turn pale only when we mention rolling stock, machine-guns.

The Premier's large-boned paws caressed his thorn; there seemed to be terror of loss in his large fingers.

Clemenceau: That's not what we're talking about. All they're willing to give . . . it might have no meaning by evening.

The hands went on smoothing down the blackthorn. Hands that had operated on Miss Plummer, New York seminarian, and imposed three children on her before she fled to American lawyers for a divorce. Hands that had known the pelt of the highest-grade tarts. Now they were uncertain as they never were with the horseflesh of the capital.

Clemenceau: The point is: you have to sign as soon as you can.

The Marshal: Of course.

Clemenceau: I called in on Monet yesterday on my way to the Senate. You're not keen on art, are you my Marshal?

The Marshal: No.

Clemenceau: I told him yesterday that things were so close to an end.

The Marshal: I suppose he's very discreet.

Clemenceau: Telling Monet is like telling God. I imagine you yourself, Marshal, have taken the time to inform *that* good friend of yours.

When the Premier was most afraid (the Marshal knew) his jokes ran to the easy mark and were most fatuous.

The Marshal: For both of us. For you as well, Monsieur.

Clemenceau: Do you know what old Monet said to me?

He said, Now we'll be able to settle down to build the memorial to Cézanne. But this morning I wonder. Nothing's sure.

A plangent sigh out of the old fellow's ample-bore, bull organs. Cut off by brassy Mordacq. Orchestrated agnosticism.

Mordacq: For that reason, all of us at the War Office trust that the Marshal will keep in mind the diplomatic realities.

The Marshal: What else?

Mordacq: Also that he will firmly understand that it is not a mystical exercise.

The Marshal: Monsieur Premier, if you don't silence him I will consider it an insult.

The Premier transferred the stick between his knees and clapped his hands.

Clemenceau: A duel, a duel.

Knowing that the Marshal could not duel, whatever his blood told him. Remembering too the years when he himself had kept the Chamber of Deputies in place with duelling pistols, until one day at Fontainebleau in 1893 he had had three shots at a deputy called Boudouaument and missed with all three and was therefore considered to have lost his fangs.

The Marshal saw the Premier's eyes glowing viscid. The glue of his memories ran there. Sentiment, sentiment.

The fire spat and returned Clemenceau to the indecisive Saturday in which he sat. He did not like it there. He dried his flaccid moustache carefully. Perhaps the upper lip it hid was sweating wildly.

Clemenceau: All jokes aside . . .

His right hand plucked and crumpled the air, a wordspinner's mannerism he'd picked up twenty-five years back, when he'd sat down in middle age to become a novelist and done badly at it.

The Marshal understood but would not forgive his helplessness this dripping Saturday. The Marshal thought, he never learned to sniff out the moment when reason should be suspended. Whereas I, alone with the enemy in the forest's eye, have sniffed it out.

Sailor Kings and Débutantes

"While [wrote the Admiral, in a memorandum for the Marshal] the British Government would certainly understand the desire of the French Army to exact payment for the insults inflicted by the German Empire in 1871, it is confident that the Generalissimo will also understand that this war has been fought on every ocean and a cease-fire (as well as an eventual peace settlement) must provide for the security, navally guaranteed, of all the 500 million and more British subjects from the southern ocean to the Orkneys . . ."

As always, the wonder of this benign imperial concept brought him to a stop and he remembered sailing round it, the empire which was not only a geographical reality but a resonant abstraction also; so that on its seas you had a sense of being not simply sailor but metaphysician as well.

He had navigated it once with Teddy, his revered king of the time. It was always temperate summer that year, for there is always summer in some limb of the empire. And the itinerary was so planned. The *Ophir* had been chartered for the voyage, and staffed by aristocratic officers.

Teddy knew Rosslyn Wemyss was illicitly related through some rutting of William IV's. Himself a sailor.

King Teddy used to wink at me when he came up to the bridge. Never trust sailors, he'd say. If you left it to sailors we'd all be related. Not that Teddy was a slouch with the women. You had to remember his mother had never allowed him any contact with the Cabinet. The one time he'd read cabinet papers she'd raised the roof. So Teddy never got used to *that* side of government even after his mother died and left him to it. His speciality was *droit de seigneur.* Carried in the *Ophir*, he exercised it amongst the well-fed daughters of rich colonies.

How long the journey took. A year. The French did not understand that: the extent of the world. All they sought was to beat the German army in set-piece battles more or less on their common frontier. In arguing with them you faced, far more than mere inadvertence, this manic obsession.

He began to write again but was distracted by memory breaking open in his belly like a pod. In Melbourne the King and Queen had disembarked from *Ophir* to travel to Brisbane by train. They left on board the officers, the crew, some officials and three ladies-in-waiting, creatures only a year or so out of the débutante pages of *The Queen*, *The Field*, *Country Life*. Mezzotint complexions now teased a little dusky by the Empire's recurring suns.

You had to be careful. A king's ship could go a little slack once the king left it. But dining was somehow a pleasanter business and you drank more and had rowdy card-games with the ladies the queen had left with you. And you danced with them, tipsily believing their nice breasts were burning holes in your mess-jacket. And one night you bent and, your head ringing, made the sumptuous suggestion: my love, have you thought of the royal bed?

The lady-in-waiting and he had both told each other, while still drunk and given to repetition, how much Teddy would have been tickled to know. Even if Queen Alexandra would have looked on it as trespass.

The Duelling Slap

That afternoon, it could be seen, Maiberling was drunk. He went about making trouble with Vanselow and von Winterfeldt who worked innocently, with slight executive frowns, at separate tables amongst the black Moroccan footstools of the saloon. *Busy, busy,* he would say. *Scribble, scribble.*

Erzberger had been writing a sort of gallows speech. He hoped to append it to the clauses. He covered with a clean sheet of paper the paragraphs he had already prepared and called to the count to sit down.

The count's answer was disconnected, mocking.

Maiberling: How much did they pay you as a director of Thyssen's?

Erzberger: Really, Alfred . . . !

Maiberling: No, come on. Tell a friend.

Erzberger: Forty thousand marks.

Maiberling: That's not much as soul-money goes.

Erzberger: Not if you're running a house in Schöneberg. But I suppose they consider it's the honour . . .

Maiberling: Do you think they'd have me?

Erzberger: If they still exist.

Maiberling: You're supposed to be the optimistic one.

Matthias could smell the class-contempt in Maiberling. There was sinew to it that had not been there last night.

Erzberger: Do you want to rest, Alfred?

Maiberling: No, Matthias. Neither rest nor work. I am mourning my good friend the twentieth century. Like all the other youngsters, about to turn his toes up in his eighteenth year.

With a wave of the hand, Matthias begged off such fulsome despair.

Erzberger: It's painful for me to speak like this. I demand better behaviour from you, Alfred.

Maiberling: You can go to hell. My behaviour, your behaviour. Behaviour's ceased to have bearing.

Erzberger: If you get drunk I won't let you sit at the conference table.

Maiberling slapped Erzberger's cheek. Not an uncontrolled gesture, not a peasant haymaker; an exact, dueller's slap, delivered from the wrist, a measured dose. Vanselow and von Winterfeldt both looked up, sat rigidly. We've heard that noise before. Points of honour in the mess. Their faces said, We hadn't expected to be diverted this way.

Erzberger remembered then: he hadn't made peace with Vanselow.

After Maiberling had about-turned and taken steps, again exactly measured, towards the far end of the carriage, Erzberger quashed the tears in his left eye and uncovered what he had been writing. Exactly like a school child who, in the face of punishment, pleads the quality of his school-work.

'Considering the discussions [the uncovered page said] leading to the armistice, we might have hoped for conditions that would have brought an end to the suffering of non-combatants, of women and children, at the same time that it assured the enemy full and complete military security.

'The German people, which has held off a world of enemies for fifty months, will preserve their liberty and their unity despite every kind of violence.

'A nation of seventy millions of peoples suffers but it does not die.'

It's very well to write it. Is it a nation? Where are the men who would have negotiated a victory, with what whore do they now huddle and are they one race with us? Are Maiberling and Erzberger one race? And what is Rosa Luxemburg doing in Berlin? Is Max still Chancellor? Is the Kaiser still darting and resisting beneath the paranoid chandeliers of the château de la Fraineuse? What are the Swabians thinking and what the East Prussians? Can Paula, Maria and Gabrielle, from the steps of the bungalow on Wansee, see reflected in the sky the red glow of Bolshevik Berlin? And what pan-German dolt of an officer is this moment loading his service revolver with a bullet for me, a bullet for the piss-pot count?

The Suicidal Horse

The Marshal lowered his face so that the steam from the pea soup stung and cleansed it.

The Marshal: And where did this happen, my lord Admiral?

Wemyss: Off the South African coast. Columbine Point is the name of the place.

Weygand: This would be during your war with the Boers?

He seemed to intimate: since that was an unfortunate affair perhaps your story is also questionable.

Rosslyn Wemyss could not prevent himself coughing. He could tell too there was a sudden radiant hostility in General Weygand.

Wemyss: That's right. Our war in Africa.

The Marshal: A horse, you say?

Wemyss: A troopship ran up on the rocks at Columbine Point. In foul weather.

The Marshal: As you said.

To show he would not repent of delays or repetitions, the admiral took his time lighting, drawing upon a cigar, inspecting its kindled tip.

Wemyss: It carried a regiment of hussars. At that time I was the humble commander of a little patrol boat. So we were able to work in close abeam ... I'm sorry, I don't know the French term ... abeam the troop ship. *Abeam* means at right angles.

The Marshal: The general and I know the term. We have sailed in Brittany.

Wemyss: Forgive me.

He took a long and uncontrite savouring of his cigar. They waited for him.

Wemyss: It was late afternoon but there was still plenty of light. The captain had lit the 'ship-aground' night lights fore and aft but the way she was heeled over we knew she wouldn't last till night. I could see the hussars on deck shooting the horses in case they broke loose from the deck stalls and ran wild. Even before I could send them a line some of the cavalry men jumped overboard but were carried to the rocks. It was frightful. They were ground up and down the rough edges until they lost consciousness. Then the currents sucked them down. I don't know if it's so in France, but we found that soldiers feared sea-perils more than going into combat. They lost all their discipline during shipwreck.

The Marshal sighed, lifting his hand concessively.

The Marshal: I never sailed to colonial wars. But I imagine you're right about soldiers. Water is not their medium.

The general, frowning a little, was not beguiled by this debate on the eccentric terrors of soldiers.

Weygand: And you saw this horse?

Wemyss: Yes. It ran free and jumped a railing to get into the sea. It must have been a fine horse to find propulsion on the sloping deck.

Weygand: They are extraordinary creatures.

Wemyss: It knew it was bound to die.

The Marshal: I think they *do* know. I think they suffer beyond the mere pain of the moment. I think like us they know they are mortal. Artillery horses are very sensitive. And, I suppose, steeplechasers.

The First Sea Lord did not like a certain gloss in the Marshal's eye and the too eager way he agreed that hussars feared water and horses foreknew their deaths. It was as if he were setting him up to be undercut by that tight-lipped little hippophile, brother Maxime.

He found it however, too late to stop telling the story. To hell with their dragoon disdain, he decided.

He looked for an instant to his staff. Hope and Marriott neutrally spooning their soup: knowing it wasn't their place to introduce anecdotes and influence the audience's acceptance.

Wemyss: It was obvious. The horse tried to commit suicide. I have never seen such a thing, before or since. It was washed to the rocks and back again at least a dozen times and each time it flung its head quite deliberately at an outcrop, and a dozen times it missed. In the end though it managed what it wanted. I saw its body go loose and its blood colouring the water. It vanished in a little while. An ominous thing, a horse killing itself. You could say, despite the conditions, quite *coolly* committing suicide.

The Marshal: Amazing.

But little General Weygand watched the cheese sideways and absorbed into himself this story of horse-suicide as if he were taking account of a libel against one of the family.

Wemyss thought, ride over the French bastard. Don't tolerate any Gallic contempt. It might rebound when the naval clauses come up again.

The Marshal kept on exclaiming.

The Marshal: Astounding. I have never seen that, not in all my years as a garrison officer of horse artillery.

Wemyss thought, where do I, tar of tars, derive this margin of fear for French scorn? Perhaps it is a vestige of the years when Scots took politics, wine, music, costume from the French.

Idly he squeezed a rind of the African orange he had earlier eaten. The acid from its pores stung his thumb. He looked full into the Marshal's gnostic eyes and at Weygand.

Weygand: Do you know horses well?

Wemyss: I keep stables, of course. I am Master of the Dysart Hunt. Like yourself, General, I have ridden steeple-chases.

The Marshal: The general was a champion, by the way.

Weygand: I have never seen a horse commit suicide. Not in battle or under the whip. If a horse could take it in its head to kill itself, what rider would be safe?

Wemyss: I can assure you my story is exact, General. Not random table-talk.

Weygand: I don't mean to suggest . . . However, suicide is the last act of non-acceptance of pain. It has always seemed to me only man had the arrogance to commit it. Perhaps you would take these observations into consideration when you next tell the story.

Does he want me to believe horses are all good French Catholics?

Wemyss punched his napkin with the knuckle of his little finger.

Wemyss: I am aware of the temperament of the horse, General. But have also had a long time to consider what I saw at Columbine Point.

The Marshal: And excellently reported it was!

But there was very little real conversation for the rest of the meal. General Weygand kept totally silent and whenever the Marshal said anything, it had about it the smell of condescension.

At the Parallel Meal

At the parallel meal von Winterfeldt turned to Erzberger.

Von Winterfeldt: Herr Erzberger, in what regiment did you do your military service?

There had been little talk. The count sat across the table emphasizing his feudal superiority by cutting his meat with long sleek motions of his knife, by masticating with high chin and both fists laid delicately on the table, by long-fingered flourishes with his table-napkin.

Feeling no more enmity, Erzberger had been a little amused by all this.

But at the general's question his belly went into spasm and he looked up furious. He thought the inane Prussian was asking, in what regiment did they tell you to ignore a challenge of honour?

Erzberger: I served in the kitchen-duty office of the 199th Swabian Incompetents. Even so I didn't belong to the officers' mess or even to the sergeants'. So I never learnt how to work off my grudges by firing antique pistols at my fellow man in some pine forest at dawn.

Von Winterfeldt: I think you are mocking me.

Erzberger stood up in his place.

Erzberger: I don't give a damn for shooting a man ritually or being shot in the same manner. If the count wishes to be so shot he should apply to the first workers' and soldiers' soviet he finds across the Rhine. I am sure a man of his title and stature will go straight to the head of the line.

The general also stood up. Holy Mother, now I'll be expected to fight both of them. The next second, Erzberger noticed the unmilitary distress in the eyes and the lay of the thin face.

Von Winterfeldt: Sir, you misunderstand me . . . I have already approached the count and demanded that he make his apologies to you. I raised the question of military service simply as a means of starting a conversation.

Erzberger whimpered and covered one eye with his left hand.

Erzberger: I beg your pardon.

Von Winterfeldt: These are monstrous circumstances. As you mentioned to the count, the waiters will report our states of mind. Please sit down, sir, and go on with your meal.

They both sat and noticed that the count continued with his mannered use of knife and fork, chewing lightly so that the set of his jaw would not be thrown out of angle. But all at once his shoulders slackened, he laid both hands palms out on the table-cloth.

Maiberling: This is damn ridiculous. Matthias understands me. Don't you Matthias?

But Matthias was aware of Captain Vanselow who stared sideways at him with eyes of sly contempt.

Maxime's True Begetter

For a quarter of an hour after luncheon General Weygand rested in his shirt and long drawers. Looking up at the vine-leafed panels of the ceiling of his cabin, he remembered that he didn't like trains, he never had as a child. The point about trains as experienced by young Maxime Weygand was that they had never carried you, say, from fond parents in Liège to a favourite aunt in Nancy. All his departures in trains had been absolute departures, journeys from one group of child-minders who had taken care to prove to you that you weren't their baby, to another pair who would sooner or later, sombrely tell you that neither were they your begetters.

He had become Maxime-nothing-at-all when born to parents whose name he didn't know in a room over a shop in Brussels. Then he was called Maxime Sagat, after his nice nurse, till a train journey to Marseilles turned him into Maxime de Nimal. He became Maxime Weygand at the end of another train journey, when an Arras accountant of that name recognized him as son. Does that mean you *actually* fathered me? Yes, the accountant told him, for the purposes of legal and financial documents, that is so.

Trains and parentage: linked questions.

Was old Weygand merely coy? Or was he paid an annuity to be legal father? When Maxime was young he yearned to have something as palpable as an accountant for his pro-creator. He couldn't think of the other possibilities with any sense of mental safety. Servants whispered about his birth. The legends spun with cyclonic speed and sucked his mind down.

That he was the son of the Mexican Empress Carlotta by her husband Emperor Maximilian or by lover I, II, III, IV, V, and so on! That he was the son of Mexican Emperor Maximilian and inamorata I, II, III, IV, V! He simply had to read the scandalmongers of the Second Empire to fill in the numerals with names. In late adolescence he concluded that you could not be outraged at the misadventures of royal parents as you would be at the adulteries of someone like old Weygand the accountant. Emperors and their Empresses moved in such spheres, a different moral galaxy. He read all the diarists, searching for a dazzling man to call father, or a picturesque lady who might have borne him.

And it wasn't such a bad thing, later, for a young dragoon officer to be the possible son of an Austrian archduke or a Belgian princess.

A young lieutenant of dragoons.

Until he met the Marshal in Lorraine, his true family had been horses. He had had the truth confirmed by the ferment arising in him when Wemyss told his tall story of the suicidal cavalry mount. It should not matter, absolutely or person-ally, if an army horse killed itself in 1900 on an African rock. But the general's impulses told him: the idea of it was as dangerous as Marxism and must not be permitted standing room in the soul.

Long ago, on visiting day at the *bon-ton* Lycée de Vanves, parents sat with their sons under cypress trees in the quadrangle. White-bloused mothers under vast summer hats lifted dishes of flan and brandy-snaps on to tables and smiled when their sons groaned with lust for the cream. Being parentless, little Maxime de Nimal (later Weygand) was allowed to look at illustrated news magazines and books with engravings laid out on a table in the junior study. He considered himself better off than the whipped-cream gluttons outside. He believed he would discover there, in the fatherless junior study, something to his advantage.

In an engraving in a copy of *Le Cid* he turned up one summer afternoon there, he saw a war-horse, abstract as a god, fluent in the midst of the affairs of war. It was what one of his schoolmasters would have called the essence of horse and it called to him saying, through my hoofs the earth is possessed. This moment reverberated in him all his life. Ten years old, he told himself this is my definite inheritance: the horse.

In the last days of the summer of '14 he'd been on a horse, leading a squadron of his regiment on reconnaissance in Lorraine, when a stumpy little general drove up, asked for Colonel Weygand, told the colonel to get down from his horse. They tell me you're a member of my staff. Weygand had dismounted and driven away to the north, the crucial flank.

It was when he heard that British admiral accuse a horse that he felt a tragic depreciation in the value of his inheritance. Why? Because I have to ride in limousines instead of on horseback? Nonsense. Because I mess about with telegrams instead of riding with dragoons? Because I don't have time to ride in the Saumur gold cup? Who leads dragoons these days and who rides at Saumur? So exactly what loss had the admiral touched and set pulsing?

The general muttered it aloud.

Weygand: What loss has occurred?

Saturday Afternoon Spin

That afternoon a message came in for Wemyss. The Prime Minister would remain by the telephone in Downing Street between seven and nine that evening. He would like to hear from the First Sea Lord on the question of re-victualling Germany.

In between memories of Teddy and exotic adulteries on the coasts of the Antipodes, Wemyss had already prepared notes on the matter. His conclusion ran:

Only the Germans can produce a catastrophic German famine. We are capable of supplying them, but failures within their frontiers, failures ideological, failures psychological, failures of good order, are the only causes which will make the Germans starve.

The telegram from London invigorated him. He told Marriott so.

Wemyss: I didn't know it. But I'd started to think like a castaway.

Marriott smiled but with a bent head. He did not know how to deal with the confessions of superiors.

Wemyss: Between seven and nine?

Marriott: Sir.

Wemyss: Presumably at nine the old Adam will get to be too much for L.G. As this bloody train is for me.

He beat the panelling above his wash-basin.

Wemyss: You can't live on a train for days. Even if it is stationary. Call my car and Admiral Hope. We're going for a Saturday afternoon spin. Ever been to Soissons?

But they found Soissons smashed. Good bourgeois bricks tumbled into the streets, and men in the perished blue of the army of 1914 picked over the mounds finding in every heap a handful of something to put in their sacks. What it was they made a handful of the admiral did not want to see. He feared they might be bagging the wrenched-out and incorruptible organs of dreams, or domestic utensils indecently fused in the heat of bombardment.

He put his hand on a corner of standing masonry and muttered. Something about this war being a triumph for the heavy gunner.

When he sat down in the car again he found his knees were jumping.

He thought, I understand my father better.

Is it Something Physical?

A quarter to four. The sun falling, peaky, an unimportant witness.

Over the duckboards von Winterfeldt and, in spite of his sense of demerit, the count carried to Weygand the document entitled *Some Observations* etc. Unsleeping last night and deserted by the count, von Winterfeldt had spent such lonely hours putting an edge on it. He seemed sure it would smooth away some of the harsher terms.

General Weygand accepted and sat some time over it in 2417D, avoiding their faces, pretending or actually suffering a sort of mental weariness. Having checked it himself and looked up with the mild relief of a schoolteacher who finds neither wrong uses of case or person nor foul words in the essay of an unfavoured pupil, he excused himself and went to the Marshal's saloon to hand the submission to him. As he walked from carriage to carriage he asked himself why he so resented the smell of hope that came from the Prussian general. To be narrow, to be peevish, that isn't the true Weygand. He remembered it was the British admiral who had put him in this state.

He resented as well the pipe-smoke thick in the Marshal's

saloon. I've lived with it too damned long. Why does he never change his brand? Always Old Breton. Fishermen smoke it.

Weygand: Their submission, Ferdinand. They're waiting in the office.

The Marshal asked for his glasses to be passed.

Maxime found and passed them.

Weygand: I think it adds nothing to the matters they've already raised.

The Marshal: Of course not, of course not.

Back in 2417D Maiberling stood up.

Maiberling: I don't suppose they'll shoot me for wandering about.

Von Winterfeldt: As you wish.

Maiberling: I understand your coolness.

Von Winterfeldt: Very well.

Maiberling began pacing.

He thought, I wonder is it something physical. Gall-bladder. Prostate. Any of them can make you silly as a duck.

From the telephone in his saloon the Marshal read von Winterfeldt's work to Premier Clemenceau in Quai d'Orsay. Then they talked about it and decided it was not a winning document.

Maiberling in 2417D was aware that rejection buzzed east–west, west–east above their heads. It was the general who would not lift his head, cock his ear.

Maiberling: I'd say he won't be back for at least another ten minutes.

It got very dark in the office car but neither waiting delegate bothered to turn a lamp on. There was a barely heard and somehow feral scraping at the door. They looked, expecting to see an invading squirrel and found Weygand incarnated there.

Weygand: The issues you raise are excellently put and perfectly understood. But the Allied command can offer you no satisfaction in their regard.

Maiberling: The end of the discussion.

He could not help but feel, perversely, vindicated.

Weygand: It would seem so. A detailed written reply will

however be handed to you as soon as possible.

Von Winterfeldt saluted and left the carriage. His style was of an officer who knows how to lose heavily at cards, who doesn't lump his despair about the mess but takes his bursting loss back to his billet and, if the code-of-an-officer-demands it, punctures it with his service revolver.

Maiberling had to run to catch up with him on the duckboards across the glade. For the count had not reacted to Weygand with the general's instant and manic dignity.

Maiberling: You see, you must rest now. All that writing's futile.

He thought damn it all, why do I feel brotherly towards the old fool?

Von Winterfeldt: Please. I don't want to hear any more about what's futile.

The last sun hung, Chinese lantern style, in the boughs of an elm. It seemed even to rock in the cold wind blowing out of the Low Countries.

Look at me, rattling over duckboards behind a soldier in glacé kid gloves, the kind old lechers wear. And being despised by this old dinosaur, yet running at his heels rather than be alone in the forest.

It's the way Erzberger says: there *was* a Count Maiberling in Sofia who was effective. And controlled. I set up the Foreign Minister with a mistress, a German mezzo-soprano. Egg-timer waist, thin ankles. The Foreign Minister of heavy-limbed Bulgaria very much wanted a girl with trim ankles. By such means, cannily arranged by Count Maiberling, all the martial demons were born from the chanteuse's womb and Bulgaria entered the war.

Von Winterfeldt broke into the count's amazement at his new and scatty self.

Von Winterfeldt: Do you think a soldier considers the question of futility? Nearly all a soldier does in peace is futile. And in war the odds mount in favour of futility.

Maiberling: You shouldn't talk that way. You're a Prussian.

Von Winterfeldt: What a childish man you are.

Upstart Socialist

Just before dinner the news came from Berlin spies, Spa spies, and intercepted telegrams, *en clair*, despatched to Swedish news editors by their German correspondents. Prince Max of Baden had given up the Chancellery to a socialist called Ebert. The telegrams vaguely delineated a seizure of power.

Weygand gave the news when the Marshal and Wemyss and their staffs came to the saloon at 7 o'clock for an apéritif. Hearing it, the Marshal said nothing. Wemyss understood the quality of the Marshal's silence. He is not shaken and still believes he has endowed the delegates across the tracks with some cosmic authority, that it cannot be eroded by an upstart socialist.

Wemyss himself talked a great deal.

Weygand thought, he's depressed and a good thing too, after all that senseless chatter at lunch.

Wemyss: What sort of socialist is he?

Weygand: Political Section say *moderate*.

Wemyss: Then . . . one hopes he can hang on.

Weygand: Yes.

The Marshal: For the moment Herr Erzberger will not be told.

Later, when the Marshal telephoned the War Office once again, old Clemenceau himself said he feared Ebert might mean a new regime, that Erzberger and his colleagues might now be mere private citizens. Paris, he said, is full of Tsarist Russians in exile. Perhaps those men over the tracks are simply the first trainload of Kaisertreu Germans in exile. I'm very depressed. I'm going home to Passy.

Clemenceau: You'll sleep well, won't you?

It was an accusation.

The Marshal: As always, Monsieur.

Clemenceau: Yes, I know, damn you. In the bosom of Jesus.

The Marshal: Aren't we all, Monsieur?

Clemenceau: That's a matter of bloody opinion.

In Passy

In Passy, in a little suburban house, he had lived alone since his bankruptcy twenty-five years ago. Even the Marshal would have admitted that for old Georges it had been a tenebral bachelor's life regulated by prostate, diabetes, the disciplines of earning a living by writing, and an eventual return to politics. Behind his virtues lay no love of abstract ethics. He had learned, almost by accident, he was a lonely and ascetic man. And it was also true that if you wanted to deal dirt in the house it was better to have no dirt in your own closet.

In the superb racy decades from 1870 he had committed enough of the conventional sins and been amazed to find that, indeed, he enjoyed more the splitting of coalitions than the parting of vulva.

Standing

At midnight all the German plenipotentiaries were sleeping or pretending to in the deep chairs in Napoleon's saloon. If they *were* asleep you might guess they dreamed of women and telegrams: the improbable arrival of either; and cert-ainly Erzberger dreamed of little Paula, desirable in a man's postal employee's uniform left vacant by a soldier, cycling round Charlottenburg with astounding messages and, in any case, never one for him.

Bourbon-Busset woke him.

Oh yes, he remembered, Count Alfred decided we ought to drink a little for the general's sake. Maiberling had come back from 2417D kindly disposed towards the general. It seemed the general was not of the Inga-killing species.

Erzberger: What?

Bourbon-Busset: The Marshal has had news.

He handed Erzberger a careful message Weygand had got ready. It told of Max and Ebert, quoting sources, saying the Marshal would communicate with Herr Erzberger tomorrow regarding the effect this information might have on Herr Erzberger's standing.

Matthias read it aloud to the others.

Maiberling: It's simple. We mightn't have *any* standing.

Vanselow: I don't understand.

Maiberling: It's simple. If this is the revolution.

Erzberger: Please don't explain it.

Maiberling: I was only answering him.

Erzberger: Please don't explain it.

A Not Inestimable Weight at the Throat

An hour later in his cabin, Vanselow found on taking off his jacket that the brown thread which held an Iron Cross at its collar had very nearly frayed through. He groaned at the idea of calling for needle and thread and repairing the ribbon in the forest.

For the first time he understood he didn't have to wear the thing. He could let the threads fray through. The Cross might fall without a sound on to carpet or into mud.

Or he could take nail-scissors and snip it away. Cutting would be difficult and the wiry thread hard to extract totally from the fabric of his uniform. But in the last days a few unexplained fibres could be permitted to obtrude.

Once it is cut away, he thought, I'll put it in an envelope and send it to someone deserving. With the note: I was awarded this Grand Cross, a not unnoticeable weight at the throat, at Easter 1915, for staff work, at a time when our flag-ship had not once sighted the enemy, and the extent of the dangers I ran were the scrimmages at the end of the seventh course in the officers' mess.

I began well on the *Holstein*. I inspected the men's food, I ordered improvements. But in the evenings we all fed like aristocrats in the mess and the bread-and-bacon sailors below could hear us sing our schnapps away. And then the admiral tells you that you are to be given the Cross. Since you are high on his staff, it's the Grand Cross for you. Refusal is an affront to the Emperor. Sixty-three officers and petty officers of *Holstein* are being so honoured. All but a few of the midshipmen. And even not they on the grounds that they were uncomradely in the mess or have liberal ideas. Probably because they are alcoholics.

He remembered the sailors sniggering on the forward deck of *Holstein* at Easter when sixty-three men who had never heard an English shell were honoured. Commander Vanselow. Lieutenant Rank.

Rank knew what was happening and said it when they were both drunk.

They had been part of an extempore pyramid formed by officers in mess-tails during the coronation-day dinner aboard *Holstein*. He and Rank had been given a place near the apex. The pyramid had not lasted long. There had been hisses and curses and someone began laughing infectiously. There was a rain of men, cascading wing collars, serge, braid, silver buttons. Rank's arm was still round him when they landed without any sense of pain. Rank landed — amongst the shouting, the hysterical recital of injuries — sombre.

Rank: We have no stature as warriors, Vansie. In my opinion the navy's just a trump-card for our diplomats to use. When they begin their bargaining.

Rank had not considered a time might come when the diplomats, unable to form *their* accustomed pyramids, might call on friend Vansie.

If I put the Cross in an envelope, Rank would be a suitable addressee. If he still had an address.

Dearest Rank,

If at Jutland a freakish shell had not lobbed down one of *Holstein*'s stern ventilators and alighted on the floor of your gunroom; if the oxygen had not been so instantly sucked up and the heat so far beyond imagining that when later we opened the lock we found you and your men all dusty and tangled together in striving like Laocoön and his sons; and if on touch this whole sculpture had not fallen to ashes – poor Rank, in the tradition of elegiasts, instantly democratized down to dust – then you would have seen a day of negotiations which began with your friend giving the navy away, a basic, reasonable and unarguable act.

Come Vanselow (Vanselow muttered aloud)! You didn't always see the Cross as an albatross around the neck, a frontal Calvary. You wore it on leave for its social potency. Your wife liked to see it on you. Only now and then did you feel its mass.

As in the summer of the award. You sat in the sun on the Station at Erfurt with colleagues from the Fleet. It was an intense season, God's last gift of a summer in the pre-war manner.

A freight train came in, a summer carnival on wheels. Open freight wagons full of bearded soldiers from France. Birch leaves and branches hung all over the wagons, bouquets of flowers exploded from the mouths of the artillery and daisies were stuck in the muzzles of the stacked rifles.

The wagons sported inscriptions. *Flea powder still accepted here. You are all finished Nicolaievich!* They were on their way to Russia.

Red Cross ladies went round the train with raspberries and the Russian-bound soldiers laughed, heads back, a carmined mash of berries behind their teeth.

Vanselow could see them nudging and pointing at the

naval officers. The others didn't care, and he could do an excellent mime of not caring. The Cross burned at his throat.

(In the forest, Vanselow thought: caring, not caring, how simple-minded of us in any case.)

As the train moved out in the lost summer the soldiers had begun to sing. No barrack-room ditty: the Red Cross ladies had made them sentimental.

> When the spring comes,
> The lilac blossoms and swallows
> Come back again.
> Courage then revives anew
> And all is well again

Departing, they had taken on holiness in Vanselow's eyes.

Now their skulls were gourds of snow in Russia. All these possible addressees for his possible envelope.

Platonic Confectionery

If he slept for as much as ten seconds that night, having gone to his bunk in his long underwear, some buffeting in the ether would spring his eyes wide-open again.

One such buffeting brought the news into the Marshal's train at half past two. Weygand received it but knew that the Marshal did not need to know it till four. The Kaiser had given up his family's call on the German throne. He had swayed away in his gold and white train from Spa without farewelling the Supreme Command. A republic had been declared and Ebert was president.

Still suffering the disquiet of the afternoon before, Weygand thought, good, they're royalist officers, just like us, those German generals. We've had to stomach a republic, mean fare, stale old Platonic confectionery. Now let those bastards eat of it.

As One Is to the Bereaved

By breakfast time there had been accretions of news: the
Berlin garrisons, for example, had placed themselves at the
disposal of the new government. The Marshal took all
Weygand could tell him at breakfast as if it were fruit that
had ripened in season. Weygand himself, by rule a rational
man, yet thought that the Marshal was wise to be tranquil,
that this was a morning on which certain leaps were necessary. It was useless to spout syllogisms.

As Admiral Wemyss did, taking coffee only.

Wemyss: That's it. Our friends no longer have power to
negotiate.

The Marshal: This business won't be decided in the
old-fashioned diplomatic manner.

That made the admiral look peevish and rather old. His
square face began to melt down into dewlaps.

Wemyss: I would like to know what other means there
are for deciding it.

The Marshal: They will present themselves.

The old argument they'd been having since they met.

The Germans were told at breakfast by Bourbon-Busset.
Just in time. For while they all still sat in silence, becoming
accustomed to the climate of an altered world, the chef and
assistant chef burst from the kitchen, argued in whispers
with the waiters in the servery, enlisted them in their
company and came forward to Erzberger. They were respectful, as one is to the bereaved.

The chef begged the Messieurs' pardons, for none of the
staff were actually permitted to speak to Their Excellencies.
He even spoke in slow, simple French: an ultimate kindness.
Then he held out a special 5 a.m. edition of *Le Matin*. How

he had got it he didn't say, someone must have rushed a carload from Paris to Compiègne and spread them round the forest, even to the kitchen-staff in the German train. Apologetically radiant, the chef indicated the headline. *The Kaiser Abdicates.*

Erzberger: May I read it?

The chef was doubtful about giving away more than headlines. The waiter said that monsieur must understand their position.

Erzberger: Please.

He had enough French to read it and as he read he passed information to the others.

Erzberger: It says Schiedemann announced a republic at midday yesterday.

Maiberling: Republic. Republic?

He sniffed the word over.

Erzberger: Why Schiedemann? They say the soldiers from the Arsenal, from Reinichendorf, Spandau and Wedding have come in and pledged loyalty to the Soldiers' and Workers' Council. They make Ebert sound like a roaring red, like Lenin's little brother. They say that the Kaiser and all his sons have skipped from the country. The King of Bavaria has abdicated and Kurt Eisner has taken the Cabinet over. Holy God, the list! The Duke of Brunswick, the Grand Duke of Hesse, the Wettins in Saxony. The Duke of Oldenburg deposed. Prince Henry of Reuss has renounced the throne in Gera. Can you take more?

Maiberling: It's only a newspaper.

Von Winterfeldt: Yes.

Erzberger: Grand Duke Wilhelm Ernst of Weimar has renounced the throne on behalf of himself and his family. As a private citizen the King of Bavaria has joined his wife Maria Theresa in Wilsennath, where she is dying or dead . . . I'm not good at participles.

He showed it to von Winterfeldt.

Von Winterfeldt: Dying.

Maiberling: We all fall down.

Vanselow felt light-headed and remembered returning from leave to Wilhelmshaven one autumn evening, approaching the dockland gate in a wet dusk, around him a hundred or more ratings coming back to the sterile fleet and blaming him out of the corners of their eyes as if he had compelled, by incantation, their return. He raised his head that night and saw the framework of Big Heinrich, the harbour crane, written against the last light like a formula for boredom, and above the gate the eagle of Prussia. Of which Heine had written, *Full of venom he stared down at me.*

Now the venomous eagles were fowl-meat. Amazing.

Old-fashioned von Winterfeldt played with a simple royalist hope.

Von Winterfeldt: Perhaps His Highness will remain on in his role as King of Prussia . . .

Maiberling: The Emperor is ex-officio King of Prussia. He can't abdicate as Emperor unless he abdicates as the other. That's the constitution.

He seemed all at once embarrassed to betray such keen constitutional insight after all his deranged behaviour. He made a shamefaced correction.

Maiberling: That *was* the constitution.

Even though they now lacked all standing they felt better for hearing such precise intelligence from Bourbon-Busset and for reading *Le Matin*'s spectacular list of abdications. The chef was astounded to see how well they suddenly began eating.

Twenty-Second Sunday After Pentecost

The Marshal and his friend Maxime drove to Mass at the chapel of the Hôtel-Dieu in Compiègne. Not knowing this, Wemyss went searching for them around the saloon and wagon-lits. He did not employ juniors on the task but went himself, wanting to feed off the Marshal's fixity, wanting too to be further annoyed by it.

In the end one of the staff found him seeking down the corridors and told him where the Marshal was.

Wemyss went and sat with Hope in the dining car. The cloth was bare on the table but spattered widely with coffee stains. I would never permit *that* in my wardroom, he thought.

Wemyss: Devotion's all very well. But while he listens to the sermon anything could happen in Germany.

At the Hôtel-Dieu it was the twenty-second Sunday after Pentecost and the priest wore green vestments. Around the choir stalls the carved standards of the guilds of Compiègne stood. The Marshal felt ecstatic here amongst the exquisite woodwork of the Middle Ages. Jeanne d'Arcq had heard Mass in this chapel and seen the same figurines. That of St. Euphrosyne, the transvestite saint of Compiègne. Jeanne d'Arcq saw the standard of St. Euphrosyne on the last morning of freedom, before the Bastard of Vandomme caught her down the hill a little and hauled her off her horse.

If woodworm had got to the Euphrosyne Jeanne saw, some craftsman had modelled a new one according to the old. The continuity of French things!

Weygand sitting at his side, he listened gratified to the priest read the Latin Gradual. *Look and see how good and genial it is when brothers live together in one heart. It is like oil poured on the head, that runs down into the beard, as it ran into the beard of Aaron.*

He thought, this isn't the rootless brotherhood Clemenceau feels for his callisthenist. This is Roncevalles brotherhood. I am a very fortunate man.

The Comic Train-Traveller

At ten Bourbon-Busset brought them a telegram from Spa, from the generals themselves. Shoulder to shoulder they massed around this direct pabulum. Any news from Spa certified their existence and must be gratefully fragmented and absorbed. Erzberger, holding the telegram, found the fingers of the others straying round its rim.

It was from General Groener and told them OHL would indicate all planned positions of delayed-action mines in recently occupied French territory. The ordinariness of it pleased them.

Maiberling: Something to work on, eh? Something to work on.

Erzberger smiled. It seemed the count had chosen to revamp his faith in the century.

Before another hour had passed three German staff-officers rolled into the glade in an open car. Under as good a sun as could be had in November they dismounted and marched amongst the thin ground mist to the officer of the guard. Bourbon-Busset went to examine them and then to speak to the Marshal. The Marshal said admit them to Herr Erzberger. But not until their boots could be heard in Napoleon III's ante-room did Erzberger and the others know they had so easily infiltrated France.

For a man who detested staff-officers, the count behaved for a while very much like a rescued member of the Spitsbergen expedition, putting his hands on their shoulders.

But they were not the kind of men to encourage handling. All three in their thirties. Caps under arms. Hair exactly groomed. No fat on them. A death squad, perhaps.

No. 1: Your Excellency, we have come to tell you something of what has happened since you left Spa.

Erzberger: Did General Groener send you?

No. 2: Not in an official sense. He permitted us to come. We are from the Strategic Offensive Office. You understand things have got slow for us since August, we are easily spared. We have travel documents and an authority to pass through the lines. I would like you to see them.

They were produced. Erzberger read them. He could feel his throat pulsing. What will it be like when they come for me and I know why, and there are no alternative explanations for their presence?

He handed the papers to von Winterfeldt who might

perhaps know more about military documents.

Erzberger: What can you tell us then, gentlemen?

No. 2: From the capital very little. I was however present at the château with Colonel Heye during the discussions between Quartermaster-General Groener and the Kaiser concerning the latter's abdication.

Erzberger: Please tell us. Everything.

The young man explained how on the morning of the abdication, OHL staff drove out of Spa to the château. There they found the Emperor raving with the unrealistic fevers his friend Admiral Muller had breathed into him. He really believed that within a week he would be at the front, living and perhaps dying like an infantry sergeant. That the love of Emperor was at the core of every soldier. As basic as the love of God or life, the Kaiser said. With my élite men, I shall crush the Workers' and Soldiers' Soviet in Cologne.

Erzberger noticed how the young man from the Strategic Offensive Office spoke of the Kaiser with little grimaces at the ends of the mouth. As if the Emperor had always been some other people's vice and hard to account for.

When the Kaiser made these fantastic proposals, the Field-Marshal looked at the floor, but General Groener read loudly the results he had got from his poll of regimental officers.

The Kaiser said, they have an oath to the colours. I am their warlord.

Groener said, these words mean nothing any more. The world's vocabulary is changing.

His Highness kept tossing his head. He said he wished his English mother had been alive to see him suffer like this. It would have consummated her perfidious life. But for that whole morning he did not leave the house. He knew it had got beyond rushing out of doors.

A little after one o'clock, the Kaiser agreed to abdicate as king of Prussia and went off to lunch, helped through the dining-room door by the Crown Prince.

"After a good lunch and a cigar," the Prince told him, "things will look a lot better."

But the event had its impetus now. In Berlin Max announced the Kaiser's total abdication and gave the seal of state to Ebert. And Schiedemann, panicked by the crowds outside the Reichstag reading-room, announced from the window a republic.

Ebert was upset, said the officer. A trade unionist he might be, but the idea of a republic made his skin itch.

The three officers smiled. There was scorn there too. As for the Kaiser who a week ago had been an evocation of the sun yet today was just a comic train-traveller.

We know about Ebert's itchy skin, gentlemen, said the young officer, because he told General Groener. After the circus in front of the Reichstag, Ebert went back to the Chancellery and sheltered in Max's office, not knowing what to do, even what telephone connected him to what place. He was fearful to pick any of them up. In the end one of them rang. It happened to be Extension 988 which, without his knowing it, connected him to Spa.

Groener was on the line. Ebert was so grateful that he told Groener about the terrible afternoon he had had and was delighted to hear Groener say that the army offered itself to him for the purpose of suppressing the Bolsheviks. So a new pact was made. The republic and the army. I am not certain that I can control events, Ebert said. Neither am I, said Groener. But we'll try.

That is all we knew (said the officer to the delegates) when we started out yesterday evening.

Young Turks

Like the count, von Winterfeldt had taken a dislike to these three élite children of OHL.

Von Winterfeldt: Do you intend to treat all republican officials as if they were ridiculous?

For all Matthias knew, the old general might really be striking out for the Kaiser's sake.

One of the officers spread his hands, a lenient movement.

Officer: If the republic can control affairs we'll be very happy. Perhaps it will be a passing phase.

Maiberling: But I want to ask you this. Are you the sort of young turks who wanted to fight to the end?

Officer: It isn't the year for that, sir.

Erzberger: Didn't Ebert . . . when he spoke to Groener . . . didn't he mention us? Our *standing*?

Officer: General Groener said nothing of it.

Matthias felt envious of Groener who had nothing but railroad maps to deal with.

Erzberger: I wish he could have managed better than that. Doesn't he understand our situation here?

Officer: We have told you what we are empowered to. If it leaves you more uncertain than you were yesterday, that's the condition of all of us.

After this cool chastisement, Matthias sent them away to have coffee.

When Blauert had led them away towards the dining car, Maiberling fell into a chair.

Maiberling: Simple soldiers. Circumspect. Respectful to their government's representatives, oh yes, no political ambitions, oh no, honest mechanics of the killing machine. Canny as river-rats.

Index finger to lips, the general hushed him.

Von Winterfeldt: I think you've said too much.

Maiberling: One mustn't anger the young masters.

At his desk, Matthias was distracted by the autumn sun which now seemed strong in the glade. He wanted to be a vacationer and stroll down the deer-tracks. It took many mid-air gyrations of his pen before he could remember what he meant to write and wrote it. The exercise wearied him. This train-bound air he thought. Then, raising his voice to chairman-level and still wincing above his notepaper, he began speaking.

Erzberger: There are two conclusions we must work by. One is that the new government wants an armistice signed— they haven't said otherwise. The second is that if the new government wants an armistice they must consider they have the power to enforce it. That's how it seems to me.

The general and Captain Vanselow took note of both conclusions but Maiberling closed his eyes.

On such principles all except Matthias went once more to speak with Weygand and the admirals across in 2417D. Erzberger was left alone and spent the time noting down remembered statistics from government white papers on Germany's hunger, Germany's diseases, the death of Germans.

The figures came slowly today. He must jolt them out of a steamy brain, part vapours to get at them. What is happening? Memory used to be my strong suit. When I was a journalist writing politics for *Deutsches Volksblatt* I was able to research and write a book on Napoleon's land confiscations in Bavaria. During the debates on corruption in German Africa I carried precise figures of fiddled accounts and dispossessed tribesmen into the Reichstag without having to copy them down, tote cumbrous notes.

The numbers he wrote down this Sunday in the forest did not assert themselves on the page in the old way.

Weight of boys at 1 yr. (he wrote) *down 41%.*

And after a long wait,

Weight of girls ditto down 32%.

He was sure that was right. Or nearly.

In Büttenhausen they say of my brother Heinrich the postman, he never forgets the smallest detail about changed addresses or anything like that. In Stuttgart they say of my brother the typesetter, it's as if he'd written the copy himself. They'd both found safer uses for their congenital memories.

In Stuttgart.

He wrote:

Stuttgart in receipt of ⅓ pre-war supply of milk.

Klagenfurt 11%.

Graz 6%.

Crick-necked Vanselow and then the other two returned from the Marshal's train. They sat about saying nothing; the count even fell asleep.

A Whisky Tipple with George

Sunday dinner, and the Marshal had no wise repented of his vision. History (he still believed) would, like black ball in corner pocket, slot down into the neat cavity of his presumptions.

Provoked this way, Wemyss took to his cabin and spent the early afternoon resting and having a whisky tipple, from a private bottle in his valise, with George Hope.

Wemyss: Did you take a nap, George?

Hope: Not really, sir.

Wemyss: Pity. It will be a long night's argument if word comes from Berlin.

Hope: I'm used to long watches, sir.

He was proud of it.

Wemyss: Indeed. Well, another crossing tomorrow, whatever happens, truce or not. Your wife meeting you at Folkestone?

Hope: No, sir. My daughter's not able to be left alone.

Wemyss: I'm sorry.

Hope: She lost a husband.

Wemyss: It's appalling. Do you know? The French picked up a signal detailing a British air raid tonight. Transmitted *en clair* by our people! The dying isn't over, George.

Hope: No.

In shirt sleeves the First Sea Lord scratched his left breast, less because it itched but as the first act in some rubric he used for coming to decisions.

Wemyss: I want to ask you something, George. I don't want to embarrass you but I know you're a good man. I don't mean good in the frightened, *pallid* way we English use it, but *really* good. Close to . . . close to . . .

Hope: God, sir?

Wemyss: That's right.

Hope: I'm not frightened of being accused of that.

Wemyss: So let me know, what do you think, George? Are those people lying? About chaos? About famine? About Bolshevism?

The blue eyes pulsed once with a certainty appropriate to Savonarola but then returned to their proper Anglican repose.

Hope: You know the beggars are lying, sir.

A Stag Over Your Shoulder

That afternoon the sun still stood quite clearly over the forest and the sentries took their trench-coats off and every now and then their fingers raked round inside their collars to wipe away mild sweat or scratch the smallest of heat itches.

Erzberger asked the count if he'd care for a walk through the woods. In spite of all the man's freakish behaviour, Matthias still looked to his company as to a last true friend.

They escaped their train and took the first path they could find. The forest made its own strange light beneath its boughs. Its breath was cold on the cheeks. There was, as well, a stag presence in the place. The tremulous could easily imagine a great beast breaking cover to gore them. This afternoon Matthias was tremulous.

Alfred Maiberling seemed tense. Perhaps he expected reprimands from his head-of-mission. As if I'd dare. As if we wouldn't end brawling like two stevedores.

At last a conversation got started.

Maiberling: What was your mother's name, Matthias?

Erzberger: Katarina.

Maiberling: Did you see much of her?

Erzberger laughed.

Erzberger: Of course. It was a small house. And Büttenhausen is full of Jews and Protestants who didn't mix much with us. Nor, to tell the truth, us with them. Yes, I saw a lot of her.

Maiberling: Servants . . . ?

Erzberger: None. *We* were the servant class.

Maiberling's high forehead struggled to ingest this alien condition.

Maiberling: You were lucky. I can tell: your little wife . . .

Erzberger: Paula.

Maiberling: Paula. She's that sort of mother, a good country mother. Who gives a damn if she lacks style? Her children won't care.

Matthias was used to the sideways compliments of the upper classes. But thought, what is this style business and who has it if Paula hasn't? And what an oaf I must have seemed when I first came up to the Reichstag from Biberach.

Maiberling: Think of my mother. She had style. She used to visit us once a day – that was her style. An administrative visit, by and large, a visit to the colonies. If we were lucky it lasted ten minutes. The nursery was a great room at the top of the house. There was one little coal fire there. I bet you spent your childhood around a great stove.

Erzberger: Yes. I did. There you are. We had nothing else.

Maiberling: We had a nanny who used to take fits. She would become very still on a chair in one of the cold corners. My older brother Erik was a real bastard. He would put a flame close to her eyes and she wouldn't move – perhaps she wanted to move, perhaps she was in a fever of fear but she couldn't do anything about it. Her eyes did not blink. Erik would make experimental cuts in her ankles with his pen-knife. When she came round she never mentioned them or tried to punish Erik. She was ashamed of having fits and didn't want to mention them by name. My mother said to us one day, if Nanny should fall down in a fit I want you children to force her jaws apart and put a pillow between her teeth. It's something Nanny does now and then. That was bloody dangerous advice, as it turned out. Nanny could have bitten our little pink fingers off. I suppose it would have all helped to make us reliable German gentry.

Erzberger felt uncomfortable to hear the count speak of his parents this way. His peasant respect for ancestors trembled in him, but he could think of nothing to say.

Maiberling: My father was high in the Foreign Office, higher than me, a friend of Holstein's in fact. We sometimes saw him on Sundays but he was more interested in his theoretical friends in Chancelleries from Tokyo to London than he was in my friendship, or in Erik's. Or even in my sister's. I *had* a sister. Called Alix. When she was nine years old Erik murdered her one evening in the nursery. He had always had what my father called unhappy leanings. Nanny slept in front of the fire, this night. Alix stood in a corner. Thoughtful. I was doing a jigsaw puzzle. Erik was whittling away at one of the peg-dolls we'd all had as children. He'd started into all our old toys with a scout-knife three evenings before and hacked away with a vengeance. He resented those things, he resented the fact we ever depended on them, invested them with personalities and so on. The night I'm speaking of, he simply stood up and put his knife into Alix's stomach. I heard her grunt. She was a correct little girl and a grunt wasn't in her usual repertoire. So I looked up from the pieces. Erik was leaning on her. I heard her say, don't. He stepped away. She sat in the corner and fell on her side. He had a whetstone in a cigar box that he used for sharpening his scout-knife and you could have shaved with that blade. He'd put it into Alix's waist and cut downwards. She was very quiet. She said, please get my mother, to no one in particular. Perhaps to God, because it would have taken God to get my mother up to the nursery at dinner-time. She told me, Alfred, wake Nanny. I went to Nanny and shook her shoulder and said, Nanny, Erik has put his knife in Alix. Erik was at the water-basin rubbing his clothes down with a face-cloth. The flow of blood from Alix amazed me. Even though I had a brother like Erik who used occasionally to slice up kittens. I didn't suspect humans carried so much blood about with them and I'd never guessed it'd leave them at such a rate. Nanny walked round the mess and put her hand on Alix's shoulder. Alix's eyes were already remote. She didn't seem to hear anything when Nanny spoke to her.

Mother and Father left a dinner at the Russian Embassy to hurry home. A dead daughter has power to claim things a live one can't. Amongst my class that's so, anyhow. Because it was an important dinner: he was always a member of the détente-with-Russia school in the Foreign Office. It would have taken murder in the family to bring him home.

Matthias felt cold, the stag breathing on his shoulder.

Erzberger: What can I say? It's the most horrible thing . . .

Maiberling: Is it? I suppose you've fought all your life to have the same advantages as me. Now you can see what my advantages were.

Erzberger: Your brother . . .?

Maiberling: My father sent him to a military school. But even the insanity of that sort of place wasn't enough to cover him. When he was fourteen he had to be put in an asylum. He's still there. It's in Potsdam.

Erzberger: But the police . . .? The little girl *was* murdered after all.

Maiberling: A Foreign Office official interested in a détente with Russia can't let people think that his children are killing each other upstairs. He talked to the highest police officials who thought he'd suffered enough without having his son tried for juvenile fratricide. He got a death certificate from a physician that said Alix Maiberling, aged nine years, had died in a fall from her nursery window. He was sole witness in the coroner's court. He said that she had always been an adventurous child and he wept and the coroner was very sympathetic. In the nursery the boards were scrubbed with carbolic and no knife allowed. I ate with a spoon until I went away to school at eleven. My parents found it easiest to assume we were all killers.

They came to open sward. A grandiose vista ran amongst the trees down hill, up hill, down and up another, past terraces to the pale masonry of the château of Compiègne.

Maiberling: Napoleon slept there. I bet he was a bastard of a parent too.

French soldiers stamped across the turf towards them, gesturing them back. *Allez. Allez.*

Erzberger would have liked very much to continue in that sunny avenue and to sit amongst the urns on the warm terraces.

Allez.

The soldiers of the French republic raked the air energetically with bayonets.

Matthias and the count turned back down the deer-path, re-entering the forest murk slowly, finding it an unseasonable element.

Maiberling: I could have forgiven my father if he'd been an insensitive man. But when I left university and was taken into the Foreign Office myself he invited me to his club and told me that a lot of Germany's problems in foreign relations rose from the Kaiser's unhappy boyhood. The Kaiser was kept in the nursery, hardly saw his mother, tyrannized by his tutor, that old pansy Hinzpeter. Hinzpeter taught him to ride by forcing him into the saddle at five years of age, withered arm and all, and lifting him off the ground and putting him back into the saddle every time he fell out. One day his mother watched the whole screaming riding lesson without making any protest. She took him from the nursery only to show him her shrine to her dead baby, and to tell him that none of her other children could make up for the loss of dear little Sigismund and to force him to look at the wax dummy of the infant she kept in a cradle and to make him pray over it. My father told me, the Kaiser is an emotional man and too much of his foreign policy is in terms of his emotional reaction to his mother. And his mother is, as you know, an English princess.

For the elder Maiberling (whom he had never met) and perhaps for his distrait son, Matthias wanted to deflect the conversation to mere politics.

Erzberger: I believe that's a perceptive assessment of the Kaiser's shortcomings.

But Maiberling had hooked his left arm round the trunk of a birch and made a fist as if to rough it up. His voice became basso and insistent.

Maiberling: That bastard who begot me! How do ordinary people feel? Their lives, their intimate bloody lives in the hands of men who don't even love their children?

Again Erzberger believed he heard hooves on the heavy earth behind him. He was too ashamed to drag his eyes, however, from the count's pathetic history.

Erzberger: What can I say, Alfred? Such a tragic life. Your sister and now your . . . your Inga.

He saw the count blush and flutter his hand in a dismissive way.

Maiberling: I expect you to be a friend, Matthias. And forgive me easily.

Clump went the mythic stag somewhere behind them, its tines at their soft backs.

Erzberger: Forgive you?

Maiberling: Inga wasn't killed. She simply dropped me. I felt myself flying apart in Spa, you see. Had to tell you something.

Matthias said nothing. The muscles around his shoulder-blades twitched.

Maiberling: Now don't carry on at me about it.

Late in the afternoon two copies of a document entitled *An Answer to Observations on the Conditions of an Armistice with Germany* arrived in the German carriages. It seemed to have a stimulating effect on the general and Vanselow. They began writing annotations on its margins.

Maiberling: You have to give it to those two. They're workers.

After dark, there was a message for Erzberger from Weygand.

As the time allowed for coming to an agreement expires at 11 a.m. tomorrow, I have the honour to ask whether the German plenipotentiaries have received acceptance by the German chancellor of the terms communicated to him and if not, whether it would be advisable to solicit without delay an answer from him . . .?

Erzberger: After dinner. After dinner will do.

Over dinner Erzberger talked to the others about an idea that had taken him from the flank in the forest that afternoon. Even through his fear of great roebucks, and his ears full of the blood of Alix Maiberling, aged nine years, the concept had filled him with a creative elation. If peace negotiations could be commenced within days of the armistice, German plenipotentiaries would be negotiating not with an insane old soldier and obsessive British sailors but with men of wider ideas. With, for example, President Wilson. Who could be trusted to understand about famine. And railroads.

Erzberger, exposing the idea to the others, watched all three faces firm with hope. If the armistice were swallowed up in peace negotiations then they would not be to blame for whatever was given away in 2417D. Onus would revert to those to whom it better belonged: the highest diplomats.

Without warning, Matthias found himself hating the three radiant and obscure men he ate with. For his blood turned perceptive in him and washed the message down to his guts: of course, you'll be used again, Erzberger. Whatever urgencies, vanities, gallantries, fatalisms betrayed you into the forest will also carry you to The Hague, or wherever the congress of peace will be summoned.

He left them at their coffee and sent a message back to Weygand. No, there was nothing from the Chancellor yet. Yes, they had requested by coded signals transmitted by permission of the Marshal that instructions should be quickly sent to them.

About nine o'clock, Erzberger sat composing a telegram to Ebert. The others were predictably employed – Maiberling at the cognac.

Weygand with an interpreter entered after knocking.

He had two telegrams. Keeping his eyes fixed with a sort of arrogant innocence he gave them to Matthias. Of course we haven't read them, said the eyes, we know how to treat other people's private telegrams.

Erzberger could not believe it: Ebert's message stood all naked and uncoded in simple German for the Marshal to read. For the Marshal to conclude: Ah, things are so sixes and sevens in Berlin, they're willing to sign anything.

The German Government to its plenipotentiaries arranging an armistice in France.

The German Government accepts the conditions of the armistice communicated to it Nov. 8.

The Chancellor of the Reich
Schluss
3,084

The second was much longer, two foolscap pages, in code. But so that he would know it must be worried out before he went into final talks with the Marshal, its tag said clearly *OHL SPA* and its signature *Hindenburg*. He foresaw Vanselow and Blauert eking it forth syllables at a time and his skin itched.

Weygand's interpreter asked whether, since the telegram ended with the word Schluss, were they to understand Ebert had been replaced by a further chancellor of that name?

Erzberger: Not at all. *Schluss* simply means *Message Ends*.

The interpreter was not embarrassed. But thanked Matthias.

Weygand: How long will your decoding take?

Erzberger: An hour or so.

Or three or four. But he could not tolerate the Marshal bedding down; so gave a sanguine estimate.

When little Weygand left, Erzberger punched a leather bolster full force. Vanselow flinched, an agile step sideways.

Erzberger: I wanted an answer. But not one they could read. Saying, give it all away, anything they ask.

In front of Matthias's lapse of control, Maiberling made a judicial face and grew analytic.

Maiberling: You have to remember: these men like Ebert and Schiedemann have been preaching the revolution for forty years. They've been going off to socialist congresses in Stockholm or Geneva, first class on trade union money, and talking about the great day that's coming. Not omitting to get themselves photographed in Skansen or Chillon for their wives. Now *the day* has come and they're frightened shitless. They're like fat curates at the second coming of Christ. They'll be guilty of a lot more silliness before they're finished.

The general put his hand gently on the Hindenburg message which Blauert held in a non-proprietary way, as if to say, let anyone with acrostic skills come forward.

Von Winterfeldt: OHL seems to be the only machine that still works.

He didn't appear very pleased at OHL's success.

Everyone, even the count, fell to work, getting notes together.

At midnight Erzberger looked up from his papers to discover the general stood by him, spying over his left arm in a friendly way.

Von Winterfeldt: I'm ready. But Blauert says it will be another hour.

Erzberger: We must let the Marshal know. We can't have him going to bed.

Von Winterfeldt: Herr Erzberger, I have never worked closely before with a member of your class.

The general's face showed no blushes for his feudal mind.

Von Winterfeldt: The army ... the army I came from ... is the worst preparation ... In any case I take such newspapers as ... *Kreuzzeitung.* Which aren't genial towards you. Perhaps you know what they say?

Erzberger: They say I was given a blank cheque to open the Propaganda-for-Neutral-Countries office and that I used it for my own interests.

Von Winterfeldt: Yes. Exactly.

By little movements of the corners of his mouth, the general begged pardon for his congenital reading habits. But Matthias went on reciting the Tory catechism on Erzberger.

Erzberger: That I'm a member of the British Secret Service. That I concocted the Reichstag peace motion with the Jesuit general on Lake Thun and then went to Rome dressed as a monk to get the Vatican's final orders ...

Von Winterfeldt: You have to remember. Some people make up these stories for political reasons. Others believe them because they're frightened.

Comfort came so creakily from the old general, as if he were using certain glands for the first time in forty years.

Erzberger therefore felt it would have been barbarous to say, *I know that.*

Erzberger: Why did you become a soldier?

Von Winterfeldt: It was the only chance you got in Prussia for looking picturesque.

They laughed together thinly. An unaccustomed chorus.

Von Winterfeldt: The price was high. I remember when I went to the military college at Potsdam. I was twelve years old. A senior cadet met me as soon as I got inside the gate. He asked me what my name was. I told him but he behaved as if I'd mispronounced it . . . my own name, mind you, that a person ought to be able to say however he likes. He instantly lashed me across the face with a dog chain. The dormitories were run by regular army corporals, good sons of Sade every one of them. Ours used to make us get down on our haunches with three concise German dictionaries under each arm. You might want to try it when you have the time. Only then if you're interested in the subtleties of pain. Mind you, I grew up to be a senior cadet in the appointed mould. I didn't ever feel a child needed to be beaten on the face with a dog chain but I certainly got used to dealing in all the average barbarities. So that when I got my commission in the hussars I was as exemplary as any other officer in freezing out of the regiment any unfortunate who didn't have *von und zu* or at least *von* before his name. I suppose that secretly I was sickened but no one would have guessed.

Awareness snapped on in von Winterfeldt's eyes. In a rush he understood he was far out on the seas of confession; and with a peasant. There was a slight trembling of the elegant structures of his face before he gave himself up to the tide.

The old Prussian's hands began working, thumbs grating against forefingers. He could have been breaking invisible bread.

Von Winterfeldt: You can imagine why I enjoyed living in Paris.

Erzberger: Yes.

Von Winterfeldt: But the French have their meannesses too.

Erzberger: Yes.

Von Winterfeldt: I think the Marshal is the worst Frenchman one could meet. The man *has* met me and knows he
has. Yet not a sign . . .

A Bitter and Zany Thing

In the small hours all the delegates' eyes were bright, no one
was petulant. Blauert handed them the deciphered clauses
one by one and they incorporated them into their papers,
working quickly, like sub-editors an hour before deadline.

An attempt [the deciphered telegram read] must be made to
get a modification of the following points in the armistice
terms.

1. The extension to two months of the time for evacuation,
the greater part of this time needed for the evacuation of the
Rhine Provinces, the Palatinate and Hesse, otherwise the Army
will collapse, as the technical execution of the terms is absolutely impossible.

2. The right wing of the Army must be allowed to march
through the corner of Maastricht (Holland).

3. The abandonment of neutral zones for reasons of internal
order, at least must be restricted to a depth of 10 kilometres.

4. Honourable capitulation of East Africa.

5. A considerable reduction must be effected in the railway
material to be surrendered, otherwise (German) economy will
be seriously endangered.

6. Army provided with only 18,000 motor lorries, 50 per
cent usable; surrender of the number demanded would mean
complete breakdown of Army supply system.

7. Only 1,700 pursuit and bombing airplanes in existence.

8. If there is to be a one-sided surrender of prisoners-of-war,
at least the present agreements as to treatment of the latter must
remain in force.

9. The blockade must be raised so far as food supplies are
concerned. Commissioners to deal with regulation of food
supplies are on the way.

If it is impossible to gain these points, it would nevertheless be advisable to conclude the agreement. In case of the refusal of points 1, 4, 5, 6, 8, 9 a fiery protest should be raised along with an appeal to Wilson.

So Hindenburg is the voice you hear exact guidance from. Never mind, Matthias. Be grateful for the reliable figures. Note them down. It would be a bitter and zany thing to give away any more than exists.

Maiberling: Honourable capitulation of East Africa? Who cares a damn about that?

Matthias was tempted to intone: for their children ask for bread and they give them honourable capitulation in East Africa.

He did not say it in case it had a bad effect on his colleagues.

The All-Hours Deity

The Marshal sat forward in his seat, dozing over his blackthorn, his big head laid sidewise on his hands.

Sometimes he woke for a little while to look out of gratified eyes and smile at both the admirals, then once more slept vigilantly. Like a fakir, a mad monk.

Wemyss played with the pages of that morning's special editions. He thought, why do I feel stale? He thought, it's the flatulence that comes when you're given too much too easily. Through little Ernst Vanselow, the dead Imperial hand would give all the fleets away, murmuring only a little.

At further occasional wakings the Marshal told them the same old news.

The Marshal: This is the second night of the war I've missed my sleep. I wouldn't do it now if it weren't the last night of all. That's not bad. That's not bad.

Sometimes Weygand brought him in memoranda freshly arrived from the Quai d'Orsay.

The Marshal: How's that old man Clemenceau tonight?

Weygand: Not as composed as yourself, my Marshal.

The Marshal: Why doesn't he telephone the great god Monet? They could talk about diabetes.

Weygand: I believe that Monsieur Monet keeps strict hours.

The Marshal: Yes, they're all Puritans at core. These libertines.

Weygand: Of course, Ferdinand.

And they looked at each other, giving off in chorus an intangible musk of joy. In being military. At having reliable prostates and an all-hours deity.

When the Marshal dozed, sleep sat on his tongue as bland as chicken-flesh.

Last Meeting

Two a.m. Erzberger sent one of the staff-officers to the Marshal's train to ask for a last meeting. The officer also carried a message for transmission and for the Marshal's eyes as well.

It read: *To be transmitted by OHL Spa to Imperial Chancellor Ebert.*

Matthias knew that if Ebert had any status it was not Imperial. But he used the word in pity for his own nervous system, and for Ebert's.

Plenipotentiary powers have just arrived. As soon as the armistice is concluded, we recommend that you inform President Wilson of this immediately by wireless and request him to institute without delay negotiations for the conclusion of a preliminary peace so as to avoid famine and anarchy. We also ask that you make arrangements through Holland's mediation for the first meeting of plenipotentiaries to take place immediately at The Hague. Only by the immediate conclusion of the preliminary peace will it be possible to mitigate the disastrous effect of the execution of the armistice terms.

Up to the present our enemies are completely without any understanding of this danger.

Erzberger

The Marshal nominated 2.15 for the session and ordered coffee for himself and the admirals.

In Napoleon's saloon the German delegates put on their coats and gloves. It was a sharp night and a thin foxy wind ran almost silently through the forest, scarcely brushing bark or leaf.

Maiberling continued to behave with dignity, but on the duckboards, behind Erzberger, he made histrionic whispers.

Maiberling: This is where we come down to it. Eh? We pay for all our little vanities. We'll never be the same men again. Our women won't recognize us.

In 2417D the Marshal and the others sat already at table. They all kept busy at their papers. Admiral Wemyss sighted a document through the lens in his right eyesocket and grunted at it a little. It might have been a proposal for some minute change in jack tars' rations.

The Marshal: Sit down, Messieurs.

He held a pen in front of him and gave it four febrile little jerks through the air, using both hands. He seemed to be pretending that he thought they might seize it out of his fingers and sign anything, at once.

The Marshal: Have you come to tell us that you are ready to sign?

Erzberger: There is information you must have first. Otherwise there will be no reality to our talks . . .

He handed across the table four copies of a digest he had made of the Hindenburg telegram. The Marshal and Weygand and the admirals received them with a scalding sort of toleration; studied them and made marks in the margins of their papers.

The Marshal: Very well, we alter Clause IV to the surrender of 1,700 aircraft.

Von Winterfeldt: The entire force?

The Marshal: That's right. The entire force.

Erzberger: We accept that.

Erzberger saw them all making ticks on their papers. Exeunt all the flying circuses. Von Winterfeldt had retracted his long neck to its shortest possible form and held his chin tucked flush against his collar. He seemed to have caught *that* virus from Vanselow.

The Marshal: And on the basis that the figures you have given us are reliable, let us write 5,000 motor lorries in Clause VII. Please don't ask for a further amelioration in this area. There will be none. I want the war to stop tomorrow. So I won't waste time with mere penultimate offers. Not tonight, Messieurs.

Erzberger: 5,000 motor lorries.

Tick, tick, tick, tick, went the Allied plenipotentiaries. Who were authentically full of power; skins crammed with it.

Von Winterfeldt: All 5,000 . . .

The Marshal: Eh?

Von Winterfeldt: All 5,000 are needed for the evacuation of the army. Which everywhere stands on enemy soil . . .

The Marshal: I thought the enemy was now within. I thought we were now united Christendom standing against the Bolshevik. No?

The Prussian general brushed the grit of this irony off the surface of his notes.

Von Winterfeldt: I am required to ask for time extensions in all directions. Particularly in the matter of time allowed for the evacuation of the army. The evacuation will have to take place by way of fourteen main rail junctions. Antwerp, Liège, Luxembourg, Metz, Nancy and so on. You are aware that in 1913 a total of four millions of passengers were passed through these junctions, west to east.

Weygand: You tell us this in your *Observations* . . . Of course, in peacetime railways never operate at capacity. We now require you to operate these lines at full capacity for a month or so.

Von Winterfeldt: The analogy between armies and ordinary passengers is a faulty one. Ordinary passengers pack their bags individually, buy their tickets, travel individually, individually feed themselves. I needn't tell you it's different with armies. All soldiers should travel in units – that's totally necessary now, for *our* army, in *our* country. Some units supervise the travel of others and ultimately travel themselves under the supervision of yet other units. The complications are four-or-five-fold. You want us to move four million men within twenty-five days not only from the territories they occupy but from the Rhineland and bridge-heads as well . . .

At the end of the table the count leaned forward in his overcoat. He had once more refused to give it up. Matthias thought, perhaps he's the sanest of all of us. For if I had a weapon resting at my left pap I would find it hard now not to abstract it and use it on the Marshal.

Maiberling: I agree utterly with General von Winter-feldt's protest. Again the problem of turning on the Bolsheviks.

The First Sea Lord groaned and threw his lens on the table.

Wemyss: The fear of Bolshevism is a greater evil than Bolshevism itself.

He could not keep out of his face his creative pleasure at this furious aphorism.

The Marshal: There may be room for a small extension.

Maiberling had passed Erzberger a note. It said – in the language of telegrams – *Essential you arrange territorial sovereignty, East Berlin Cycle Club.* Erzberger, reading it, felt mad fear prickling in his larynx, lest the count might not be joking, lest his mind – under the early morning bludgeon-ing – had shrunk to concern for the bike-riders of Friedrich-shafen.

But for all those hours he could not be quit of Maiber-ling's suggestion: that in a dream that lay just beyond the corner of the coming second they were the executives of two rival East Berlin cycling clubs, planning a meet for the Paladrome.

Meanwhile the official Erzberger worked well.

Erzberger: The First Sea Lord might like to hear a brief index of the spread of soviets in Germany. On November 5th revolution and the formation of soviets occurred in Kiel, Lübeck and Brunsbüttel. By November 7th . . . last Thursday . . . these had been joined by Wilhelmshaven, Cüxhaven, Bremen, Hanover, Hamburg, Oldenburg . . . I won't go on with the list. By Friday, Leipzig, Cologne, Frankfurt, Munich, Magdeburg and so on. By yesterday, Berlin, Posen, Breslau, Stuttgart . . . There has been communication and collusion between the various soviets.

Wemyss: Soviet is merely a word to play with. If I were as depressed as some Germans, I'd play with it too.

Von Winterfeldt: It is more than a word. For that reason we need more machine-guns than Clause IV would leave us.

The Marshal: You can use rifles.

Von Winterfeldt: I am sure the Marshal is not serious. Through their seizure of a number of barracks the revolutionaries are in possession of a quantity of armoured vehicles and machine-guns.

The Marshal: There may be a small final adjustment of the figure for machine-guns.

In the silence they heard a poilu cat-call another in the forest, and an hour had gone.

Meanwhile the Marshal said he would let a half-thousand German officers, hiding in the forests on the borders of Mozambique, capitulate honourably. It seemed to amuse him to do it.

And the debate circled on four pivots: time, machine-guns, rolling-stock, blockade; time, machine-guns, rolling-stock . . .

Erzberger: I have the following information from my study of German statistics and of such reliable outside authorities as the Swedish Medical Association and the Red Cross. Milk and fat are in acutely short supply in the cities. Stuttgart, I know, receives one-third of its pre-war supply of milk. Klagenfurt 11%. Graz 6%. Dr. Ingmar Beck of Sweden reports a form of infantile scurvy rampant in the industrial suburbs of Berlin. Five thousand cases were reported in September in the capital alone. The available milk, he reports, will not cure the disease because of the impoverished quality of stock-feed. Dr. Martin Vantzius of the Dutch Red Cross speaks of a new strain of tuberculosis which he calls acute tuberculosis. It is deadly amongst adolescents, and in many cases the disease shows its first symptoms and kills its victim all within the space of the one season. During the summer months therefore the death rate of children two to sixteen years increased 60% on its 1914 figure. You might well discern the effects of acute tuberculosis if I told you the death rate of children eleven to sixteen years has increased 95% on its 1914 figure, the death rate of children six to ten years 55%. In the sixteen years to twenty years area the rate is 120% over that of 1914. I see a trebling and quadrupling of these rates if the blockade does not stop, if the merchant marine is not permitted to perform its function, and if we are deprived of our rolling-stock. There is for example, no fuel for the coming winter. The Ruhr coal production has fallen sixteen million tons and it seems there will not be a Ruhr left to us soon.

Across the table the Marshal trembled with simple-soldier probity.

The Marshal: That is not for us to discuss. Continue with your case.

Erzberger: There are as many as one and a half million children with rickets in our cities, but the number is difficult to define exactly, because of internal chaos. What is known is that the weight of boys at one year is down 41% and of girls 32%. These figures appal one all the more when it is remembered that the middle-class can afford to buy their children black-market food, so that hidden behind the percentages must be thousands of infants from the working masses who weigh a third the weight of a normal one-year-old and who will not see the new year. I know it is not your purpose – any more than it is ours – to wage war on such people. In their name I say there is no justice in a continued blockade.

The First Sea Lord's facial pouches turned pink. There had, it seemed, been a lapse in taste.

Wemyss: Anyone can talk of innocents. *I* can talk of innocents.

He held his hands up none the less, above the level of the table, to show that he had made a record, on his paper, of Erzberger's figures.

Wemyss: You say there's no justice. You sank ships without discrimination and now say there's no justice. My God you're hot, you fellows.

Erzberger: I should also speak of the thousands of vagabond children – twenty thousand in Berlin.

Wemyss: My God, we'll have Peter the Hermit soon.

His hand patted the table in a brittle way that said: These pats could be blows, and I turn into a northern barbarian.

Wemyss: You sank our ships, sir. Everyone's ships. Do I talk to you of the child-corpses of the *Lusitania*?

The Marshal did not miss the opportunity to point up his own freezing composure.

The Marshal: These figures, Herr Erzberger. Do you have any official documents to certify them?

Erzberger: They are from memory.

The Marshal: Do you have any official documents to certify your memory?

Erzberger: You force me to say my memory is a byword in the Reichstag. Your political section might be able to advise you of the fact . . .

Before he was cool and ready, the First Sea Lord rushed back.

Wemyss: You look pretty sleek to me, Herr Erzberger. Your colleagues' *Observations* mentions citizens of Berlin who manage to eat only 100 grams of meat a week. This statistic, I would venture to say, does not include you.

Erzberger: At the Hotel Bristol and Adlon you can buy a good meal. The best hotels and nightclubs are kept well supplied as a propaganda measure, so that visitors to the country, influential Swedes for example, will believe the abundance of the Bristol is typical of the entire country.

Wemyss: The advertising succeeds rather too well in your case.

Erzberger: We all know that we belong to a class of

people who would manage to get food even in extreme circumstances. If Britain were this morning in the position of Germany I would not expect to see the First Sea Lord emaciated.

From his executive Erzberger felt inane reverberations of applause. Wemyss too felt the outer ripples break against his jaws. He closed his eyes and disciplined his breathing. Opening them, he became a calmer and more dangerous man.

Wemyss: We do not know what the situation in Germany is and we do not believe that you necessarily have a clear concept. We are prepared to deal with famine. The British War Cabinet has detailed a hundred thousand tons of British shipping to carry foodstuffs to the north German ports.

Maiberling: Foodstuffs.

The count's lips were shuddering. Everyone pretended not to notice.

Wemyss: Powdered milk and eggs. Flour. Canned and frozen meats.

Maiberling: Canned meats.

Matthias prayed, Christ silence the count.

Wemyss: These ships will sail under naval escort as soon as the new German government establishes its authority in its seaports. They will continue to ferry foodstuffs until the need passes. So I shall not tolerate talk of innocents dying. Innocents come readily to hand as soon as a military nation runs into problems. Might I simply add that if the German government does not quickly create order along its seaboard, the Royal Navy very soon will.

Maiberling: Powdered eggs. We need our rolling-stock. You can't distribute powdered eggs in a handcart, you know. Not from Hamburg to Munich. Not a chance.

The Marshal: The surrender of locomotives and wagons in the specified number is a strategic necessity.

Erzberger: I cannot see that. It is an economic punishment. It is not provided for in President Wilson's points.

At the mention of that remote platonist of the prairies, a film fell on the eyes of the French generals and British admirals. They looked like men who had been unexpectedly reminded that at the age of fourteen they had learned physics or history from a scholarly man of endearing naïvety.

Count It Five O'clock

See, at four o'clock, little Vanselow make his ordained bid to save the fleet. Putting the question with the same futile courage as a small-hours suicide choosing the second in which to pull the trigger. Since, said Vanselow, the German fleet had not been defeated on the high seas it should not all be disarmed, interned, confiscated. Admiral Wemyss turned his large face towards the protest. The left eye was nearly closed, the right so large behind the monocle that you might have thought it painted on the lens.

Wemyss: If you'd wanted that attended to, you had but to sail out.

Vanselow's left hand twitched like a rabbit. He covered it with his right.

Prosit, Lieutenant Rank. You were right in the wardroom of *Holstein* when the pyramid fell.

Towards the end of the night the air grew thin and feverish. Though he had an illusion of breathlessness, Erzberger talked, wooden and fluent, about prisoners-of-war.

The Marshal: No. That's a settled matter. It's nearly five o'clock you know. If we hurry things along, we can have the last shot fired at eleven.

General Weygand cradled the amended document in his arms in such a way as to show Matthias and the others that the improvements had been written into the text, the old figures scratched out in ink. Amend 14 days for clearing invaded territories. Make it 15. Cross out 25 days for evacuating the Rhineland, write in 31. Cross out 10,000 lorries in 15 days, write in 5,000 in 36. Cross out 30,000 machine-guns. Write in 25,000. Write in that the return of German prisoners-of-war shall be settled at the conclusion of the peace preliminaries.

Give two copies for signature to the Germans. They all sign both; even that little lock-jawed nothing of a sea-captain signs. When the documents are returned to the Marshal's side of the table only he and Wemyss sign. Generalissimo of earth. Generalissimo of water.

It was ten past five.

The Marshal: We shall count it five o'clock, gentlemen. The armistice will operate from eleven.

Erzberger sought leave to read and append the document that said a nation of seventy millions suffers but does not die. He read it and the interpreter who had not known what *Schluss* meant directed it, fragment by fragment, on to the table, in front of the Marshal's chest.

The Marshal: All right.

Then he, his pet general, the admirals, simply walked out.

The Maiberling Thesis

At the breakfast table the count chattered across the condiments at mute von Winterfeldt.

Maiberling: You've seen it now. Behaviour, professional or unprofessional, didn't have any meaning.

He seemed elated, as if he had proved some Copernican vision of the arrangement of things.

Matthias drank coffee and was quiet and somnolent and, for a small while, tranquil. No need to debate whether I should become a target. Now I *am*. The only question left is the dodging of bullets.

Posterity Reserves Its Gratitude

Where the Marshal and Wemyss sat, telegrams and decrees were written. Telephones quavering with the voices of politicians were brought to them.

The Marshal composed a telegram.

> After resolutely repulsing all the assaults of the enemy, you have won the greatest victory in history and rescued the most sacred of all causes, the liberty of the world.

The Marshal: You won't edit this, Maxime. Not a word.

Weygand: Very well, Ferdinand.

The Marshal: You may well be my encyclopaedia. You may be the encyclopaedia editorial board as well. But you won't touch this.

Wemyss refused to smile any more than fractionally at this show of fraternal teasing. It was strange that he felt lightened less on account of the success of the naval clauses than of never having to spend a weekend with the Marshal again. There would be no invitations to Brittany next summer. If the Marshal mentioned him at dinner-tables on summer evenings it would be as a glum and parochial Englishman. Whose parish was, whimsically, the sea. And who spoke of the sea as if *it* were the centre, and the western war its flank.

The Marshal, bent on disarming him, read a sentence of the telegram aloud.

The Marshal: Posterity reserves its gratitude for you . . . What does posterity *do*, Maxime? Should we say *it reserves* or should we say *it will reserve*?

Weygand: That's a question.

The Marshal: Posterity doesn't exist at the moment. It

will exist. In ten or twenty years. But not now.

Weygand: However, Ferdinand, *posterity,* the noun, is the present name for a future reality. When the reality arrives it will no longer be posterity but will go by other nouns.

The Marshal: I begin to see.

Weygand: Posterity has existence in the present as an abstract force.

The Marshal: I wouldn't want to make an error of grammar.

Weygand: There is surely no noun with which you cannot use present tense.

The Marshal: So *posterity reserves* is correct?

Weygand: Exactly.

The Marshal: My encyclopaedia.

Admiral Wemyss gave the last of his telegrams to Marriott. It congratulated the fleet which lay this morning in the Firth of Forth in sight (if the sun rose clear) of his childhood coasts. The professional officers would be depressed. No Trafalgar had come their way. The ratings would be happy and in nine months' time there would be navy bastards born to the loose girls of Methil and Burntisland.

In the first of the light an army lorry carrying two photographers and all equipment backed down the track until level with the windows of 2417D. The Marshal, Weygand, the admirals, bunched around one of the small tables. Weygand had supplied the Marshal's copy of the truce to put on the table and a pen for the Marshal's hand. Wemyss was crushed so close to the gnomic Frenchman that the piquancy of sweat, heavy tobacco and shaving soap stung his eyes. So he gazed up at the lens, with the same glazed geniality as, at five years, he had projected when photographed on the knees of fishermen at Issambres. And the Marshal. Because he had not been to bed and the light was thin he looked thinner than he was. His brows cast a long shadow over his face when the phosphorus flashed. The oblique flash caught all his age lines and put a membrane of heroic exhaustion over what his face was trying to say: For all of you and for France my vocal will has triumphed single-handed over Germans and frocks. A claim that even on such a day as this would seem to some (though not many) in Paris to be extreme and even pathological.

The Marshal: There is to be another photograph when we leave. Will you travel with me, Lord Wemyss?

Wemyss flinched. The unwelcome intimacy was not yet finished.

Wemyss: That would be most generous of you.

The Marshal: We can both hand over the text to the Tiger.

Wemyss: You're too kind.

The Marshal: No. I have ordered a car for 7.30. You mustn't think me rude. I shall probably doze all the way up.

Wemyss thanked God that sleep was part of the old man's performance.

Saining

Now he wanted to clear his head of the static fug of the Marshal's train. He and George Hope fetched their overcoats and went for a stroll. The mist uncoiling in the forest reminded him of his family's mythology.

Wemyss: Did you know, George, that the elm was a resurrection tree with the Druids?

Hope: Indeed Rosy? No, I didn't.

Wemyss: I wouldn't know it myself. Except, when we were brought home from London all wrapped up and newly born, an old lady called Meg McLeod used to force her way into the castle and swing a burning elm-bough over mother and child three times. I can't remember it. But old Meg called it 'saining'. I wonder what it meant?

Hope: There's a lot of that sort of thing goes on even in the home counties.

Wemyss: Trees are strong magic, George. I was always a bit uneasy in forests. When I was a child.

The long toe of Hope's shoe went far ahead and crushed something in the mauve mud ahead of them. The exotic conversation perhaps.

Hope: You must be very proud, Rosy.

Wemyss: Oh yes, oh yes.

Hope: You have every right. Every right.

Wemyss: I was well-supported, George. The mundane things will be harder. Talk about sailors' soviets! We've got 'em, George. Call them committees if you like, *soviet* is a loaded word. It would be too unfortunate if we had a sailors' strike.

Hope: The marines, Rosy.

Wemyss: Send them in, you mean?

He thought, if ever I have to, I hope you're still with me, unflinching in the front office.

Wemyss: One has to admit, George. One and eightpence a day for seamen. Damn awful pay.

Hope: We could all complain, sir. Admiral's pay hasn't gone up since '55.

Wemyss: Imagine George Hope on strike. Imagine.

Hope: Indeed.

Wemyss: Still. It would be nice to be able to announce a pay-rise on the way. For all hands.

Hope: Mightn't that seem to be playing up to them?

Wemyss: We don't play up to people, George.

Hope: It's just that in the new world, Rosy, I can see trade unions running mad.

The First Sea Lord found that he himself was grinding away at the mud conclusively with his boot. He thought, I wonder what *I* understood of the blazing elm circle over my head? Chagrin rose in him.

Wemyss: Imagine those chaps trying the *starving-children* line?

Their Talk Had Solemn Rhythms

Long after the generals and the admirals drove away, Matthias sat working on a report for Ebert and at another table von Winterfeldt wrote observations down for his masters. The habits of work protected them in a forest which threatened, on the Marshal's departure, to become as notional as forests in dreams. You could not help believing that minds trying to dwell on the woods this morning, under the thin sun, would fail to get purchase, would fall out of their accustomed notches. Vanselow and Maiberling evaded this hazard quite well by sleeping. Blauert kept to a deep lounge chair. Chained to his wrist a brief-case, and in it the signed document itself as well as maps to illustrate all its terms. He was to be flown to Belgium from a field at Tergnier — Weygand had said that. But it seemed no plane was available for him till noon.

As for the train, Bourbon-Busset had told them it would be two hours before it was flagged out of the forest.

While Matthias worked, more staff-officers arrived from Spa.

Somehow they had got passes from Groener's office and radioed and white-flagged their way through the lines and been treated seriously by the French. Erzberger wished Groener's office had not been so careless with its travel permits.

They were very spruce young men. Blauert, who still waited for his aeroplane, introduced them to Erzberger. They carried no particular news but seemed unshaken by their journey. One of them said that they would leave the train and let Herr Erzberger get on with his work. Erzberger said leave the train and go where? Camp under an elm? No, use that end of the saloon.

For a minute or so Erzberger watched them all, the young professionals, the men who had come yesterday, this morning's group. Their talk had solemn rhythms. Occasionally someone laughed but only briefly. They lacked, to a degree that Erzberger found indecent, any suggestion of belonging to an endangered army.

Their talk, however restrained, annoyed von Winterfeldt. Erzberger was surprised to see the general get up and begin snorting.

There may have been old regular's envy for their General Staff carmine-striped pants and golden buttons, so untarnished in these last hours of war.

In the end he did not speak up to them. Only to Matthias.

Von Winterfeldt: You see. The General Staff. Yesterday they dropped their potentate. But they're lasting well, don't you think? Tomorrow they'll pick up some other divinity.

Erzberger: But now a republic! No more divinities.

Von Winterfeldt: Can you believe, Herr Erzberger, that you're truly going home to a republic?

And Matthias tried the tension in his belief and found it slack.

Von Winterfeldt: I see these things. I see them with an outsider's eyes because my wife is French and an intelligent woman. They used to make her drink beer on Wednesday mess-nights. Like any fat frau.

At half past eleven sentries boarded the train, sealed all windows and pulled the blinds down. The engine, which Erzberger could hear sighing steam half the morning, dragged them away in an instant. Erzberger who disliked haphazard departures and thought that you only truly saw a place when you were leaving it, peeped out of the half-inch aperture between blind and pane and saw Blauert step into a French army vehicle, his black case strapped to his wrist. He seemed to carry it without sense of onus.

No quick journey. There was much traffic on the line. The stations crowded. Behind the windows the pallid delegates did not care to peep out and see whether it was soldiers or refugees cheering and singing and baying threats; or sight-seers drawn by rumour to view this train amongst all the others. In some places they could hear sentries ordering people back.

By early afternoon it had become so wearing that Matthias and the others sat all together in a knot.

Matthias Erzberger's Final Forest

It is against all feeling to leave Matthias without conducting him to his final forest. The journey is quickly fulfilled.

He reached the capital on Wednesday. The republic eked its existence daily forward between poles. For one pole the conservative wing, swelled by thousands of inveterate ex-officers. For another, the deep socialist and authentic reds.

Politics wasn't a remote art as in stable government. You didn't practise it through memoranda, secretaries and public officials. It was an act of immediate and hourly contrivance. Most of all, you went yourself and talked with people. You were a sort of transcendental shop-steward or drygoods salesman.

This style of work appealed to Matthias Erzberger, gave him a sense of forcing a mould upon time, instead of being himself moulded by it. So the fatalism was soothed which he had suffered from during the armistice days. And might suffer again any day he was left idle.

Maiberling had fewer demands on his time. He stayed in the country and when he came to Berlin was escorted by two large young men, former sergeants in the Bavarian infantry. Flinching, he would call them his Praetorians.

In the summer of 1919 Erzberger became vice-chancellor and, more fatally, a reforming finance minister. He denied all the old kingdoms: Bavaria, Saxony, Prussia and the others, by taxing Germans directly from Berlin. As a means of freezing army pay he froze army promotion.

He enacted other reforms that are best enquired of from historians.

All at once he was the darling target of respectable conservatives and their bastard brothers of the secret parties, the private armies.

Karl Helferrich, who had once been a finance minister, began tearing at him in articles published by *Kreuzzeitung*. Each article was headed *Away with Erzberger*. Later the articles were gathered into a booklet of the same title. In the vicious journals of the north Erzberger and the others were called 'the November criminals'. When Matthias first heard the term his predestinarian guts said, there it is, a stage in a process that can't be begged off.

Helferrich's people stole his tax returns. Helferrich indicated irregularities; said that while a director of Thyssen's Matthias had warned a shipping and engineering subsidiary of some government intention; accused him of perjury.

On such grounds a priest giving consecrated bread in a parish church in Weimar came to Erzberger, recognized him from his photograph in maligning papers, refused him the Eucharist.

Paula Erzberger: You can't sue a priest. My love.

Erzberger: You can sue Helferrich.

The trial began in the new year. The galleries in the dim court-room in Berlin-Moabit were full of those young men who called themselves *the disinherited of 1918*. They cheered Helferrich, his counsel and his witnesses. They cat-called and yowled at Erzberger and his counsel. The judge threatened to clear the galleries if the noise continued. The noise continued. He never cleared the galleries. Similarly, when Helferrich called old members of the Imperial cabinet they were fetched by clerks and bowed into court. When Erzberger called ministers of the republic they were bawled for by ushers.

On 26 January it was like midnight when the court adjourned. Erzberger went to his car, stepped in and sat by his secretary. His lawyer talked to him through the lowered window. All their speculation went up in vapour.

One of the young men from the galleries stepped to the

lawyer's side, bent past the wound-down pane, had a Mauser in his hands and fired twice. The noise horrified Matthias. There was no other keen pain. A bullet went into his right shoulder but the one that would have killed him was deflected into the upholstery by his big rustic watch-chain.

The boy's name was Hirschfeld. Yes, a former subaltern. At his trial his defence lawyer compared him to Cicero gunning for Catiline. He got eighteen months.

In March Helferrich was found guilty of making false accusations and fined the nothing sum of 300 marks. Erzberger, it was found, was guilty of impropriety, perjury, the mixing of business and politics. There, the court said. He deserves to be denied sacraments and to have Mausers pointed at him.

He resigned his portfolio. Friends and doctors told him to rest and let the psychopaths forget him. It was a tender, wistful summer for Matthias Erzberger. He scarcely campaigned but was returned in the June elections for the Swabian constituency of Biberach. He thought, at least down there in my home valleys there's still a sort of political temperate zone.

In the House he kept his silence. At home he was most tender with fragile Paula. Their infant Gabrielle played on the shingles at Swinemünde that hazy summer. *(Erzberger: Thank God she's got your hips.)* His damaged shoulder foretold thunderstorms. His elder daughter Maria wanted to go to Holland and become a Carmelite. They argued about it. He had always taken nuns for granted. They were other people's lost children. There was so much ripeness in her that he hated her to go as a tithe.

By the summer there were a few hints in political columns that he might be seeking a place in the cabinet. He found reasons to feed to Paula but thought it best not to tell her as well that working short hours disgruntled him. He told her, and seems to have four-fifths believed himself, that he would not be further menaced. The assassins of Walter Rathenau at midsummer had said that they shot him because he was part of the Jewish industrial and cultural plot. There, Matthias said, they have moved on from fantasies of November criminals to Jews.

There was time, he said, to think about it. He had them booked into three Black Forest hotels for July and August. First, Jordanbad. Firs and sharp air and apolitical locals in braided shirts.

On 8 August on to Beuron by village taxi. A dear old yokel at the wheel. On 19 August to the Sisters of Charity pension at Bad Greisach and nut-brown people in peasant knickers.

The Mother-Superior asked to see his watch-chain.

Mother-Superior: A miracle.

Erzberger: Perhaps not in the strict sense.

Mother-Superior: How do you know?

Erzberger: Indeed. How do I?

Mother Superior: And all because you simply wanted taxes collected.

She made his policies seem the sunny apex of good sense.

He walked every day, often with Paula. But there were many wild thunderstorms.

On 25 August for example a falling conifer broke down powerlines, and candles had to be lit in the pension lounge. A guest began playing old mountain songs on the piano and everyone, the nuns too, began singing in the dusk. Erzberger sang in baritone, Gabrielle on his knee. Candlelight sat bland on her baby-broad face and on her father's.

That evening a friend called Herr Diez arrived in Bad Greisach by feeder-train from Freudenstadt. Herr Diez was also in the Reichstag. He and Matthias went to a tavern and got mildly tipsy.

The next morning Matthias and Diez planned to go walking up the mountain road towards Kneibis.

Paula made him take an umbrella because there would be more thunderstorms.

Paula: Admit it. You can feel it in your shoulder.

Halfway up the hill they could see the Kinzig flowing cobalt between the lazy clockwork towns.

They got to the top, sat a while, talking politics. No one was on the road except two young climbers.

Who, when they got to Diez and Erzberger, called greetings, put their packs down and took army pistols from them.

Erzberger had forgotten his dream of 1918. All he had was the normal sense of *déja-vu*. Impelled by it he opened his umbrella. Diez hit them with his. But Erzberger yielded to his supine nub and blotted them out with black silk.

Through this false hemisphere he was shot in the chest and forehead. He walked the little way to the edge of the road and fell ten metres down the embankment. They slid after him and shot him in the lung, the stomach, the thigh. He was still quite conscious and, while they loaded again, tried to hide behind a fir tree. Here they came and put into him the last three of the eight shots he suffered.

Then they mounted the embankment, picked up their haversacks and disappeared in the wood.

Diez, bleeding from the chest, took the news to Bad Greisach.

The body was left *in situ* all night to enable senior police to determine the circumstances of the crime. That, anyhow, was the reason police gave for leaving Matthias's corpse all the high-summer night in the forest. Not that they caught the killers. It was twenty-seven years later, in a season of retribution, that they were caught and tried and sentenced.

The autopsy in Oppenau showed that the victim's heart and kidneys were gravely enlarged and that he would not have had long, in any case, to live.

THOMAS KENEALLY

SCHINDLER'S ARK

Winner of the 1982 Booker McConnell Prize

SCHINDLER'S ARK

'An extraordinary achievement'
Graham Greene

'Brilliantly detailed, moving, powerful and gripping'
The Times

'A magnificent book, powerful, harrowing and beautifully written'
Sunday Express

'Swift, cool and brilliantly successful'
Books and Bookmen

'Thomas Keneally has done marvellous justice to a marvellous story'
Sunday Times

'Keneally is a superb storyteller. With SCHINDLER'S ARK he has given us his best book yet, a magnificent novel which held me from the first page to the last'
Alan Sillitoe

ALSO AVAILABLE FROM CORONET BOOKS

THOMAS KENEALLY

☐ 33501 7 Schindler's Ark   £2.95
☐ 33783 4 Confederates   £2.95

MORRIS WEST

☐ 26587 6 The Salamander   £1.75
☐ 27638 X The Clowns Of God   £1.95
☐ 32051 6 McCreary Moves In   £1.50
☐ 32052 4 The Naked Country   £1.50

JAMES CLAVELL

☐ 20446 X Tai Pan   £2.95
☐ 26877 8 Noble House   £3.50

All these books are available at your local bookshop or newsagent, or can be ordered direct from the publisher. Just tick the titles you want and fill in the form below.

Prices and availability subject to change without notice.

CORONET BOOKS, P.O. Box 11, Falmouth, Cornwall.

Please send cheque or postal order, and allow the following for postage and packing:

U.K.—45p for one book, plus 20p for the second book, and 14p for each additional book ordered up to a £1.63 maximum.

B.F.P.O. and EIRE—45p for the first book, plus 20p for the second book, and 14p per copy for the next 7 books, 8p per book thereafter.

OTHER OVERSEAS CUSTOMERS—75p for the first book, plus 21p per copy for each additional book.

Name ....

Address ....

....